MW00457481

GHOST COACH

ALSO BY ROBERT VAUGHAN

The Tenderfoot

On the Oregon Trail

Cold Revenge

Iron Horse

Outlaw Justice

Western Fiction Ten Pack

The Founders Series

The Western Adventures of Cade McCall

Faraday Series

Lucas Cain Series

Chaney Brothers Westerns

Arrow and Saber Series

The Crocketts Series

Remington Series

...and many more

GHOST COACH

LUCAS CAIN
BOOK THREE

ROBERT VAUGHAN

WOLFPACK PUBLISHING
— EST 2013 —

Ghost Coach
Paperback Edition
Copyright © 2024 Robert Vaughan

Wolfpack Publishing
701 S. Howard Ave. 106-324
Tampa, Florida 33609

wolfpackpublishing.com

This book is a work of fiction. Any references to historical events, real
people or real places are used fictitiously. Other names, characters,
places and events are products of the author's imagination, and any
resemblance to actual events, places or persons, living or dead, is
entirely coincidental.

All rights reserved. No part of this book may be reproduced by any
means without the prior written consent of the publisher, other than
brief quotes for reviews.

Paperback ISBN 978-1-63977-186-8
eBook ISBN 978-1-63977-185-1
LCCN 2023951070

GHOST COACH

Lucas Cain referred to himself as a rambling man, and his unwillingness to settle down in any particular location was proof of that appellation. He was a deputy U.S. Marshal. Although he received no official pay, that didn't mean he was without compensation. His arrangement of the position meant that he was eligible to collect a bounty on those outlaws for whom a reward had been posted. He was, in reality, a bounty hunter, but with the authority of an officer of the law.

With his purse fat from his most recent adventure, Lucas began a journey that was without specific purpose or destination. He was riding his horse, Charley Two, and finding a good camping site that offered graze as well as water for the horse and himself, he decided he would stop.

Lucas lay out his bedroll, made a circle of stones, then began gathering firewood. He had started a fire when he saw a couple of riders approaching. The riders were making no effort to conceal their approach, so Lucas felt no sense of alarm. However, he was alert should a challenge develop.

"Hello, the camp," one of the riders called out.

"Hello," Lucas replied.

The two men continued on to within a few feet of Lucas then stopped to wait for an invitation to dismount.

"We've got bacon that we'll cook up and share, if you'd be willing to share some coffee," one of the riders said.

"Sounds like a pretty good deal to me," Lucas replied. "Dismount, and join me. I'm Lucas Cain."

Both riders dismounted, then the one who had been vocal stuck out his hand. "I'm Ezra Karg, this is my brother, Wyatt."

Lucas shook hands with both men. "You gentlemen headed anywhere in particular?"

"No, we have no idea where we're going," Ezra said.

"We don't even know where we are," Wyatt added.

"I can help you with that," Lucas said. "You're in New Mexico." He paused for a moment, then added, "I think."

Ezra laughed. "Well, it's good to know that we'll be sharing a meal with a kindred soul."

Their supper consisted of coffee, fried bacon, and biscuits.

"It's not that we don't know why we're goin'," Wyatt said. "We know the why, it's just that we don't know where we're goin'."

"What?" Lucas said, puzzled by the strange comment.

"What my brother's tryin' to say is, we're private detectives, and we've been hired by the citizens of Colorado City, in Mitchell County, Texas, to find four men who escaped jail and killed the sheriff, his deputy, and the judge. They also stole four horses from the livery," Ezra said.

"You say they hired you, so now you're the sheriff and deputy?" Lucas asked.

"No, we're private detectives. You're familiar with the Pinkertons?" Ezra asked.

"Yes, I know of the Pinkertons," Lucas replied.

"Well, we're like them, just not as large," Ezra said.

"Or famous," Wyatt added.

Ezra laughed. "We're not famous at all."

"When you say they hired you, is that in addition to the bounty?" Lucas asked. "I assume there's a bounty."

"Yes," Ezra said, nodding his head. "The county paid us five hundred dollars to look for them, and we get that money whether we find them or not. And, of course, if we do find them, we'll collect a bounty."

"How much?" Lucas asked.

"Two thousand dollars," Ezra said. "Five hundred dollars each."

"Would you like some help in finding them?"

"I don't know if you want to get mixed up in this, Lucas. These are dangerous men. Like I said, they killed Sheriff Baylor, Deputy Boyle, and Judge Stone. You don't understand. You could get hurt, or even killed."

Lucas took out his badge from his vest pocket. "I understand, all right."

"No, no I don't think you do understand," Wyatt said. "You see, we're going after the reward. I don't think they'd be willing to pay if a lawman was involved."

Lucas chuckled. "That's because you don't know what kind of lawman I am."

"What do you mean?" Ezra asked.

Lucas explained the arrangement he had which

allowed him to have the authority of an unpaid lawmen, while acting as a bounty hunter.

"Well, sounds like you might be helpful after all," Wyatt said.

"Do you have the names of the men we're going after?" Lucas asked.

"Oh yeah. Cyrus and Caleb Dilbert, they're brothers. Bud Newman and Moss Kelly," Ezra said. "They also know us."

"They know you?" Lucas asked.

"Yeah, we're the ones who brought them in, in the first place."

"They escaped a hanging," Wyatt said, continuing the story. "They'd already been found guilty and sentenced to hang by Judge Stone. The gallows had been built, and they were supposed to be hung on the day after they escaped."

"There sure were a bunch of pissed off people back in Colorado City," Ezra said. "Just about everyone in the entire county had come into town to see the hanging, only there wasn't one."

The three men shared stories and background information far into the night, doing so because, as Lucas told the others, the better they knew each other, the easier it would be to work together.

Lucas was still awake well after midnight. As he listened to the snoring of the other two men, he wondered if he had made the right choice in teaming up with them.

Finally, Lucas came to a decision. He had nothing to lose, so why not get involved?

After his brief time of contemplation, Lucas put all conflicting thoughts and considerations aside. He would go into this with a one hundred percent dedication to the mission. And now, having come to that conclusion, he drifted off to sleep. Soon his snores joined those of the Karg brothers.

———

THIRTY MILES SOUTH, Cyrus and Caleb carried on a quiet conversation as Bud and Moss slept fitfully.

"Here's the problem," Cyrus said. "We ain't got no money, ceptin' what little bit we took outta the pockets of them three we kilt. Hell, we ain't no better off now 'n we was a' fore we escaped."

"Really? You mean you warn't bothered none when you clumb them thirteen steps up to the gallows? You didn't mind it when they put the noose around your neck, and you was all right with fallin' through that trap door, so's that the knot broke your neck?" Caleb asked.

"Caleb, what the hell are you a-talkin' about? You know they didn't none of that stuff happen," Cyrus replied.

"Ah-ha. So we are better off now than we was before we escaped," Caleb replied.

"Oh, well yeah, I mean if you're goin' to put it like that, we're a lot better off."

"Let me ask you this, Brother. Before we was put 'n jail, what kind of job did we have?"

"What do you mean? We didn't have no kind of job a'tall."

"Really? Then, I don't understand. How did we have money to buy food, to have a few drinks in a saloon, maybe get us a woman from time to time? Where did we get that money?"

"Come on, why are you askin' me such dumb questions? You know we stole all the money we ever needed."

"Did gettin' put in jail make you forget how to steal money?" Caleb asked.

"You know it didn't."

"No, I don't reckon it did. And I'm pretty sure Bud and Moss can remember, too."

A big grin spread across Cyrus's face, though in the dark, nobody saw it. "Then all we got to do is steal some more money."

"You catch on fast," Caleb said hitting his brother on the arm.

"Come on, Caleb, don't be teasin' me, now. I know Mama and Papa always told me I was slow, but you was always on my side."

"I guess I was, Little Brother. And if you do ever' thing I tell you to do, well then I'll stay on your side."

WHEN LUCAS, Ezra, and Wyatt rode into Laguna, Texas, they saw a town with one street, a scattering of businesses and homes lined up on both sides.

One low adobe building with a door and two windows had a wooden sign that identified the building as the city hall. Dismounting, the three men tied off their horses out front.

There were three men. The man nearest the front door looked up. He was quite thin, with a prominent Adam's apple, a weak chin, a prominent nose, and glasses that enlarged his eyes.

"What can I do for you gentlemen?"

"Are you a lawman?" Lucas asked.

"City clerk. Name's Martin Taylor."

"Well, Mr. Taylor, we'd like to talk to the sheriff, or

city marshal, or whoever you have acting as a lawman," Lucas said.

"That would be Marshal Curtis," Taylor said, pointing to a very overweight person sitting behind a desk.

Lucas, Ezra, and Wyatt stepped over to the desk.

"Marshal Curtis, I'm Deputy U.S. Marshal Lucas Cain. These two gentlemen, Ezra and Wyatt Karg, have been hired by the good people of Colorado City, over in Mitchell County. They're looking for four men who killed their marshal, his deputy, and the judge who had sentenced them to hang. They escaped the gallows."

"I thought you said you were a U.S. Marshal," Curtis said.

"I am, and the three of us will be working together."

"What do you need from me?" Curtis asked.

"The men we're looking for are the brothers, Cyrus and Caleb Dilbert, and the two men with them, Bud Newman and Moss Kelly. Have you heard anything about them? Are they in your area?"

"I got a telegram tellin' about the killings, but that's all I know," Curtis said.

"All right, we thank you for your time, and if you would, keep your eyes and ears open."

Lucas had long ago learned that the best source of knowledge of any town could be found in a saloon. In some of the larger towns, this would require visiting several. But Laguna had only one saloon, the Dusty Trail.

There were no swinging batwing doors like the kind they were used to when entering a saloon. Rather, the door to the Dusty Trail was hung with beaded strings, which clacked as the three men pushed inside. There were only six men in the saloon, counting the bartender.

"Well now," the bartender said, by way of greeting. "Haven't seen you fellers before."

"No, we just arrived," Lucas said.

"Stayin' or passin' through?" the bartender asked.

"We're just passing through," Ezra said.

"We're gettin' to be just real busy here, ain't we, Dooley?" one of the saloon customers said. "They was them four men come through here warn't no more 'n week ago."

"Four men, you say?" Ezra asked. He took a folded paper from his pocket and showed it to the bartender. Lucas noticed that it was a wanted poster for Cyrus Dilbert. "Would this look like one of the four men you're talking about?"

"Yeah. I'll be damn," Dooley said. "That feller's worth five hunnert dollars, 'n he was just standin' here right in front of me."

"I don't suppose you have any idea where they went from here, do you?" Lucas asked.

"Nope, no idea at all."

"I can tell you this, though." This was from the customer who had mentioned seeing them. "I watched 'em leavin' town, 'n they was a-goin' east."

2

It was a couple of hours past nightfall when the Dilbert brothers, Newman, and Kelly rode into the town of Murita. There were several streets in the town, those running east and west, parallel to the railroad, and those running north and south, at right angles to the railroad. Businesses and private homes flanked both sides of the roads and streets, but no street was better represented than Corsicana Street where downtown businesses pushed all the way out to the sidewalk.

The first place they stopped was the Silver Spur Saloon, and even as they were tying off their horses, they could hear a tinkling piano as well as laughter and dozens of boisterous conversations.

"Sounds like we've picked the right place to have a beer and find out where we might get some money," Cyrus said.

"Yeah? Well right now, as far as I'm concerned, the most important part of this stop is gettin' a beer," Caleb said.

"A beer is where I'm startin'," Bud agreed.

The four men got their drinks, then found a table in a back corner of the saloon. Two of the girls wearing practiced smiles came toward the table.

"Get outta here," Cyrus ordered, waving the women away. "We got business to discuss, 'n we don't have time for the likes of you."

The girls' smiles were replaced by an expression of surprise, and they turned away heading for another table.

"Damn, never thought I'd see you turn away a pretty girl," Moss said.

"By my calculations, we have six dollars and twenty-five cents," Cyrus said. "Now, just how far do you think that would go with one of those girls?"

"I can understand that," Bud said.

"Which brings us to where we are," Caleb said. "How do we get some money?"

Moss laughed.

"What are you laughin' at?" Caleb asked.

"I can answer one of those two questions," Moss said. "I don't know where, but I know how we're gonna get money. We're gonna just take it."

Cyrus laughed. "Well, you got that right, anyway."

The others joined him in laughter.

"So, what do we do now?" Bud asked.

"Now we need to decide on the where," Caleb said. "Where we will go for our," Caleb paused for few seconds before he added, "job?"

As Lucas, Ezra, and Wyatt approached the little town before them, it rose from the ground—not as clearly defined buildings, but more like hills, and ridges. As they came closer, they understood the illusion, because every building was of adobe construction, so it blended perfectly with the environment.

As they rode through the town it would have looked empty, except for a man sitting in a chair in front of one of the structures. He had his arms folded across his chest, his head bowed, and a sombrero was pulled down over his eyes.

"Let's try that place," Ezra said, pointing to one of the buildings. The sign in front of the building read *Rosita's Cantina*. When they went inside, a man and woman were sitting at a table. They were the only two people in the building. The man got up and walked over to the bar, then around behind it.

"*Si, Señor?*"

"Beer?" Lucas ordered.

"No beer, *Señor*. Tequila."

Lucas looked at the two men with him, and they nodded.

"All right, tequila."

The bartender put three shot glasses on the bar and began pouring the tequila.

"What is this place?" Lucas asked.

"*Rosita's Cantina. Esa es Rosita en la mesa.*"

Lucas looked over at the table the bartender had pointed out. Rosita, who looked to be in her mid to late forties, had a hard face, and a more than ample-sized body.

"No, I meant what is the name of this town?"

"Greiton, *Señor*."

Lucas looked at the two brothers and smiled. "We're in Texas. That means they've got a lot of room to run from us."

MEANWHILE, the Dilbert brothers, Newman, and Kelly were making plans to address their serious lack of funds.

"I'll hit the gun store," Caleb said. "Cyrus, you take the Emporium, Bud, you go to the leather goods store, and Moss, you'll be in the apothecary. We'll hit all four of 'em at exactly the same time. Take no more than one minute to get the job done. If you can't get anything in a minute, come outside anyway. We'll all leave town together, that means you absolutely have to get the job done in one minute. Does ever'body understand that? One minute."

Nobody questioned Caleb's authority. It was understood that for four people to act together, someone must assume the leadership role, and Caleb had no difficulty doing so.

After finishing their drinks, they went outside into the bright sunlight. They had already tied off their horses, in front of the targeted businesses.

"All right, let's go," Caleb said, holding up his finger. "One minute."

They walked to the four targeted stores, then stopped just out front. Everyone looked toward Caleb, who paused for a brief moment, then brought his hand down in a signal.

WITH CALEB:

There was only one customer in the gun store when Caleb went inside. He was standing at the counter, across from the proprietor. The customer was holding a silver-plated revolver and a gun belt and holster. Every bullet loop was filled.

"You did a great job with this, Johnny" the customer said.

The proprietor chuckled. "I don't know why you wanted a gun like that. It's somethin' a gunfighter might wear."

"I just wanted it," the customer said as he ran his hand over the barrel.

"Well, that's a good enough reason for me."

Caleb walked right up to the two men. Neither of them noticed that he had drawn his pistol, and was holding it down by his side.

"I'll be right with you, sir, as soon as I've finished with this gentleman," the proprietor said.

"You're finished with him now," Caleb said, bringing the butt of his pistol down on the customer's head. The man went down, and quickly, Caleb grabbed his gun and holster, then raised back up.

"Here! What is this?" the shocked proprietor asked.

"This here is a robbery. Empty your cash drawer."

WITH CYRUS:

There were four people in the Sanderson Emporium, in addition to the salesclerk. Two women were shopping, comparing yard goods. There were two young girls, about eight or nine years old, and they were laughing as they made their own comparisons.

Cyrus stepped up behind one of the little girls, reached around to grab her, and pulled her toward him. He held a pistol to her head.

"Mama!" the little girl called out in fear.

"Sir!" one of the women gasped.

"If either of you call out, the girl dies," Cyrus said.

Cyrus dragged the little girl, who was now whimpering, over to the counter.

"Sir, what is the meaning of this?" the man behind the counter asked.

"Give me every dollar you've got in the store and do it in a hurry, or I'll kill the little girl, then I'll kill you."

"Mama, he's going to kill me," the little girl called out.

"No he isn't, sweetheart, because Mr. Sanderson is going to give him all the money he has."

WITH BUD:

The store smelled of leather, old and new. Bud walked through the saddles, panniers, boots, bridles, and whips. At first the store seemed to be completely empty. Then he heard someone call out.

"I'll be with you in a minute."

The person who had called was in the very back, putting some saddles on sawhorses for display. Bud walked up to him. The proprietor looked up with an irritated expression on his face.

"I told you I'd be with you in a minute." The irritation that was on his face, was also in the tone of his voice.

"You'll be with me now," Bud said, pointing his pistol at the man.

"Here, what is this?"

"It's a robbery," Bud said. "Take me to your cash drawer, and empty it."

WITH MOSS:

There was a customer standing at the counter talking to the druggist. The customer had a stethoscope sticking out of his pocket, which told Moss that he was a doctor. Moss stepped behind the doctor, then stuck his pistol into the doctor's back.

"Give me all of your money, or the doc dies," Moss said.

"No, please!" the druggist said. "He's the only doctor in town."

"Well then, you'll want to do what I say, won't you?" Moss said.

"All right, all right," the druggist said. He pulled open the cash drawer.

"Good, that's just what I…" Moss stopped in midsentence when he saw that, instead of money, the druggist had pulled out a derringer. The pistol was so small, that Moss didn't notice it at first glance.

The druggist pulled the trigger, but he was so anxious that he jerked the gun as it fired, and the bullet, instead of hitting Moss in the head as he had wanted, took off Moss's earlobe. The pain caused Moss to react, reflexively. He shot both the druggist and the doctor, then he leaned across the counter and emptied the cash drawer.

Caleb's instructions were followed by the other three, because within a minute of the beginning of the operation, all four had returned to their horses.

"I heard gunfire. Who fired their gun?" Caleb asked.

"I didn't have no choice," Moss said. "The son of a bitch shot me." He displayed his ear.

"Let's get out of here," Caleb said, as they heard the shout of, "Robbery! Help, I've been robbed!"

The first call was joined by a second, then a third.

The four men galloped out of town looking back to see that no one was following them.

3

After riding hard and fast from Murita, the four robbers made camp for the night, on Duck Creek. It wasn't until then, that they counted their money.

"Eight hunnert 'n seventeen dollars," Caleb said. "Nothin' we can retire on, but it'll keep us goin' for a little while."

"I don't know if it's worth an ear though," Moss said. He had torn off the tail of his shirt and was holding it against his bleeding ear.

"It wasn't a whole ear, it was just an earlobe," Bud said.

"Ear, earlobe, there's no difference in the way it hurts," Moss said.

"You can still hear, can't you?" Caleb asked.

"Yeah, but that don't mean it ain't hurtin'."

"Where to now, Caleb?" Cyrus asked.

"No place special, as long as we can stay ahead of the law," Caleb said. "Let's head sort of to the northeast from here."

"How're we goin' to know what way's northeast?" Bud asked. "We ain't got no compass."

"Which way will the sun come up in the morning?" Caleb asked.

"Well, it'll come up over here," he said, pointing.

"And which direction is that?"

"Hell, it's east, on account of the sun always comes up in the east."

"If that's east," Caleb said, "then that's north." He pointed.

Bud smiled. "Then that must be northeast," he said, pointing in the direction.

"Now you see there, Moss? Bud ain't near as dumb as you thought he was."

"What?" Moss said, obviously flustered. "I ain't never said no such thing."

Moss pulled the cloth from his ear and looked at it. It was saturated with blood. He threw it aside, dipped another piece of his shirt into the creek, and held it against his ear.

"Looks to me like the bleedin' is all but stopped," Caleb said. "By tomorrow morning it'll be stopped for sure."

Lucas, Ezra, and Wyatt rode coming to Murita and it was fortuitous that they did. They heard talk of the four simultaneous robberies and knew, without further discussion, that these were more than likely the four men they were looking for.

"Well, I'll tell you this," they overheard in a saloon discussion, "they ain't necessarily all that good 'a shots. Hell, the one that robbed the drugstore shot Amon

Cruthers and Doc Presnell 'n didn't kill either one of 'em."

"Yeah, 'n from what I hear, he damn near got his own ear shot off," another added, laughing at the concept of someone getting his ear shot off.

"Let's go talk to the city marshal," Lucas suggested.

Marshal Ollie Lynch looked more like a banker than a law officer. He was thin, with a very closely cropped mustache, and he wore a suit, rather than the denim and cotton shirt that would more likely identify him as a person of action. He was reading a newspaper when Lucas and the other two entered his office, and when he saw them coming in, he removed his reading glasses.

"What can I do for you, gentlemen?" Lynch asked.

"I'm Deputy U.S. Marshal Lucas Cain, these are my associates, Ezra and Wyatt Karg. We are looking for Cyrus and Caleb Dilbert and Bud Newman and Moss Kelly."

Lucas chuckled. "They were here yesterday."

"What do you mean they were here yesterday? How do you…?"

Marshal Lynch paused in midcomment. "I'll be damn. You're talking about the men who robbed our town, aren't you?"

"Exactly," Lucas said.

Lynch stroked his chin. "Well, there was four of 'em, that's for sure. I guess I just didn't put it together when ya first asked about it. So, what do you intend doing about it?"

"If you don't mind, we'd like to talk to anyone who had any interaction with them. We heard some talk over in the saloon. Someone said your doctor and the druggist were both shot but they're still alive. If they're up to it, do you think we'd be able to talk to them?"

"I don't see any problem with that. Neither one of 'em was hurt as bad as the man who was shot. The apothecary's open this morning same as always and Doc Presnell has already seen old lady Malloy. I swear, that old lady has more aches and pains than the whole town all put together."

Lynch took the three down to the doctor's office. Currently, the good doctor didn't have a patient.

"Before we start getting into the questions, Doctor, how are you doing?" Lucas asked.

"All right, under the circumstances," Dr. Presnell replied. "The bullet just grazed me. I'm getting along better than Amon is."

"Amon is the druggist?" Lucas asked.

"Yes. And don't get me wrong, he should make a full recovery."

"How about telling us what happened?" Lucas asked.

Presnell told the story, adding what seemed to be a few embellishments, but it made for an interesting story.

THERE HAD BEEN several of the townspeople who had seen the four robbers gallop out of town on the Wild Horse Road.

"I don't think we'll be able to actually track them on the Wild Horse Road," Lucas said. "But that's where we'll start."

It was getting close to nightfall when Lucas pointed to a thicket of trees ahead, just off the road.

"We may as well spend the night there, then get a fresh start in the morning," Lucas said.

"Yeah, I'm ready to stop," Ezra said. "I'm so hungry that my stomach is mad at my mouth for not eating."

Lucas chuckled. "Your stomach is mad?"

"It must be. It's growling."

Lucas and Wyatt laughed.

The three men made camp, secured their horses, and began gathering wood for a fire.

"Look, there's a fire ring." Ezra pointed to some rocks that encircled the black remnants of what had been a campfire.

"Well, then we know this is a good place to camp, don't we?" Lucas said. "You guys fry some bacon and I'll get the coffee started."

Carrying the coffeepot in his hand, Lucas went down to the stream to get water. Just as he leaned over he saw a bloody rag lying on the bank of the creek.

"Ezra, Wyatt," he called. "Come here, you need to see this."

Both men came quickly. "What have you found?" Ezra asked.

Lucas didn't answer verbally, but he pointed to the bloody rag.

"Hmm, a bloody rag," Wyatt said.

"Yeah," Ezra said. "Like something you would hold up to your ear, if you got the earlobe shot off."

"They were here, weren't they?" Wyatt asked.

"It would seem so," Lucas said.

Forgetting about supper for the moment, the three men searched the camping area for any clues. The bloody rag proved the robbers had been here recently. Now the question was where did they go from here?

They looked around until they found where the horses had been secured.

"Look at this," Wyatt said, pointing to a distinctive print left on the ground.

"Ah-hah! One of the horses has a tie-bar shoe," Ezra said. "Let's see where this horse went."

"Boys, they went that way," Lucas said when they got to the road. "Let's eat your bacon and get started on their trail."

Following the tie-bar shoe, they arrived in Big Spring. There, they lost the exact horse's print because of the normal traffic of the town.

"What do we do now?" Wyatt asked.

Lucas smiled as he pointed to a saloon. "The best place to get information," Lucas said.

"Makes sense to me," Ezra said. "Since there are four saloons, should we split up?"

"I don't think so. Since you two brought these men in, they would recognize you and they'd know you're looking for them. It would be four against one," Lucas said. "We'd best stick together."

"That's a good point," Wyatt said in agreement.

When they went inside, they saw how busy the saloon was. Every table was full, the bar was nearly full, and there were even some standing by the side wall, but the three found a place to stand that was close to the end of the bar.

"What'll you have?" the bartender asked as he ran a wet and stinking cloth over the bar, wiping up the residue of a spilled drink.

"I'll have a beer," Lucas said.

Ezra and Wyatt indicated that they would have the same.

"We're looking for someone," Lucas said.

"Who?" the bartender asked.

"Four men," Ezra said. "They escaped jail on the very day they were to hang. And they killed three during their escape."

"What are their names?" the bartender asked.

"Cyrus and Caleb Dilbert, they're brothers. The other two are Bud Newman and Moss Kelly."

The bartender shook his head. "Those names don't mean anything to me."

"I didn't expect that they would. But one of them you would remember if you saw him. He just had half his ear shot off."

The bartender chuckled. "Yeah, someone like that would sure stand out all right."

One of the many customers that happened to be in the saloon at that moment, was Bud Newman. He was sitting at a table near the piano, so he was lost in the crowd, and not noticed by either one of the Karg brothers.

Bud called one of the bar girls over.

"You want another drink, honey?" the girl, whose name was Lola asked with a wide smile.

Bud stood up, and walked away from the table, standing in such a way that put the piano between him and the bar.

Lola followed him, with a questioning expression on her face.

"I know those three men who just came in, and I know who they're looking for," Bud said. "I want to tell 'em somethin', but I'm afraid to. The men they're lookin' for, are real dangerous, and if they was to find out it was me who told on 'em—why I'd be shot as sure as grass is green. I'll give you two dollars to give 'em a message, but don't do it till I'm out a here."

"What about me? Wouldn't I be in danger if I do what you say?" Lola asked.

"How would it put you in danger? Do you know Cyrus or Caleb Dilbert, or Bud Newman or Moss Kelly?"

"No."

"Then, if you don't know 'em, and they don't know you, what's the harm?"

Lola smiled. "You're right," she said, taking the two dollars from him. "What do you want me to do?"

Bud told Lola what he wanted her to pass on to the Karg brothers and the man who had come in with them. "But make sure you wait about ten minutes after I'm out of here before you tell 'em."

Lola watched Bud move through the crowded saloon, avoiding the three men at the bar he had pointed out to her.

Leaving the saloon, Bud hurried over to the Westside Saloon where he saw Caleb, Cyrus, and Moss sitting at a table playing cards.

"We've got to get out of this place," Bud said.

"Why?" Caleb asked, as he pushed out a chair. "Sit down and join our game."

"I just saw them Karg brothers—the ones who brung us in back in Colorado City, and they got the law with 'em. You know they're a-lookin' for us."

"Let's go," Caleb said as he drained the last swallow from his drink.

"We'll go west," Bud said.

"What do you mean, go west? Why?"

"Because I told one of the bar girls to give me ten minutes, then tell 'em she seen us leavin' town, headin' east."

"You say you told her to wait ten minutes?" Caleb asked.

"Yeah."

Caleb laughed. "That's perfect," he said. "We'll go east."

"No, we can't. That's the direction I gave the girl to tell 'em," Bud protested.

"Exactly. And they'll ride right into our ambush," Caleb said.

———

WHEN THE MAN who had given Lola the money had been gone about ten minutes, she walked over to the bar. She saw that one of the three men was wearing the badge of a U.S. Marshal.

"Are ya'll looking for four men, and one of 'em has a wounded ear?" she asked.

"Yes," Lucas replied. "Do you know anything about them?"

"I know that when they left town, they were headed east."

"Thanks," Lucas said. "I guess we've got some work ahead of us."

4

Caleb stopped and looked around. He pointed ahead, to a curve in the road. "Once we get on the other side of that curve, nobody comin' up the road from this direction will be able to see us."

"What are we goin' to do?" Moss asked.

"What do you mean, what are we goin' to do? We're goin' to find us a spot to hide in, then when they come 'round the curve, we'll kill 'em."

"It warn't just the Karg brothers I seen," Bud said. "I know there was a U.S. Marshal with 'em."

"Well ain't that great. He's sort of like a rabbit comin' into a trap. We'll kill all three of 'em."

"Yeah," Moss said with a wide smile. "I like that."

As Lucas, Ezra, and Wyatt rode east on the road, Lucas saw a sharp turn to the left, just ahead. From where they were now, they would have no way of knowing what was just beyond the curve.

Lucas held up his hand as a signal to stop.

"What's wrong?" Wyatt asked.

"I don't like the looks of that curve in the road up there," Lucas said. "I've got a bad feeling about it."

"Like what? Like an ambush or somethin'?" Ezra asked.

"Exactly."

"Well, what are we going to do?" Wyatt asked. "We can't just sit here."

"If we can't see them yet, that pretty much means they can't see us either, doesn't it?" Ezra asked.

"Right," Lucas replied. "Ezra, you're a genius."

"I'm glad I could help you out," Ezra said. He chuckled. "But just what bit of my 'genius' did it for you?"

"It's like you said, they can't see us yet, so they have no idea we're here. So, what we're going to do is," Lucas said as he pointed to his left. "We're going to cut the turn. There are trees between us and them, so we'll be able to come out on the other side."

"Ha! I like that!" Wyatt said.

"Well, let's get this show started," Lucas invited. He turned Charley Two off the main road, then started across the field. Ezra and Wyatt joined him.

"Bud, take a look around the curve, and see if anyone's comin'," Caleb said.

"Why do I have to?" Bud replied.

"Because I told you to."

"What if someone's comin', and they see me? Won't that give it away that we're a waitin' on 'em?"

"If you want to be a part of this, just do what the hell I

tell you to do," Caleb said, his irritation reflected in the tone of his voice.

"All right, all right, I'll look," Bud said, begrudgingly.

Bud left the trees where the four of them were waiting, then walked down to the curve, and took a look down the road. The road was clear. He walked back to the tree line.

"As far as I can see there ain't nobody comin'," he yelled back to the others.

"Well, if you really told that little old girl what you said you did, you know damn well they'll be comin' after us, so we'll just wait right here until they come along," Caleb said.

IT TOOK Lucas and the two brothers about fifteen minutes to cut across the curve. Instead of approaching from the direction where the outlaws would be expecting them to appear, they were coming toward their hiding spot from the opposite direction.

"Look," Ezra said, pointing. "There are their horses."

"Then they've got to be close by," Lucas said.

Within a couple of minutes, Wyatt pointed them out. "There they are, just back in the tree line," he whispered.

"Draw your guns, and be ready," Lucas said.

The three men drew their pistols, then walked their horses very slowly until they reached a point where the trees offered no protection for the waiting men. The men were still looking in the opposite direction, unaware of the danger that approached from behind.

"You men drop your guns and turn around with your hands up!" Lucas ordered.

"What the hell?" Caleb said. "Shoot 'em, shoot 'em!"

All four of the outlaws turned quickly, and were able to get a shot off, but all four missed.

Lucas, Ezra, and Wyatt returned fire. For a moment, the isolated area was filled with the sound of gunfire, but very quickly, all four of the outlaws went down.

"Either of you hit?" Lucas asked as he approached the bodies.

"We're good," Ezra said. "Do you think they're dead?"

Lucas checked each of the four bodies. "They're dead. Let's get 'em on their horses. I expect we'll have to take the bodies back to Murita to collect on 'em."

"They have to go to Colorado City," Ezra said. "That's where Wyatt and I will collect the rest of the fee the town owes us. We can collect the bounties there, too, so you may as well come along with us, Lucas."

"Sounds good to me."

It took them a day and a half to reach Colorado City. Colorado City was a small town to be a county seat, but it had earned that position by virtue of the Missouri Pacific passing through.

As the three men rode into town with the four escaped prisoners belly down over their horses, the few people who lived there came out into the street to shout out congratulations to the Karg brothers. They wondered who Lucas was, but because he was riding with Ezra and Wyatt without any restraint, they were sure he wasn't a prisoner.

"Here's the sheriff's office just ahead," Ezra said. "But since the sheriff, his deputy, and the judge were all killed, I don't know who's there now."

When Lucas and the brothers dismounted in front of the sheriff's office, they were met by a tall, gray-haired man. The man was wearing a badge.

"Hello, Emerson, are you the sheriff now?" Ezra asked as he dismounted.

"I'm just acting as sheriff until we can elect a new one," Emerson replied.

"Lucas, this is Bernard Emerson. He's a retired Texas Ranger, and this is Lucas Cain. He's a U.S. Marshal," Ezra said.

Lucas extended his hand, and Emerson took it.

"Lucas is going to share the reward with us," Ezra said.

"Well, after the Murita holdups, the state added to the reward. It's up to four thousand dollars, now," Emerson said. "But you all know it'll take a few days before it can be paid."

"That's all right," Lucas said. "It'll be good to spend a few nights in a hotel room, instead of sleeping out on the ground."

"We don't have a hotel, but you all are welcome to stay in the jail cell if you'd like," Emerson said. "We don't have anyone in jail now, so you won't be crowded."

Lucas smiled. "That's good enough for me."

The town held a celebratory picnic that evening, with most of the townspeople attending. Nearly everyone made it a point to personally thank Lucas, Ezra, and Wyatt for ending the menace of Cyrus and Caleb Dilbert, Bud Newman, and Moss Kelly.

Two days later the reward of four thousand dollars was paid. Lucas's share was fifteen hundred dollars. The increase in his share was proposed by Ezra and Wyatt because, as they explained, they were also receiving a fee for their services, in addition to the reward.

As they were counting out the money, a boy of about fourteen came into the sheriff's office.

"Hello, Abe, what can I do for you?" Emerson asked.

"I've got a telegram for Mr. Ezra Karg," he said.

"I'm Ezra Karg." Ezra held up his hand.

Abe handed Ezra the telegram, and Ezra gave him a quarter. The quarter was considerably more than the usual nickel tip, and Abe smiled in appreciation.

"What is it?" Wyatt asked.

"McKnight-Keaton has a job for us, back in Fort Worth."

"Probably want us to trace down a lost shipment."

"It won't pay as well, but then, nobody will be shooting at us, either," Ezra said.

"And since our office is there anyway, I say we take it," Wyatt said.

"Lucas, since you're just rambling around, to use your words, you may as well come with us to Fort Worth."

"I think I'll take you up on that," Lucas said.

"HEY," Wyatt said the next morning. "Why don't we catch the train to Fort Worth?"

"You getting tired of riding, Little Brother?" Ezra asked.

"No, I'm just, uh, thinking of the horses is all."

"Well, I'm tired of riding, and I think catching the train is a great idea," Lucas said.

The next train that would have a stock car for the horses would leave at seven o'clock that evening. There would be another one at nine o'clock the next morning.

"What do you think? Do you want to catch the train tonight, or the one tomorrow morning?" Ezra asked.

"Either one is fine with me," Lucas said.

"I say tomorrow morning," Wyatt said.

"Good enough," Ezra replied.

The three of them bought tickets for themselves and their horses, made arrangements to board the horses in the depot corral, then headed for the saloon to, in Ezra's words, "cut through the dust."

It was relatively full for this early in the day, but there were a few empty tables and they chose one.

Wyatt walked over to the bar to get three beers, when another man came over to the table. He was about six feet tall, clean-shaven, with blue eyes and closely cropped brown hair.

"Ezra Karg," he said. "I thought that was you when I saw you come in."

"Hello, Deke, what are you doing here?"

"I'm after those four men you took in that ran out on the hangman here." He pulled out a dodger and handed it to Ezra. "The reward's up to four thousand dollars."

"You're too late," Ezra said as he looked over the piece of paper.

"Too late? What do you mean, too late?"

"We three have already split this reward," Ezra said. "They won't be gettin' away this time."

"Dead, huh?"

"Yep. Deke, this here is Lucas Cain," Ezra said. "And this is Deke Pauly."

"Lucas Cain," Deke said, as he extended his hand out over the table. "Well, I'll be damn, we meet at last."

"So we do," Lucas said. "I've heard about you, people keep comparing the two of us."

"They do indeed, and I admit to being flattered by being compared to you," Deke said.

"So, what are you goin' to do now, Deke?" Ezra asked.

"I'm not sure, I guess I'll just check out all the wanted posters 'n see where I want to go next."

"We're headed for Fort Worth. Why don't you come with us?" Ezra asked.

"No, that would be too many of us fishing in the same pond." Deke looked over and saw Wyatt coming toward the table, carrying three beers. "I will join you for a drink though, if you don't mind."

"Sure thing," Ezra said. "Wyatt, go get another beer. It's the least we can do since we took his bounty."

The four men visited until supper, then after breakfast the next morning, Deke walked down to the depot with them, to see them off.

5

STATE PENITENTIARY—HUNTSVILLE, TEXAS

As Lucas Cain and the Karg brothers were in route to Fort Worth, Rufe Sawyer was in a prison yard with three other prisoners—Moe Godfrey, Chris Dumey, and Amos Coleman.

"You three'll be gettin' out of here next week," Sawyer said. "So, here's the thing. It won't be long 'til I get out, too, so don't none a one of you be a-doin' nothin' 'til I get out, then we'll all join up again 'n we'll start in 'a makin' us some money."

"Why is it we can't do nothin' 'til you get out? How are we goin' to live while we're waitin' on you?" Godfrey asked.

"I got a place up north of Denton. It ain't much, but we can hang out there 'til you get out, Rufe," Coleman said. "Why hell, we might be able to pick up a dollar or two."

"Don't you do nothin' on your own, it'll be somethin' dumb, 'n like as not you'll get caught, 'n that'll mess up ever' thing. Anyway, you'll be gettin' twenty dollars apiece when you get out. That ought to hold you for a month, especially if you're stayin' at Coleman's place."

"What've you been thinkin' we should do to get some money?" Dumey asked.

"I been thinkin' of some things," Sawyer said. "I don't want to say nothin' yet, but I'll be thinkin' more about it in the time that I've got to go in here."

"You men," one of the guards shouted at them. "Yard time is over. Back inside you go."

As THE TRAIN rolled into the station, Lucas saw a sign hanging from the roof of the depot building.

FORT WORTH
Population 14,327

"I wish you would come work with us. We'd make you a full partner," Wyatt said, as they were getting off the train.

"Well, I admit that the offer is tempting, but I think I'd like to just keep on by myself. That way, if I happen to really make a mess of things, I'm the only one who would have to pay for my mistakes."

"I can understand that," Ezra said. "But if you ever change your mind, you've got a place with us."

"Thanks," Lucas said as he led his horse off the stock car. "But for now, I'll just say so long."

The three men shook hands and parted company.

"So, here we are in Fort Worth. What do you say, Charley Two, do you think we might want to spend some time here, or are there too many people?"

Lucas always referred to his horse as Charley Two out of respect for his first horse named Charley. Since he spent so much time traveling alone, he had come to regard Charley Two as more of a traveling companion than a beast of burden, and he often spoke to his horse believing that to be better than talking to himself.

"You know, Charley Two, I think we might be able to make a little money here," Lucas said. "But we have to get ourselves set up, first."

Stopping in front of the sheriff's office, Lucas tied Charley Two to the hitching rail, then stepped inside. He saw a man of about forty that he assumed to be the sheriff, sitting behind his desk writing something.

"Sheriff?" Lucas said.

The man looked up. "Damn, you startled me, I didn't hear you come in," the man said. He cleared his throat. "What can I do for you?"

"I'm Deputy U.S. Marshal Lucas Cain." Lucas stuck his hand out.

"Sheriff Michael Moore. What brings a U.S. Marshal to Fort Worth?"

"Nothing in particular, it depends on who you've got paper on, and what the rewards are."

"Rewards? What do you mean rewards? Law officers can't collect rewards."

"They can if they aren't otherwise compensated," Lucas said. "I'm not your ordinary lawman. I work without pay and my only compensation is in the bounties that I can collect."

"Mister, I've never heard of a U.S. Marshal who works without pay. What kind of scheme are you trying to pull, here?"

"Here's my badge," Lucas said, taking a silver star from his pocket. "And here's my letter of appointment."

The sheriff took the letter from Lucas, then picked his spectacles up from the desk and fitted them on before holding the letter up so he could read it.

To whom it may concern:

Know all by these presents that the bearer of this letter, Lucas Cain, holds the appointment of deputy U.S. Marshal. This appointment gives Marshal Cain jurisdiction, without limit, anywhere within the borders of the United States.

Further, Marshal Cain is serving without compensation, thus authorizing him to collect bounties when such are offered.

Jason Caldwell
U.S. Marshal
Austin, TX

"I've never heard of such a thing," Sheriff Moore said.

Lucas smiled. "I would be surprised if you had. Not even Marshal Caldwell had ever heard of the idea when I proposed it to him. But, after doing a little research he determined that it was legal."

"If I understand this, you are actually a bounty hunter," Sheriff Moore said.

"'I suppose you could say that, but I have the authority of a U.S. Marshal," Lucas explained.

"Hell, the bounty itself gives you all the authority you need."

"What's your opinion of bounty hunters?" Lucas asked.

"Not very high, I'm afraid to say. To me…"

"Unless he's a lawman, wearing a badge," Lucas said.

Sheriff Moore stared at Lucas for a moment, then

laughed. "I'll be damn," he said. "That's about the smartest thing I've ever heard of. So who are you after now?"

"Well, nobody at the moment. The Karg brothers and I brought in the Dilbert brothers and their two compadres. They were stirring up quite a bit of trouble out in West Texas."

"If you brought them fellas in, I'd say you're pretty flush with cash right now," Sheriff Moore said.

Lucas chuckled. "Let's just say I'm not going hungry, or at least I won't be after I pick up a bite to eat."

"Do you have a place to stay?"

"Not yet. I'm thinking for the next few days I'd get a place, preferably a boardinghouse, rather than a hotel. I'll want to look over all your wanted posters and see if there might be one that I think would be a fit."

"It might be good to have you around at that," Sheriff Moore said. "Have you already picked out a boardinghouse?"

"No, I haven't. Do you have any suggestions?"

Sheriff Moore smiled. "As a matter of fact, I do. It just so happens that my aunt runs a boardinghouse. And it's really convenient for your horse, too. She's only about half a block from the livery."

When Lucas stepped into Mama Cay's Boardinghouse a few minutes later, he saw a room that looked like the parlor of a house. It had two sofas, four padded chairs, a table and two chairs facing each other over a checkerboard, and a fireplace that wasn't currently being used. There was a heavyset woman with gray hair sitting on one of the sofas darning a pair of socks. She looked up as Lucas entered.

"What can I do for you, son?"

"Are you Sheriff Moore's aunt?"

The woman smiled. "Bless Mickey's heart, he never forgets to recommend me to new people. Yes, I'm his aunt, but you can call me Mama Cay, everyone does. So, you're wantin' a room?"

"Yes, ma'am."

Mama Cay put the sock down and walked over to the table. She opened the door to a nearby cabinet and brought out a book, then picked up a pen.

"And you would be?" she asked.

"Lucas Cain."

"And would you be a permanent resident or a temporary lodger?"

"Temporary," Lucas replied.

"How long?"

"I don't have any idea how long I'll stay."

Mama Cay chuckled. "Like a tumbleweed, huh?"

Lucas chuckled as well. "You might say that."

"You got any bags?"

"Just my panniers."

"That'll be five dollars a week, and you'll have to pay the first week in advance."

Lucas gave her a five-dollar bill.

Mama Cay made an entry in the book, then stood. "Come along, I'll show you your room."

Lucas followed her up the stairs.

"Your room has a window that looks out over the street. I hope you don't mind that."

"No, I think I'd like it."

There was a key already in the lock, and Mama Cay took it out and handed it to Lucas, then she opened the door. The room had a bed, a soft chair, a small table by the bed, and another by the chair. There was a dry sink on which sat pitcher and a large porcelain basin.

"There are two privies out back, one for men and one

for women, both of them marked. There's a bathing room at the end of the hall. It's used by both men and women, so be sure and lock the door when you use it."

She gave Lucas the room key. "Your board includes meals—breakfast is at seven, dinner at twelve, and supper at six."

"I probably won't take too many meals here," Lucas said.

"It's still five dollars a week whether you take your meals here or not. Any questions?"

"No, I think you've covered everything, thank you."

FOR THE NEXT few days Lucas wandered around the town, from the livery to the general store, the doctor to the apothecary, restaurants to saloons, learning the town, meeting people, and getting known.

Lucas was having breakfast in the dining room of the El Paso Hotel, when a familiar voice called out to him.

"Lucas Cain!"

"Jim! Jim Barnes!" Lucas said. "Wow, I haven't seen you in a coon's age. You were the one who helped me get Dan out when the *Sultana* sank."

"That was me," Jim said with a big smile, as he extended his hand.

"Have you had breakfast?"

"Just now."

"Why don't you take a seat and have a cup of coffee with me? Last time I ran across you, you were farming up in Kansas," Lucas said. "What brings you to Texas?"

"Well, I sold my farm, and got enough money to buy a ranch and a starter herd of cattle just a ways north of here. It ain't a big ranch. I don't run more 'n five hundred head. Only thing is, as of this morning, I've only got about three hundred head. I'm a thinkin' a couple of sons of bitches run off two hundred of my cows," Jim said as he ran his hand through his hair. "I come in to see the sheriff, but the deputy says he got called down on the Trinity this morning. He don't know when he'll be back."

"I can look into it for you," Lucas said.

"You'll look into it? Oh, wait, that's right, I almost forgot you're a bounty hunter now. But, Lucas, we better let the sheriff try, because I sure as hell can't afford to pay you to get my cows back."

"You already paid the bounty," Lucas said.

"What do you mean?"

"You helped me save Dan's life. Anyway, I'm not the ordinary bounty hunter. I'm also a deputy U.S. Marshal, and that means I can go anywhere I need to go. I'm not limited by county lines, but Sheriff Moore can't leave Tarrant County."

"Oh, damn, Lucas, if you could do that, I'd be way grateful."

"You said you think you know who did it?"

"I don't just think I know, I for sure know who did it. It was Farris Broome 'n Perry Edwards," Jim said.

"How are you so sure?"

"Because the two of 'em worked for me, and when I found out two hundred of my cows was gone, Broome and Edwards were gone, too."

"Could it be possible that they're trying to track down your cows?" Lucas asked.

"No, 'cause if they was goin' after 'em, they would've told me."

"What about your other hands? Wouldn't one of them have told you about it?"

"Broome and Edwards are the only two I had

working for me. They weren't that dependable, but they worked cheap. I guess you could say that I was a penny wise and a dollar foolish. I never had any thought they would do something like this, though," Jim said.

"All right, I'll see what I can find out," Lucas said. "I'll start this morning."

"I'd like to go with you, if you don't mind," Jim said.

"They're your cows. I'll be glad to have you come along."

The first place they went after Cain finished his breakfast was the Fort Worth Stockyard. There, they spoke to the purchasing agent.

"Two hundred head, you say? I can't say I've seen any cows with your brand coming through," Loomis Smithfield, the purchasing agent said.

"Have you got any idea where else they might sell these cows?" Lucas asked.

"I'd say Denton," Smithfield replied.

"Denton? I didn't know they had a purchasing agent there," Jim said.

"It's fairly new, just within the last few months or so."

"Mr. Smithfield, I thank you for seeing us this morning," Lucas said.

"Well, you're welcome, but I'm afraid I wasn't that much help to you."

"You told us where the cattle aren't, and if you're looking for something, that's always helpful. And you steered us to Denton."

"I wish you good luck in finding your cows, and Jim, you know your cows are always welcome here," Smithfield said.

"Assuming I can get 'em back," Jim said with a chuckle.

"So, we go to Denton now?" Jim asked, once they left

Smithfield's office.

"How far is Denton from your ranch?" Lucas asked.

"A little over forty miles, I'd say."

"More than likely, we won't have to go all the way to Denton. If they moved the cows sometime during the night, we'll catch up with them before they get there."

"What if Broome and Edwards don't want to give 'em up?" Jim asked.

"We'll deal with that problem when it comes up."

WITH THE STOLEN HERD:

"Ha!" Broome said. "See this sign?"

"Yeah, what about it?" Edwards asked.

"It says Roanoke that way." He pointed. "That means we're in Denton County and Sheriff Moore ain't got no jurisdiction up here. If Barnes told 'im we took his cows, whenever Moore starts after us, he'll have to stop right here."

"You know what we ought to do? We could just wait on the sheriff, and when we see him have to stop, we can just heckle 'im."

"Or, we could go on up to Denton, sell the cows, get the money, and get the hell out of here," Broome said.

Edwards laughed. "I say we do it your way."

"We'll get at least four thousand dollars for these here cows, maybe more," Broome suggested.

"What are you going to do with all that money?" Edwards asked.

"Hell, that's an easy question to answer. I'm goin' to move on up to Colorado, and spend ever' dollar on women and whiskey."

"IT'S PRETTY easy to follow them," Lucas said. "Unless there are two herds going from Tarrant County to Denton."

"Yeah, two hundred cows do leave a clear trail. Lucas, what are we going to do when we find them?"

"We're going to ask, real nice, that they bring the cows back."

"Real nice?"

"While we're pointing our guns at them."

"That'll work," Jim said, with a little chuckle.

It was just after noon when Lucas and Jim caught up with the herd. As they got closer, they saw that there were two riders behind the herd, moving from one side to the other to keep the cows moving.

"That's Broome and Edwards, all right. They haven't even seen us," Jim said.

"I'm sure they think they've gotten away with it. And seeing as they're your only two hands, they think they know for sure, that nobody from the ranch will be coming after them. And now that they're out of Tarrant County, they think Sheriff Moore and Deputy Campbell won't be comin' after them either," Lucas replied.

"How are we going to handle this?" Jim asked.

"You take the one on the right, I'll take the one on the left."

Lucas and Jim rode up behind the two men who hadn't bothered to look around. They were right on them, when Lucas spoke to them.

"You two men take out your guns and hand them to us, butt first," he said.

"What the hell!" Edwards shouted.

"Do what I told you, or get shot," Lucas said.

Edwards took out his pistol, and holding it by the barrel, handed it to Lucas, butt first. Broome did the same thing with his gun, handing it to Jim.

"Mr. Barnes, this here ain't nothin' a'tall what it's lookin' like. This mornin', me 'n Perry here seen that some cows were missin', 'n what we done was, we come out a-lookin' for 'em, 'n we just now found 'em. We was bringin' 'em back to you," Broome said.

"Oh, yeah, I can see that, seein' as you've got the herd going north, and the ranch is south," Jim said.

"How are we going to get these cows turned around?" Lucas asked.

"That's no problem. Before I had any hands working for me, I had over two hundred head. Whenever I would bring them into Fort Worth, I would do it all by myself. We'll just ride up on the right side and put a little pressure on the cows in the front. Do that, and they'll start drifting to the left. Just keep the pressure on 'em 'til they turn all the way around. Then we'll drop behind 'em, and push 'em on back to where they belong," Jim said. "But what are we goin' to do with Broome and Edwards?"

"I've got a pair of handcuffs. I'll handcuff them together," Lucas said as he opened his saddlebag. "That way they'll have to ride side by side, and if one of 'em decides to ride off, he'll have to drag the other one with him. I'll keep 'em in front of me while we're taking your cows back home."

Lucas cuffed the two men together, then watched them climb awkwardly into their saddles.

"All right boys, let get these cows movin'."

The frowns on the faces of Broome and Edwards made a sharp contrast with the grins of Lucas and Jim.

6

C arol Jean Barnes was cooking supper when her nine-year-old son, Ernie, came running into the house, yelling.

"Ma! Ma! Pa's back! He found the cows!"

Carol Jean went to check on what her son was telling her, and sure enough, there was Jim and the cows. She saw Broome and Edwards, but she also saw a man she thought she might know. She was surprised to see that Broome and Edwards appeared to be holding hands. She thought that odd, but when she looked closely, she saw that they were handcuffed together, and the man with Jim was guarding them.

Lucas waved his gun at the two prisoners. "Get down. I'll take the cuffs off, and you can go one at a time to the privy."

"I'm first," Broome said, once he was free.

Lucas stepped back from them but kept his pistol in his hand.

"Pa, Pa, you found the cattle!" Ernie said, running out

to meet him. As he did so, he ran between Lucas and Edwards.

"Ernie, get back!" Jim called.

Jim's warning was too late. From somewhere, Edwards produced a derringer. He put one arm around Ernie's neck, and in the other hand, held a pistol to Ernie's head.

"Where'd you get that pistol?" Jim asked.

"You shoulda checked my saddlebag. I was just lookin' for the chance to use it, and this boy here just gave it to me. Now, both of you, drop your guns by the time I count to three."

"You do realize, don't you, that if you kill the boy, I'll kill you," Lucas said.

Edwards grinned an evil grin. "Yeah, but I don't think you're goin' to let this boy be killed."

"Ernie!" Carol Jean called, her voice reflecting the terror she felt at seeing a gun pointed to her son's head.

"I'm goin' to commence a-countin' now. One—two —"

Edwards's counting was interrupted by the sound of a gunshot. Carol Jean screamed, thinking her son had been shot, but the one that went down was Edwards, with blood spewing from the hole where his right eye had been.

Broome was returning from the privy at that moment, and Lucas turned his still-smoking gun toward him. Broome threw his hands up in the air.

"No, no, don't shoot! I ain't a-goin' to do nothin'."

Carol Jean ran out to wrap her arms around Ernie, and pull him to her.

"Oh, Ernie, you were so foolish to do that."

"I'm sorry, Ma, I was just happy to see Pa. I won't ever do nothin' like that again."

Jim chuckled. "Son, I hope you don't ever have the opportunity to do anything like that again." He walked over and put his arms around his son and his wife.

"Carol Jean, this is Lucas Cain. You remember him, don't you? He stopped by our farm up in Kansas."

"I thought I recognized him. He was on the *Sultana* with you."

"Yes, he was. He also helped me find the herd."

"And he saved our boy's life," Carol Jean added. "There's no doubt in my mind, but that Edwards would have killed Ernie."

Jim nodded. "I think you're right." Jim turned toward Lucas who, while listening to them, was keeping vigil over Broome. "Lucas, come have dinner with us."

"Jim, you don't plan on having…him come in, do you?" Carol Jean asked.

"Of course I do. Like you said, he saved Ernie's life."

"No, I'm not talking about Mr. Cain. I mean," she said, pointing, "Broome."

"Broome doesn't have to come in," Lucas said. "I've got enough rope to tie him to a tree for six months, if I have to. And if the invitation is open, I'd love to have dinner with you."

AFTER A FRIENDLY DINNER, Lucas took a piece of the roast beef, and a couple of slices of bread out to Broome. "Thought you might be hungry," he said. He untied Broome's hands.

"What about untying me from the tree?" Broome asked.

"I will when we're ready to go."

"Where are you taking me?"

"To jail, of course."

"You can't take me to jail, you ain't the sheriff."

"No, but I'm a deputy U.S. marshal," Lucas said with a smile.

While Broome was eating, Jim helped Lucas drape Edwards across his saddle. Then Lucas untied Broome and put a loop around Broome's neck.

"What the hell? You ain't plannin' on hangin' me, are you?" Broome asked in a frightened voice.

"Not unless you try to ride away from me, then you'll hang yourself. Now, get mounted."

"Those are my horses, by the way," Jim said.

"I thought they probably were," Lucas said. "I'll bring them back to you."

"Actually, that won't be necessary, I'll bring them back myself. I think I should go into town so I can swear out a charge against the two of them for cattle rustling."

"That's a good idea, and you can also back me up on how I came to shoot Edwards."

"I'll do that," Jim promised.

LATER THOSE CITIZENS of Fort Worth who happened to be outside, were witness to a strange parade riding down the street. There were four horses in column. The rider of the first horse had a rope around his neck. The rider of the second horse was holding on to the end of that rope. The rider of the third horse was holding a lead to the fourth horse. That horse had no rider, but it did have a body draped across the saddle.

Sheriff Moore and Deputy Campbell had already gone home for the night, but Deputy Morgan, who as the jailer and had a room at the jail, was there.

"What have we here?" Morgan asked, when he saw the three men coming in. He recognized Broome and Jim Barnes, but he didn't know the third man. That man was holding his gun level against Broome.

"Burt, Broome here, and Edwards outside, stole two hundred head of my cattle. Marshal Cain helped me recover them."

"You say Edwards is outside?"

"Yeah, he's lyin' belly down across his saddle. We'll be takin' him to the coroner."

"All right, I'll put Broome in a cell while you take care of Edwards. I'll get Sheriff Moore and meet you back here."

An hour later, with all their business with the sheriff taken care of, Jim went back home and Lucas stepped into the Cattle Drive Saloon. This was his first visit to the saloon, so he had a good look around to check it out. The bar was well furnished, four hand towels hung from polished brass towel rings, whiskey bottles sat on a glass shelf, their number doubled by the reflection in the mirror.

Lucas ordered a beer, and when it was set before him, he picked up the mug, then blew some of the white head off the golden liquid, before turning his back to the bar to examine the room. Nearly all the tables were full, the customer base of cowboys and merchants, being served by half a dozen attractive young women in revealing dresses.

It had been a tiring day, so after a nightcap of a single beer, Lucas went back to his room at Mama Cay's. He went to sleep quickly and slept soundly for the night.

LUCAS HAD THOUGHT there would be no reward for Broome and Edwards, so he was pleasantly surprised the next morning, to learn that the Tarrant County Cattlemen's Association had a standing policy of rewarding two hundred dollars to anyone who could locate and return stolen cattle.

Lucas accepted the reward, then rode back out to Jim's ranch. He was met at the door by Ernie.

"Mr. Cain!" Ernie said excitedly. "You saved my life. That was a really good shot!"

"Yeah, I'm sorry about that. I didn't mean to shoot— the gun just went off."

"What?" Ernie replied with a look of shock on his face.

Lucas laughed. "I'm just teasing you, Ernie. There's no way I was going to let Edwards hurt you. Is your pa here?"

Ernie turned his head and shouted. "Pa, Mr. Cain is here! He wants to see you."

"Well show him in," Jim said.

Lucas followed the young man into the house, where he was met by a smiling Jim Barnes.

"Lucas! What brings you out here? Oh, I know. It's Carol Jean's cooking, isn't it?"

Lucas laughed. "Well, your wife is a damn good cook, but it's something else that brought me out."

"Oh?" Jim asked with a look of confusion on his face.

"Here, this is for you," Lucas said, handing Jim five twenty-dollar bills.

"What? What's this?"

"It turns out that the Cattlemen's Association has a standing policy of rewarding two hundred dollars to anyone who recovers stolen cattle. Here's your half."

"Oh, don't be silly, Lucas. It was my cattle we recovered."

"No, you were with me, so half the money is yours. Don't tell me you can't use it. You either take it, or I'll give it to the next drunk I see."

Jim laughed. "All right, I'll take it if you'll have dinner with us."

"I was hoping you'd invite me," Lucas replied with a broad smile.

SOMEWHERE IN WISE COUNTY, TEXAS

Harley Mack Crawford was a big man—six foot, three inches tall. He was over two hundred pounds, and most of it was muscle. Crawford and a man named Jerry Seabaugh had stolen twenty cows and were now using a running iron to alter the brands.

"How much you reckon we'll get for these cows?" Seabaugh asked.

"Won't make any difference to you, you won't be gettin' none of it," Crawford replied.

Seabaugh looked up from his task at hand. "What the hell do you mean I won't be gettin' none of it? I took as big a chance as you did."

"Yes, but you owe me five hunnert dollars, 'n we'll likely only get around seven hunnert dollars for the cows. We ain't likely to get no more 'n that, so I'll take it all, then I'll say you don't owe me no more, which is a good deal for you 'cause if you think about it, that means I'm givin' up my share."

"Are you talkin' 'bout that poker game we was

playin'? We was just playin' for fun, there warn't no actual money been bet."

"It was real for me, and you owe me five hunnert dollars," Crawford insisted.

"The hell I do!" Seabaugh shouted, and he shoved the gleaming red hot branding iron into Crawford's face, twisting it as he did so.

Crawford yelled in pain and covered his face with his hands.

"I guess that'll learn ya!" Seabaugh shouted while cackling in glee.

Though the pain in his face was almost unbearable, Crawford pulled his pistol, pointed it at Seabaugh, and shot him in the face. Seabaugh was dead before he hit the ground.

BACK IN FORT WORTH, Lucas stepped into the Cattle Drive Saloon. He spent a lot of time in saloons, even though he was a moderate drinker. The purpose of his frequent visits was because saloons were a great source of information. Most of the time he didn't even have to ask questions, all he had to do was sit there, nurse his beer, and listen in on the conversations. Those conversations would often make him aware of any recent criminal activity that had taken place, and sometimes they would even name the perpetrator, and provide information as to where he might be found.

Today, however, his saloon visit consisted of one beer, which he drank slowly as he enjoyed a conversation with one of the bar girls, Lucas having just bought her a drink.

The girl's name was Larue, and she was a pretty

thing, but Lucas couldn't help but think she would be even more attractive in normal street clothes.

Lucas put a dollar on the table.

"You want me to get us another drink?" Larue asked.

"No, that's for you," Lucas said as he stood. "I have to go."

Larue's smile was genuine, not the pasted-on smile of her chosen profession. "Why, thank you, honey. That is sweet of you."

7

WITH HARLEY MACK CRAWFORD:

There were two reasons why everyone was staring at Harley Mack Crawford when he rode into Wayland with Seabaugh. One was the terrible looking, puffed up, red-and-blue scar on his left cheek, and the other was the body thrown across the saddle of the horse trailing behind the rider.

Crawford stopped in front of the sheriff's office, then went inside.

"Sheriff, how do I get the money for an outlaw that has a bounty on him?"

The sheriff chuckled. "Well, the first thing you do, is you bring in the outlaw."

"I already done that. He's belly down over the horse outside."

"Who is it?"

"It's Jerry Seabaugh. There's a reward out for him, 'n for Harley Mack Crawford. I almost had 'em both, but Crawford got away."

The sheriff followed Crawford out to the front of his office. The body draped across the horse had drawn many of the town's citizens.

"How will I know it's Jerry Seabaugh?" the sheriff asked.

"It's Seabaugh all right, Sheriff," one of the citizens of the town said. "Take a look at his left hand. His little finger is missing."

"Yeah, that's right. That is one of the distinguishing features, isn't it? All right, Mr. uh, I didn't get your name," the sheriff said.

"It's Kincaid. Adam Kincaid," Crawford said.

"Well, Mr. Kincaid, follow me to the bank, and we'll pay the reward. I believe it's for five hundred dollars."

"Yeah, and the reward for Crawford is seven hundred and fifty. I'm sorry he got away."

Crawford turned to the man who had validated the corpse as Jerry Seabaugh.

"Come to the bank with us, then we'll go to the saloon and I'll buy you a drink," Crawford invited.

"Sounds good to me," the citizen said.

Half an hour later, with five hundred dollars in his pocket, Crawford and the citizen, who identified himself as Rosco Kingsly, were having a drink. They were approached a few times by some of the girls who were plying their trade, but as soon as they saw the terrible scar on Crawford's face, they turned away.

"I'm curious, how did you know that was Seabaugh?"

"Because the son of a bitch used to work for me. The reason he didn't have a little finger, is because I shot it off."

Crawford chuckled. "Why did you do that?"

"I own the leather goods store here, and I don't take my money to the bank but ever' few days. One time when I was home tallying up my receipts, Seabaugh was watchin' me. All too close if you ask me. I shot at him, hit him in the hand, then sent him on his way. That was two years ago, and I never saw him again, before today."

"You keep your money at home?"

"It's not because I want to, but my wife keeps the books for us. She don't like coming to the shop, and I do whatever she says."

"Yeah, I can see that," Crawford said.

Kingsly glanced up at the clock. "Damn, it's near suppertime. I'd better get home, or Mable will take a frying pan to me." He laughed and Crawford joined him in the laughter.

"Say, here's an idea. Why don't you come have supper with us? I've got two reasons for that. One is that you can be my excuse for being late, and that'll keep Mable from goin' after me. And the other is she cooks so damn much that we have leftovers for three days. And as good a cook as she is, I don't look forward to three days of leftovers."

Crawford laughed. "Sure, I'd be glad to come, if your wife doesn't take one look at this face, and throw me out."

"I've been wondering about that. How did you get that nasty scar? However you got it, it had to hurt."

Crawford put his hand to the scar. "It still hurts. Seabaugh give it to me. I caught him using a runnin' iron to change the brand on some cows what he had stoled. I'd planned on taking him in alive until that happened. I had no choice but to shoot 'im. He was goin' after my eyes."

"I don't think a soul would question you, or find fault with that," Kingsly said.

Crawford followed Kingsly home.

"She'll prob'ly be in the dining room workin' on the books. Like as not, she's got money spread out all over the table."

Crawford followed Kingsly into the dining room. There was a short, not particularly attractive woman sitting at the table, posting numbers in a book. She looked up as Kingsly and Crawford came into the room. Putting her finger on the nose bridge of her glasses, she pushed them up.

"Who's this?" Mable asked.

"This is Mr. Kincaid. He brought Jerry Seabaugh in to the sheriff, today, so I invited him to have supper with us."

"Supper's ready, I'll just have to clear the table," Mabel said.

"That won't be necessary," Crawford said. "I'll eat after."

"You'll eat after what?" Kingsly asked.

"After this," Crawford said. He pulled his gun and shot Kingsly right between the eyes.

Mable observed the slaughter of her husband in shocked silence. When Crawford turned the gun on her, it was almost welcomed. She didn't want to live without Rosco.

When Crawford saw the look in Mabel's eyes, he almost withheld the shot, but he knew it would be illogical to stop now.

He pulled the trigger, and Mable fell forward onto the table.

Crawford gathered up all the money from the table and counted it. It came to two hundred twelve dollars and thirty-five cents.

Crawford chuckled. He had come into town with eight dollars. He would be leaving town with over five hundred dollars. And with the food Mable had already prepared, he didn't even have to spend the thirty-five cents on supper.

FORT WORTH—THREE WEEKS LATER

Leaving the saloon, Lucas walked down to the sheriff's office to check the reward posters, and to see if there had been any recent criminal activity within the area.

Sheriff Moore was reading the paper, and when he saw Lucas, he smiled. "Here's some good news for our fair city," he said. He handed the paper to Lucas. "Take a look."

Good News for Fort Worth

On the 8th instant, William Kirby, Mason Poppell, and Woodrow Knox, leading businessmen of Fort Worth, were dispatched to Eastland by the Fort Worth Board of Trade, to invite the owners of the Eastland County Cottonseed Oil Mill, to consider expanding their operation to Fort Worth.

Word has come by telegraph, of the success of their mission. It is the pleasant responsibility of the Democrat Gazette *to report the success of this endeavor. Because of the effort of these gentlemen, Fort Worth will soon have a cotton-seed oil mill.*

"That's really good news for the city," Sheriff Moore said.

"Yeah, I can see how it would be," Lucas replied.

"I tell you what, why don't we have a drink to celebrate? My treat," Sheriff Moore invited.

"No need for you to be buying it," Lucas said. "I'm happy enough just to have a drink with a friend."

"Now, damnit, that wasn't the answer I wanted," Sheriff Moore said.

Lucas looked confused. "What? You invited me to join you for a drink and I accepted."

"You do remember me offering to buy your drink, don't you?"

"Yes, and I turned it down."

"See, there you go," Sheriff Moore said, pointing his finger at Lucas. "That's what I'm talking about. You shouldn't have just turned it down; you should have offered to buy me a drink."

Lucas laughed. "Here's an idea for you," Lucas said. "Why don't I buy you a drink?"

"Oh, you don't have to do that."

"Sheriff, you are the beatin'est thing," Lucas said. "You just said that I…"

"All right, if you insist," Moore said, interrupting Lucas in midcomment.

Lucas laughed.

Since the main reason to go to the saloon was to visit with others, Lucas and Sheriff Moore stood at the bar, holding their beer as they exchanged greetings.

"Did you hear what happened in Wayland?" one of the customers asked.

"No, what happened there?" Sheriff Moore asked.

"There was this feller named Kingsly. Him 'n his wife was shot dead."

"Where did this happen?" Moore asked.

"I told you; it was in Wayland."

"No, I mean where in Wayland?"

"Oh, it was at Kingsly's house."

"Do they know who did it?" Lucas asked.

"No, they don't have the slightest idea who done it."

"Too bad they don't know who killed that family," Sheriff Moore said to Lucas as they were walking back to the sheriff's office. "I've got a feeling that if you knew who it was, you'd be on him like a duck on a June bug."

"I've got a feeling we'll find out," Lucas said. "And when we do, you're right, I will go after him."

THE SUBJECT of Lucas and the sheriff's conversation, Harley Mack Crawford, was in the Cactus Saloon in Eastland, Texas, when he overheard some of the others talking.

"Three of 'em there, are businessmen from Fort Worth."

"What are a bunch of muckety-mucks from Fort Worth doing here in Eastland, anyway?" one of the men asked. "Fort Worth is a lot bigger than we are."

"Ah, but we have something they don't have."

"What's that?"

"Why, the cottonseed oil mill, of course. Fort Worth wants Gillespie to put one in over in Fort Worth."

"Who is it that's over here?"

"William Kirby, Mason Poppell, and Woodrow Knox. They're 'bout the richest people in Fort Worth, and you better believe they brought a lot of money with 'em."

"Yeah, well if they get the mill, they'll be taking a lot of money back with 'em."

After leaving the Cactus Saloon, Crawford looked up Cole Rogers and Gene Hanson, two of his acquaintances, to pitch an idea to them.

"Damn, Crawford, what the hell happened to your face?" Hanson asked.

"Seabaugh stuck a brandin' iron in my face," Crawford answered.

"What the hell did he do that for?" Hanson asked.

"Let's just say that we had a difference of opinion," Crawford said.

"Yeah, well did you stick it back in his face?"

"No, I shot 'im."

"Did you kill 'im?"

"That's what happens to the people I shoot."

Rogers chuckled. "Remind me never to piss you off."

"Yeah, that might not be a good idea," Hanson said. "So, what do you have in mind for these Fort Worth businessmen?"

Crawford smiled. "We're goin' to take a train trip."

"I ain't got money for a ticket," Hanson said.

"I'll buy the tickets."

8

F ort Worth was in a celebratory mood. A banner was stretched across the street.

WELCOME FORT WORTH COTTONSEED OIL MILL

Similar signs decorated the windows of all the stores and businesses, and the atmosphere was almost like it would have been if a circus had come to town. Happy people were wandering up and down the street, greeting each other effusively, taking advantage of the free lemonade and sandwich stands that had been put up along the street.

The children were the most effusive of all, and they ran from one storefront to the other, totally beyond the control of their frazzled parents.

"When will Bill Kirby and the others get here?" Earl Volker, of Volker's Jewelry Store asked.

"They'll be comin' in on the three o'clock train," Al Sikes said.

"I hope the town settles down then. I don't like all

this commotion. Not only is it bad for business, I'm always afraid somebody will take advantage of all the commotion to run in here, smash the glass, grab some jewelry, and disappear in the crowd."

"You don't have to worry about that while I'm here," Deputy Ray Campbell said with a sense of self-importance.

"I'm going to count on that, Ray," Volker said.

EASTLAND, TEXAS

During the week they spent in Eastland, the three Fort Worth businessmen made quite an impression spending money like it was water. Now, it was Saturday morning, and the three men, clutching success, were ready to go back to Fort Worth.

"Mason, would you come on, for crying out loud?" Knox asked. "You know damn well everyone back in Fort Worth is waiting for us, and I don't want to miss the train."

"Don't you worry about me, Woodrow," Poppell replied. "I just have to get something for Donnie. He thinks every time I leave town, that I'll bring something home to him."

Kirby laughed. "Well, don't you buy him something every time you leave the house?"

"Yeah," Poppell replied with a guilty laugh. "Here, this pocketknife will do. His mother won't like it, but I'm sure Donnie will."

When the three businessmen walked down to the depot for the one-hundred-mile ride back to Fort Worth, they were met by a reporter for the *Eastland*

Journal. The attractive woman wanted to know all about their time in Eastland, particularly their thoughts about the town.

Several of the townspeople were gathered around them, feeling privileged for being present to hear the interview.

"Carolina's put in the paper how Gillespie made 'em squirm," one of the men called out.

"Don't you be tellin' Miss McKay how to do her job," one of the others said. "She's near 'bout the best reporter in the whole state of Texas, 'n she don't need you to be tellin' her nothin'."

"That's them over there," Crawford said, pointing to the Fort Worth businessmen, and the dozen or so people gathered around them.

"You're sure they've got money?" Rogers asked.

"Yeah, I'm sure. I seen it in the paper. They're takin' money back to Fort Worth so's they can put it in the bank and that way the cottonseed oil mill will have 'em a bank account."

Crawford watched which car the three businessmen boarded, then he, Rogers, and Hanson took the same one. They sat in the back of the car keeping an eye on the three men who were sitting in front. The train left the station with a jerking start which quickly smoothed out. By the time they left the city limits of Eastland, the train was picking up speed, and within a few minutes it was out in the open country, traveling at a speed of forty miles per hour.

CEPHUS MCKAY, owner and publisher of the *Eastland Journal*, took the first copy from the press and read the story.

Cottonseed Oil Mill to Expand to Fort Worth

William B. Gillespie announced today that negotiations have been successfully completed for a second cottonseed oil mill to be built in Fort Worth. William Kirby, Mason Poppell, and Woodrow Knox were the esteemed businessmen representing Fort Worth in the business arrangement.

The new cottonseed oil mill will have its manager and employees from Fort Worth, but it will be owned by William Gillespie, so that indirectly, Eastland will benefit by the expansion of the mill.

Satisfied with the content and setting of the story, McKay continued the print run.

"Papa, Mama wants to know when you'll be home for supper," Maggie McKay asked, as the twelve-year-old came into the shop.

"As soon as I get this press run finished. It won't be any later than six o'clock."

"Can I help?"

"No, Maggie, that won't be necessary, you just tell your mama when I'll be home."

"You always let Carolina help," Maggie said. "She's the one that writes all the stories."

"Carolina is older than you. Besides, you help. You help a lot."

"I'll just be glad when you let me do everything she does."

Cephus chuckled. "It seems to me, like you and your sister are trying to put me out of a job."

As the train sped toward Fort Worth, Harley Mack Crawford thought about how they were going to do this. The train would have to cross the Brazos River before it reached Fort Worth, and there was a stagecoach way station there. And because the way station was part of Crawford's plan, they would have to get the money before they reached the river.

"When are we goin' to do it?" Rogers asked.

"We'll keep an eye on 'em to see when we get a chance to make our move," Crawford said.

"What about the others in the car?"

"When they see our guns, they'll be too scared to do anything. Look at 'em. Three women, seven kids, and an old man who has to be eighty years old."

"But there's two more back there, and they look like cowboys," Hanson said.

"Yeah, but we'll have our guns in our hands, they won't," Crawford said.

"Gentlemen, I have an idea," Kirby said to the other two who had made the trip to Eastland with him.

"All right, Bill, you've got our attention," Poppell said.

"Yeah," Knox said. "What is this great idea?"

"The mayor's office," Kirby replied.

"The mayor's office?" Knox said. "What about it?"

"Getting this cottonseed oil mill for the city is a big thing. Everyone in town is going to know our names. Any one of us could run for mayor and be elected."

"Yes, but which one of us?" Poppell asked.

"We can draw straws or something," Kirby said. "It

doesn't make any difference which one of us it is. We can all three benefit from it."

Knox nodded his head. "A good idea."

"I like the idea, but I don't want it to be me. I'll work to get whichever one of you runs, elected," Poppell said.

"You sure about that, Mason?" Kirby asked.

"Yes, I just want the benefits of one of us being mayor. I don't think I'd much like the work that goes with the position," Poppell said, with a quiet laugh.

"You know what, Bill, it was your idea, so you run," Knox said. "Mason and I will support you."

"You two are sure about that?"

"Yeah," Poppell said. He smiled. "And then, in after a couple of years of being mayor, you'll be ready to run for governor."

"Governor?" Kirby asked.

"William Ross Kirby, governor of Texas. How does that sound?"

A big smile spread across Kirby's face. "Gentlemen, this calls for a drink. Let's adjourn to the parlor car."

"*Adjourn* to the parlor car. Listen to him, Woodrow. He's already talking like a governor."

The three men laughed as they got out of their seats and started forward.

"THIS IS WORKIN'" out real good," Crawford said. "We're almost to the river, 'n it looks like them three are goin' into the parlor car. That means we won't have to do nothin' in front of any of the passengers."

Crawford, Rogers, and Hanson waited for a minute, then they got up to follow the three businessmen.

WILLIAM KIRBY, Woodrow Knox, and Mason Poppell ordered drinks, then Kirby turned toward the other two and lifted his glass. "To our success, gentlemen, with the sure and certain knowledge that no other three men from Fort Worth would have been able to accomplish what we just did."

"And to the next mayor of Fort Worth," Poppell added.

"Here, here," Knox said.

The three men lifted their drinks.

"Should we throw the three glasses down so that no lesser toast could ever be drunk from them?" Knox asked, with a broad smile.

"Oh, I think not," Poppell said. "I'm afraid they'd kick us off the train, then we'd have to walk all the way back to Fort Worth."

Crawford, Rogers, and Hanson came into the parlor car, just as Kirby and the other two lowered their glasses. Kirby saw the three men enter the car.

"Gentlemen," Kirby said, greeting them with a great smile. "My name is Bill Kirby, these two gentlemen are Woodrow Knox and Mason Poppell. And you would be?"

"Crawford is the name. This is Hanson and Rogers."

"Well, Mr. Crawford, Mr. Hanson, and Mr. Rogers, step up to the bar and have a drink, on us. We're celebrating."

"What are you celebrating?" Crawford asked.

"We're celebrating getting a cottonseed oil mill for Fort Worth."

"And, getting Mr. Kirby, here, elected to the office of mayor of Fort Worth," Knox added.

"Are you gentlemen from our city?" Poppell asked. "If

you are, you will be the first ones we will ask for your vote for William Kirby."

"We ain't from Fort Worth, but we got us somethin' to celebrate, too," Crawford said.

"Oh? What's that? Tell us, and we'll celebrate with you," Kirby invited.

"We're celebrating you three gentlemen giving us all your money."

"What?"

Crawford, Rogers, and Hanson pulled their pistols. "Empty your wallets there on the bar."

"Here, what is this?" the bartender demanded.

Crawford turned his pistol toward the bartender and shot him. Then he turned his attention back to the three businessmen. "That should show you that we mean business. So I'm going to ask you just one more time to empty your wallets on the bar. Do it now."

With shaking hands, Kirby, Poppell, and Knox did as they were directed.

"Rogers, you and Hanson, keep your guns on them while I gather up the money," Crawford ordered.

"What the hell, now they know our names," Rogers said.

"It won't matter," Crawford said.

"What do you mean, it won't matter?"

Crawford turned back toward the three businessmen. "Because there won't any of 'em be left alive to tell."

Crawford shot one of the businessmen, Rogers and Hanson shot the other two.

Crawford looked at three men lying on the floor, then he, Rogers, and Hanson left the parlor car, but didn't enter the following car. Instead, they remained on the vestibule.

"How much longer?" Hanson asked.

"It shouldn't be much longer. The train will slow down before getting on the bridge to cross the river," Crawford replied. "Then it won't be going any faster than a walk. We can get off real easy then."

MASON POPPELL WAS LYING on the floor with the other two. "Bill, Woodrow, are either one of you alive?"

Poppell didn't get an answer, so when he scooted across the floor to examine them, he learned that both were dead.

"Bartender? Bartender? You alive?"

"Yes," a weak voice replied.

"Hang on, we're going to have to tell the authorities what happened," Poppell said.

"I'll try," the bartender said.

STANDING on the vestibule with the other two, Harley Mack Crawford grabbed hold of the post that supported the overhanging extension of the car. Thus secured, he was able to lean out, and get a good look ahead. He saw the copse of trees and knew the stagecoach way station was just on the other side.

"Get ready, boys, here it comes," Crawford said.

As Crawford knew it would, the train slowed, and the three men hopped down, doing it so easily that they remained standing. They stepped out into the trees so as not to be easily seen by anyone in the train as it passed them by.

"How much did we get?" Rogers asked.

"I ain't counted it yet," Crawford said.

"Well, count it, I'd like to know, too," Hanson said.

Crawford counted the money, his smile growing broader the longer he counted. "Boys," he said. "What we got here is three thousand, one hunnert 'n twenty-one dollars."

"Damn, I don't think I've never even seen that much money," Rogers said, his smile matching that of Harley Mack Crawford.

"You think we'll be able to catch the stagecoach here?" Hanson asked.

"We damn well better be," Crawford said. "Come on, let's go catch the coach and get outta here."

It was less than half a mile to the stagecoach way station. There, three people were waiting for the next coach: two men and a woman. Crawford and the other two had no problem with getting a ticket.

9

O n board the train, Sidney Cowell, the conductor, was walking through all the cars, informing the passengers of the upcoming stop.

"Fort Worth in ten minutes, folks," he said repeatedly as he passed through the cars.

"How long will we be there before we go on to Dallas?" a woman passenger asked.

"We'll be in Fort Worth for half an hour, and we'll be in Dallas no more'n a hour later."

The conductor passed through all the cars. "Fort Worth in ten minutes," he continued to call.

Cowell saw that the three businessmen hadn't returned to their seats from their visit to the parlor car, and he was aware they would be getting off in Fort Worth, so he decided to step in to let them know. He knew that they had negotiated some sort of business deal that they were pleased with, and he suspected that they might have gotten a little drunk from celebrating too much. He didn't want them to be so distracted that they would miss their stop.

Opening the door, he stepped inside.

"All right folks, we'll be…" Cowell stopped in midsentence, shocked by the scene before him. The three businessmen were lying on the floor. At first he thought they may have passed out drunk, then he saw blood on the floor.

"Good Lord, what happened here? Turner, are you here?" he called to the bartender.

"Help." The call was weak, but Cowell heard it, and he hurried around to see Turner lying on the floor behind the bar.

"Turner, what happened?"

"There were three of 'em," Turner said. "Crawford and Hanson. I don't remember the other name. Check on the others. One of them is still alive."

Cowell returned to the front of the bar to check on the three who were on the floor.

"Not anymore, Dale," he called back to the bartender. "All three of 'em are dead."

LATER THAT SAME DAY, Lucas decided to return to the sheriff's office just to visit for a while. The sheriff wasn't there, but Deputy Campbell was.

"How's Broome doing? Is he giving you any trouble?"

"No, it seems like all he's doing is sleeping," Campbell said.

"Have they set a court date for his trial yet?"

"Not that I know of."

"Well, I'll sure be there to testify, and I know that Jim…"

The door opened then, and Sheriff Moore came into the office, interrupting the conversation. "Cain, good,

I'm glad I found you here. You might want to get down to the depot."

"The depot? What are you saying, Sheriff? Are you suggesting I should leave town on the next train?" Lucas asked with a chuckle.

"You know the article you read about Kirby, Poppell, and Knox saying that they were getting a cottonseed oil mill to come into town?"

"Yeah, it seems like just about everyone in town is talking about it."

"They're dead. All three of 'em."

"How? What happened?"

"They were coming back by train, and somebody that was on the train robbed and killed 'em. I've ordered the train be delayed so we can talk to all the passengers. I'd appreciate it, if you'd come down to the depot with me so you could help us out."

"I will," Lucas said as he joined the sheriff.

The train, which should have left the Fort Worth station fifteen minutes earlier, was still sitting on the track in front of the depot. Because the fireman had to keep the steam pressure up, the steam had to be vented. There was almost a rhythmic pattern to the gushing sounds that permeated the depot area.

The train had been emptied of passengers, and now almost a hundred people were standing around in groups, or else sitting where they could find a place. Sheriff Moore and Deputy Campbell began interviewing the passengers, one at a time.

"Has anyone spoken with the conductor yet?" Lucas asked.

"No, not yet," Sheriff Moore said. "Why don't you start with Sidney Cowell? I saw him inside the depot."

"All right, I will."

Lucas found the conductor sitting on a bench in the depot. He had a mustache and was wearing glasses. His conductor uniform was tailored to his thin body.

"Mr. Cowell, I'm Marshal Cain. I'd like to talk to you, if you don't mind."

"No, I don't mind, but I've already talked to Mr. Dorsey, the station manager."

"I know, but if he and I hear the same story, we may each have a different perspective. That helps us to see the whole picture, so start from the beginning."

"Well, Mr. Kirby, Mr. Poppell, and Mr. Knox were excited because they had done some big business deal. They were talking about how much money it was going to bring to Fort Worth. And from the way they were talkin', there wasn't a soul on the car that didn't know about it."

"They were probably carrying on too much about it, and that most likely is what put it in Crawford and Hanson's mind to kill 'em and take what money was on 'em."

"Crawford and Hanson? They're the killers?"

"Yes, and there's one more, but Turner couldn't remember his name."

"Who's Turner? Is he out here?"

"Turner's the bartender in the parlor car and he's not here now because he got shot too. He's down at the doctor's office."

"How badly was he wounded?"

"It's pretty bad, I would say, but the doctor thinks Dale will probably pull through it."

"The two men you said were the killers—do you remember seeing them on the train? Can you describe what they looked like?"

"Oh, yeah, I remember seeing 'em on the train. After

the three businessmen went into the parlor car, Craw-ford and Hanson followed right behind them. But, as I said, there were actually three of them, it's just that Dale could only remember two names. I can pretty much tell you what all three of them looked like. Only thing is, I won't be able to put a name to a description, because I don't know who is who."

"All right then, just give me what you've got."

"One of them was a big man, your size, or maybe even a little bigger. The other two were smaller. The biggest of the three men had what looked like a burn scar on his cheek, it was an ugly thing, all puffed up about the size of the palm of your hand. The third one didn't have any tag in particular I could tell you about. If you talk to Dale, though, he might be able to tell you a little more."

"Thanks, Mr. Cowell. You've been a big help."

LEAVING THE DEPOT, Lucas walked down to the doctor's office. The door to the surgery room was open, and Lucas looked in. The doctor was looking down at the man on the table.

"Hello, Doc, I'm Marshal Lucas Cain, working on the train robbery case. Would it be all right if I talked to your patient?"

"He's pretty groggy, but you might get something from him," the doctor said.

"Thanks."

When Lucas went into the back room of the doctor's office, he saw the patient lying on the operating table.

"Mr. Turner, can you talk to me?"

"A little bit, I guess."

"Mr. Cowell said you saw the men who did this."

"Yes, I saw 'em, 'n I heard their names, too."

"The conductor said you could remember only two names."

"That's what I told him, but while the doc's been workin' on me, the third name come to me. It's Rogers. Crawford, Hanson, and Rogers. And Crawford's got a real bad mark on his face."

"You've been a big help, Mr. Turner."

LATER THAT DAY, all the passengers had reboarded the train and were underway once more. Some were disgruntled over the delay, but most of the rest looked upon the whole incident as necessary.

After leaving Dale Turner, Lucas returned to the sheriff's office.

"The names of the three men who did this were Crawford, Hanson, and Rogers. Turner didn't get any first names, but the one with the scar everyone remembered is Crawford."

"That would, more 'n likely be Harley Mack Crawford," Sheriff Moore said. "But we don't have any information on him that says anything about a scar."

"The way the conductor described the scar, it was more than likely a recent burn."

"That's probably true. I better get the word out so the dodgers on Crawford can be updated."

Leaving the sheriff's office, Lucas returned to the depot, to talk to the station manager.

"We've got all three names now," Lucas said. "But none of them got off here. The conductor said that the last time he saw them, was shortly before they reached the Brazos River. The train doesn't stop there, does it?"

"No, this was a through train, nonstop from Eastland to Fort Worth."

"Eastland?"

"Yes. Actually, one of the lady passengers said she saw them get on the train in Eastland. She remembered it, because one of the men had a badly scarred face."

"Then that's a good place to start. When is the next train for Eastland?"

"That would be nine o'clock tomorrow morning."

"Will it have a stock car for my horse?"

"If it doesn't, I'll put one on for you," Dorsey said.

"Good, you do that. I'll be buying a ticket to Eastland. How much for my horse?"

"I won't charge you or your horse," Dorsey said. "Your work will benefit the railroad."

10

Harley Mack Crawford, Cole Rogers, and Gene Hanson were camped on the Brazos River.

"One hundred and twenty-one dollars," Crawford said. "That's all the hell we got."

"I thought you said we had three thousand, one hunnert 'n twenty-one dollars," Rogers said.

"I thought we could cash the bank draft, but it's made out to the cottonseed oil mill account," Crawford said. "That ain't somethin' we can use. For us, it's only good for startin' a fire."

"Hell, if we divide what we got, it ain't no different from a cowboy's wages," Hanson said. "I thought you said we was goin' to make some money."

"Yeah," Rogers said.

"Don't worry about it," Crawford said.

"What do you mean, don't worry about it?" Hanson asked.

Crawford smiled. "Bank drafts ain't the only way you can get money from a bank."

WITH CHARLEY TWO safely in his own stock car, Lucas boarded the last in the line of passenger cars, choosing it because it was the closest one to which the stock car was attached.

It would be about a three-hour ride from Fort Worth to Eastland, so Lucas leaned back in his seat, pulled his hat down over his eyes, crossed his arms across his chest, and drifted off to sleep.

"Oh, there you are," a woman's voice said. "What kind of brother are you to get on the train before I did? I wondered what happened to you."

Lucas woke up, pushed his hat back from his eyes, and saw that a young woman had just sat beside him. She was pretty with dark hair and brown eyes.

"What?" he asked.

"Please, sir, just go along with it. You're my brother," the young woman said in a quiet, frightened voice.

The front door of the car opened, and two men came in. They were dressed as cowpunchers, and there was a swagger to their walk.

"There she is, Wally. Sittin' back there with that old man. Darlin' what you doin' sittin' there with grandpa?"

Lucas felt the young woman beside him flinch and draw in a sharp breath of fear.

"Come on, let me show you what me 'n Wally can do for you."

The man reached out toward the woman, as if to grab her by the neck of her dress.

"No, please!" the woman beside Lucas said, and she tried to draw back from the intrusive arm.

Lucas reached up and grabbed the man's wrist and twisted it so rapidly, causing the man to let out a yell of pain, and when Lucas let go, he grabbed his right wrist with his left hand. He was grunting in discomfort.

"Mister, you ought not to have done that," the other man called out. He started to draw his gun but stopped, when he saw that Lucas already had his pistol out, pointing at him.

"Take your gun out with your thumb and forefinger," Lucas ordered. "Then, bring it here, and give it to my sister, butt first."

Wally did as he was told.

"Now, get your partner's gun out, and hand it to my sister, the same way."

"What are you going to do with our guns?" Wally asked, as he pulled his partner's gun from its holster, then handed it to the young woman.

"You're going to get off at the next stop, then wait until the train starts to pull out and I'll toss the guns out to you."

"But the next stop ain't where we're gettin' off."

"Well, I plan to throw these guns out the window at the next stop whether you're there or not. So, if you want to see 'em again, I'd recommend that you get off the train. But for now, I want you out of this car."

The two men, one of whom was holding his wrist, left the car. When they were gone, everyone else in the car applauded.

"Oh, thank you, sir. Thank you so much," the young woman said. "I won't intrude on you any longer." She started to get up.

"You might want to stay here until the next stop. Just in case they don't believe me when I say I'm going to throw their guns out. They may decide to come back in here."

The young woman laughed. "Oh, I think you made it

pretty clear to them that they're not welcome. But as far as my sitting here, do you mind if I stay here until we get to Eastland? I'd feel more comfortable."

"I'd welcome the company," Lucas said. Then he smiled. "The only problem is my parents always kept it a secret that I had a sister, so I don't even know your name."

The young woman laughed. "My name is Carolina McKay. And before you ask, no, I'm not from the Carolinas, but my mother was born in Asheville. They never told me I had a brother, so I don't know your name, either," she added with another little laugh.

"Lucas, sis. Lucas Cain."

"Well, Lucas, I thank you," Carolina said. "I was afraid something like that might happen. Those two got on the train in Dallas and started bothering me right away. It finally got so bad that I left the car to come in here, and well, you saw what happened. And now, thanks to you, it's over."

As Lucas was talking, he was also punching the shells out of the two pistols, so that both guns would be empty when he tossed them out.

A short time later, the conductor stepped into the car to announce the next stop. "Parker! Next stop, Parker! If this is your stop, get ready." The conductor pulled out his watch. "Five minutes to Parker."

"How long will we be there?" one of the passengers asked.

"There'll be no standing time in the station, so everybody just sit still if you're goin' through."

"Excuse me, sir," Lucas said when the conductor passed by. "What were the names of those two men who were bothering Miss McKay?"

"I don't know anything but what I heard them say.

One was called Wally, and the one who did all the talking, was called Pike."

At that moment, the one the conductor had identified as Pike stood just outside the car, tapping on the window.

"Give us our guns back, you son of a bitch!" he shouted.

Lucas opened the window. "Don't be in such a hurry. I'll give them back as soon as the train starts to move again."

The two men glared at Lucas until, once again, the train got underway. As soon as it began to move, Lucas held the guns out the window.

"Die, you bastard!" Pike shouted, as he and Wally began pulling the trigger, only to hear the hammer click against an empty chamber.

"You two have a nice time in Parker," Lucas called, as the train began to pull away from the station.

Carolina laughed. "Oh, you have no idea how good that made my heart feel."

With the train underway again, Lucas and Carolina carried on an easy conversation as they continued on to Eastland. During that time, Lucas shared with her that he was a deputy U.S. Marshal, though he didn't tell her of his unique arrangement that allowed him to wear the badge.

Carolina explained that she was the daughter of the publisher of the *Eastland Journal*, and that she had been to Dallas to call on her grandmother.

"You must come to our house for supper tonight," she said.

"Oh, I'd hate to just barge in on your folks like that."

"Oh, don't be silly. Dad's always bringing someone over for supper at the last minute. My mother is used to it. But, I have to warn you—my dad will probably ask you if you want to buy an ad."

Lucas smiled. "All right, if you're sure it won't be any trouble, I never turn down the opportunity to have a home-cooked meal. Give me the address, and I'll be there."

"Why don't you come to the newspaper office with me, so I can introduce you to my father?"

Lucas nodded his head. "I can do that, but first, I'd like to take care of Charley Two."

"Charley Two?"

"My horse."

"Your horse?" Carolina chuckled. "The way you said the name, I thought it was a friend."

"Charley Two is my friend," Lucas answered. "In fact, he's probably my best friend. We tell each other everything."

Carolina laughed again. "Well, I guess that's what a friend is for."

No more than half an hour later, the train pulled into the depot at Eastland. After he stepped down onto the depot platform, Lucas walked back to the stock car and waited as the ramp was lowered. Then he climbed up into the car and brought Charley Two out.

"Well, old boy, how did you like your train ride?"

Charley Two snorted at Lucas and nodded his head, as if protesting his accommodations.

"Well, come on, Charley Two, I know you think you're people, but you're a horse. And horses can't travel first-class."

Carolina laughed. "You said you and your horse talked to each other. Is it always like that?"

"Not always. This is just bantering back and forth.

Sometimes Charley Two and I have deep, philosophical conversations."

"Ha! I'd like to listen in on one of those," Carolina said.

"You should, you might learn something. Charley Two has a keen, analytical mind. We don't always agree on things though, and sometimes we have quite an argument."

"I'm sure you do," Carolina said, laughing again.

It was a two-block walk from the livery to the newspaper office. The name of the newspaper, *The Eastland Journal*, was painted on the front window.

When Lucas followed Carolina into the newspaper office, he experienced the familiar sensory inputs of any newspaper office he had ever visited: the smell of ink, the sight of the web press, the composing table. It brought back memories of his wife. She had been a journalist for the newspaper in Cape Girardeau, Missouri, and because she had worked there, he had been a frequent visitor to the office.

Such memories were bittersweet, though. On the one hand, he took pleasure from remembering the happiness he and Rosie had shared, while on the other hand, being here, in a newspaper office, brought back the pain of her dying.

"Papa, I'm home!" Carolina called.

The man Carolina had summoned now appeared. He was just a little beyond middle age, with gray hair and a gray mustache. He was wearing glasses and an ink-stained apron.

"Hello, Carolina," the man said. "How was your trip?"

"It was wonderful," Carolina replied as she hugged her father. "Grandma sends her love, by the way."

"Well, it's always good to have my mother send her

love," he replied with a chuckle. He turned his attention toward Lucas. "Yes, sir, may I help you?"

"He's with me, Dad."

"Oh?"

"Dad, this is Lucas Cain. He's a U.S. Marshal, and this is my dad, Cephus McKay."

Cephus extended his hand, and Lucas took it.

"It's good to meet you, sir," Lucas said.

"The pleasure is mine," Cephus said, though there was a questioning expression on his face.

A young girl, who looked a little like Carolina, came up from the back of the pressroom to join them. She smiled and looked from Carolina to Lucas.

"And this is my little sister. Maggie's the baby of the family," Carolina said, with a teasing smile.

"Huh-uh, I'm no baby," Maggie said. "I'm thirteen years old."

"Not quite thirteen," Carolina corrected.

"Well, I will be in two months," Maggie insisted.

Carolina turned her attention back to her father. "Dad, I invited Lucas to supper tonight. And before you say anything, let me tell you how I happened to meet my brother."

"Your what?"

Carolina told the story of what had happened on the train, and how she had pretended that Lucas was her brother. By the time she finished the story, all four of them were laughing.

"Of course, you're welcome for supper tonight," Cephus said. "I think it's about time Ethyl met her son. You will accept our invitation, won't you?"

"I'd be honored to come," Lucas said.

"If he's your brother, he's my brother too," Maggie said.

"That's fine with me," Lucas said. "I wouldn't mind having a little twelve-year-old sister."

"I'm almost thirteen," Maggie insisted.

"All right, an almost thirteen-year-old sister," Lucas corrected with a little laugh.

"Mr. Cain, I believe Carolina said you are a U.S. Marshal?"

"Deputy U.S. Marshal."

"What brings you to Eastland?"

"As it turns out, I was going to come see you anyway, even if I hadn't met Carolina. Do you know anything about a man named Harley Mack Crawford?"

"More than I want to know. And yes, I got word by telegram that Crawford and a couple others killed those men on the train." Cephus shook his head. "Such a shame. Those three were here to make a deal with Bill Gillespie to put a cottonseed oil mill in Fort Worth."

"Will the deal still go through?" Lucas asked.

"Hard to tell," McKay said. "This Crawford you're talking about. I know he's been in trouble here in Eastland enough times that the sheriff put wanted posters out on him, and I know that for sure, because I printed them."

"Do you have a description of him?"

"Only that he's a big man. They say he's six feet, three inches tall. About your size, I would reckon."

"Thanks, I appreciate that," Lucas said. "That'll give me something to go on."

When Lucas and the others got to the McKay house, Cephus greeted his wife. "I see you're looking at our guest," he said. "Ethyl, I'd like to introduce you to Carolina's brother."

"What?" Ethyl said with a gasp.

"Carolina, you'd better tell your mama the story,

before she gets the broom after me," Cephus said with a little laugh.

Carolina told the story of what happened on the train, and how she passed herself off as Lucas's sister, and how he handled the two men who had accosted her.

Ethyl smiled and nodded at the story. "Well, then all I can say is, I'm glad Carolina had a big brother to protect her."

Lucas was pleased to see that supper was chicken and dumplings, his favorite fare.

AFTER LEAVING the McKay house that evening, Lucas checked in to a hotel, then found a saloon to visit.

He stood at the bar for at least an hour and was about to leave when he recognized the two men from the train.

"Pike, lookie there!" Wally said, pointing toward Lucas. "That there is the son of a bitch that was on the train!"

"Yeah, 'n our guns ain't empty now," Pike said, making a grab toward his pistol.

Wally was drawing his gun as well.

Lucas's reaction was automatic, and even though both Wally and Pike had cleared leather before Lucas even started his draw, Lucas's gun was in his hand in a flash. He fired two times, and both men went down. Only Wally had managed to get off a shot, and it was a reflexive action as he was going down. The bullet from his gun punched a hole through the floor.

The whole thing happened so fast, that nobody in the saloon had any time to react to it, until after the fact.

"Damn, did you see that?" someone asked.

"Beatin'est thing I ever seen," another added.

As the others in the saloon gathered around the two fallen men, Lucas turned back to the bar, and lifted his beer to his lips.

"Damn, you're a pretty cool fella, ain't you?" the bartender said.

"It doesn't help anything to get too excited," Lucas answered.

"No, I guess not. Did you know them two?"

"One is Wally, and one is Pike. That's all I know, and I'm not even sure which is which."

The bartender chuckled. "Well you sure got 'em pissed off, not to know 'em any better."

"They were accosting a young lady on the train, and I intervened on her behalf."

"Well, you must have been successful."

The sheriff came into the saloon then and seeing a group of men standing just inside the door and looking at two bodies on the floor, he stepped up for a closer look.

"All right, somebody want to tell me what happened here?"

"Damndest thing I ever seen, Sheriff," one of the men said. "These here two," he pointed to the two on the floor, "come in here, 'n they was a-cussin' 'n yellin' soon as they come in. Both of 'em went for their guns, drawin' against this here feller," he pointed to Lucas. "But he outdrawed 'em 'n shot 'em both down."

"Anybody else see it that way?" the sheriff asked.

"Yeah, that's how it happened all right," another said, and all the others put in their own concurrence of the events.

"All right, Mister, looks like you're in the clear. What's your name?"

"I'm Deputy U.S. Marshal Lucas Cain."

"Sumbitch! I've heard of you." He stuck out his hand. "I'm Sheriff Quinton Dozier. What are you doing in Eastland?"

"I'm after Harley Mack Crawford, and a couple of others named Rogers and Hanson. I don't know their first names."

"I heard what they did to them three Fort Worth businessmen that was on the train. I hope somebody catches up with 'em."

"I will," Lucas said confidently.

11

PALO PINTO, TEXAS

Forty-four miles northeast of where Lucas Cain was standing, the three men he was looking for, Harley Mack Crawford, Cole Rogers, and Gene Hanson, were having a drink in Gordy's Saloon. They had purposely chosen a table in the farthest corner so they could have a discussion without fear of being overheard.

"We'll go in one at a time," Crawford said. "Cole, you'll be first. Go up to the teller 'n get change for a twenty-dollar bill. Gene, you come in last, 'n stand at the table, like you're fillin' out a deposit slip or somethin'. I'll go see the bank manager like I got business with him, then I'll bring him out with my gun stuck in his back. When you two see me a-comin' out with the manager, pull your guns. Cole, you keep an eye on the teller, make sure he don't try to go for a gun under the counter or nothin'. Gene, you keep an eye on the door, 'n if anyone comes in, you keep 'em from tryin' to go back outside once they see what's goin' on."

"How about the real gettin' of the money?" Rogers asked.

"I'll take care of that," Crawford answered.

"How much you reckon there is in this bank?" Hanson asked.

"Hell, it's a bank, Hanson," Rogers said. "Banks have lots of money."

HALF AN HOUR LATER, the three men entered the Bank of Palo Pinto. There were two tellers, one of them was a man, and the other a woman. A customer was at the woman's window, so Rogers went to the other teller.

"I'd like you to give me some change for this twenty-dollar bill if you would, please," he said, presenting the bill.

"Yes, sir, and how would you like that? Two tens, four fives, or twenty ones?"

"I don't know. Two tens, I reckon."

Crawford came in bumping into the other customer as he was leaving.

"I beg your pardon," the man said.

"Yeah," Crawford said. He went back to the bank manager's office, just as the teller gave Rogers two tens.

"You're the bank manager?" Crawford asked.

"Yes, Lowell Dempster at your service. What can I do for you?"

"I got a big deposit to make, and I'd feel just real good if you was to watch me while I make it."

"Of course, I would be happy to," Dempster said, getting up from behind his desk.

When they left the bank manager's office, Crawford jabbed his gun into Dempster's back.

"What you feel in your back is a gun. And now, you're gonna do ever'thing I say."

"Oh, my!" Dempster said in a frightened voice.

ROGERS WAS STILL STANDING in front of the teller's window. Crawford hadn't shown up with the bank manager yet, so Rogers knew he needed to stall a little longer.

"Better make that four fives," Rogers said.

He got the four fives too quickly, so he asked for a ten, one five, and five ones.

"You know what, why don't you make that a five and fifteen ones?"

"Mister, would you please make up your mind?" the frustrated teller demanded.

At that moment Crawford came out of the bank manager's office, with his gun sticking in the man's back.

"This is a holdup!" Crawford shouted.

Hanson and Rogers pulled their guns as well.

"Heavens! What is this?" the teller who was making change for Rogers called out.

"Are you plum deaf or somethin'? You heard the man —it's a bank robbery. Get one o' them money bags, 'n start fillin' it."

"But, what about your change?" the frazzled clerk asked.

"Stick it in there, too," Rogers said. "And you might as well give me back my twenty."

"Oh, my," the teller said as he started filling the bag Rogers had given him.

At that moment the front door opened, and a man

and woman came into the bank. Hanson turned his gun toward them.

"Here, what are you doing?" the man called out, his voice reflecting both his anger and fright.

"Get in here, both of you," Hanson demanded with a wave of his gun, "and don't even think of gettin' out of here."

"Now, you tellers empty the safe for us."

The two tellers did as they were ordered.

With two money bags full, both tellers and Dempster lying on the floor having been knocked out, Crawford cautioned the customers to stay in the bank for five minutes before leaving.

"We got a friend on the roof across the street. If anybody comes out sooner, he's got a rifle and he'll kill ya."

EASTLAND, TEXAS

Lucas followed Sheriff Dozier down to his office.

"Travis Hastings over there is my deputy," Dozier said, when he and Lucas stepped into the office. The deputy was peeling an apple.

"Now, the names of those other two men you were talking about are Cole Rogers and Gene Hanson."

"So you do know them," Lucas said.

"Yeah, I know who they are. They ain't a damn one 'em that's worth the gunpowder it would take to blow their nose."

"Since you say you know them, would you happen to have any reward posters on them?"

"Yes, I've got some dodgers with their pictures on 'em, if you want to take a look."

Dozier opened a desk drawer and began running through a stack of wanted posters.

"Here they are," he said, selecting three of the posters and handing them to Lucas.

"These are the same ones that Sheriff Moore has." He put his finger on the poster for Crawford. "This one needs updating, though," he said.

"What do you mean, updating?" Sheriff Dozier asked.

"Crawford has a severe burn scar on his left cheek."

"Really? Damn, that's good to know."

"Sheriff Moore is getting the word out about Crawford's scar to as many as he can."

"Sheriff, I think we got somethin' about that," Deputy Hastings said as he began going through a stack of telegrams that were on a nail.

"You say you know all three of these men," Lucas said. "Do the others have any distinguishing features?"

Dozier laughed. "There ain't none of 'em what you would call distinguished, but I know what you're talking about. Cole Rogers, when he opens his mouth, you can see that he's missin' his front two teeth. Hanson is redheaded."

"I see the reward is higher for Crawford than the other two. Is he the ringleader?"

"Well, I don't know that for sure, but I expect he is. He's four or five years older than the other two, and he was in prison for a couple years. He's probably got more experience than the other two, and even though it's bad experience, it's still experience."

"I think you're right about experience. Well, I can't think of anything else to ask you, so I guess I'll go down to the Cactus and have a beer," Cain said.

The Cactus was quite a ways from being a first-class saloon. The bar was of rough-cut lumber. There was an unpainted plank, attached to the wall holding six or seven bottles. The mirror behind the plank was so dirty, it barely made a reflection.

The bartender moved down to Lucas, and wiped the bar with a smelly, wet rag.

"What'a ya want?"

"I'll have a beer," Lucas said. "In a clean glass," he added.

"Kind'a picky ain't ya?" the bartender asked. He reached under the bar then extracted a mug and held it out for inspection.

"That'll do," Lucas said.

Lucas drank his beer slowly, and listened to the others talking, but so far, there was no string of conversation that got his attention. Then, just as he was about to leave, Sheriff Dozier came into the saloon.

"I just got a telegram from the sheriff up in Palo Pinto," he said. "The bank was robbed by three men. One of the men had a really bad scar on his cheek. It had to be Crawford and his men."

"How far is it to Palo Pinto from here?"

"I'd say about forty miles," Sheriff Dozier replied.

"If I get an early start tomorrow, I could get there before the bank closes."

DEKE PAULY HEARD about the bank robbery in Palo Pinto, and was going to go check it out, when he learned that Kit Chiles, the wanted man he was going after, had been seen in Decatur. Since he was closer to Decatur than he was to Palo Pinto, he decided to take a train up to Decatur to see if he could catch up with Kit Chiles.

The train trip turned into a pleasant interlude when Pauly went into the parlor car where he met up with three attractive young women. The women were also going to Decatur where they had been hired as bar girls. Now, it seemed, they were practicing their trade on Pauly.

"More wine, Mr. Pauly?" the redhead asked as she got up from the table and reached for the bottle.

"Thank you, Lucy, that's kindly of you," Pauly answered, holding his wine glass out.

"I'm Letty," the redhead said as she giggled, and filled his glass.

Smiling, Deke looked across the table at the blonde. "Then you must be Lucy?"

"I'm Lana."

"I'm Lucy," the brunette said.

"Then I propose a toast to Letty, Lana, and Lucy, three of the most beautiful…"

Suddenly the engineer applied the brakes for an emergency stop. Wine splashed from Pauly's glass. Letty, who had not yet sat down, was thrown to the floor while Lucy and Lana braced themselves to keep their seats. Almost immediately, bullets came crashing through the windows.

"Down on the floor!" Pauly shouted as he shoved the two women off the seat.

Drawing his pistol, Pauly started toward the back of the car.

"What are you doing? Where are you going?" Lucy asked.

"This will only take a minute," Pauly replied, holding his hand out to calm them. "Please, enjoy a glass of wine."

"Enjoy a glass of wine? *Enjoy?* Are you crazy? Someone is shooting at us!" Letty said.

"They're shooting through the windows, because the bullets won't penetrate the sides of the car."

"He's right," Lana said. "Listen! The bullets are hitting the car but none of them are getting through."

Pauly stepped out onto the back platform. He could see six men standing in the bubble of light projected from the windows of the train. Two men went down under his opening fusillade.

Bullets flew and popped into the night. The four men who were still standing, retreated into the darkness.

With the attack broken up, Pauly hurried to the front of the train to see if any of the crew had been injured. The engine was venting steam as if impatient to be underway. The engineer was in the window, backlighted by the glow of the firebox. Behind him could be seen the array of valves, pipes, levers, and dials.

"Anyone hurt up here?" Pauly called to the engineer.

"No one hurt up here," the engineer answered.

"What caused the sudden stop?"

"Sure 'n would you be for lookin' down the track, now, and tellin' me what you see?" the engineer suggested.

Looking in the direction the engineer indicated, Deke saw a fire in the middle of the track.

"T'was burnin' like the devil's own inferno it was, a few moments ago. I hope you'll be for pardonin' me for stoppin' like I did, but I could 'na take the chance of runnin' my train through it. Not without knowin' what was on the other side."

"You did the right thing," Pauly said.

At that moment a figure materialized out of the darkness between the engine and the fire. "Mr. O'Leary," he called. "No damage to the track. It's just some burning brush, is all. We can push right through it."

"Fine job, lad," O'Leary called back. Then he called out to Pauly. "Sir, if you'd be for returnin' to your car, I'll get us underway before those heathens who stopped us take a notion to return. We'll be in Decatur right soon."

"If you don't mind giving me a moment, Mr. O'Leary, I would like to take my horse off the train and stay here while you go on."

"You're serious, you want to be leavin' the train here?"

"Yes, sir, if you'd let me."

"Well, I don't know why you want to do that, but I reckon you have earned the right to do it. If this is really what you're a-wantin'."

"Thank you. I'll step into the car and tell some friends goodbye, then I'll take my horse down and be out of your hair."

"After what you did for us, Mister, believe me, you weren't in anybody's hair," O'Leary said.

Pauly waved, then returned to the parlor car. When he stepped inside, the women were laughing and talking as if at a party, and indeed they were having a fine time, for they had taken his advice to enjoy the wine. One bottle was gone and they had started on a second, which put them well on their way to being tipsy.

"Ah! Our gallant hero has returned," Letty said, lifting her glass toward him. She sloshed some of the wine on herself. "Oops!" She laughed.

"I wish I could join you, ladies, but I'm going to have to leave the train here."

"Leave the train? Why on earth would you do that?" Lana asked. "Why, we're in the middle of nowhere. There's nothin' out there."

"Oh, but there is. I shot two men, and they're still out there."

"But if they're dead, why would you want anything to do with 'em?"

The three women laughed.

"It wouldn't be right just leavin' a couple of bodies exposed like that. Wolves, coyotes, even buzzards would have a field day with 'em," Pauly said.

"So what, that's good enough for 'em," Lucy said.

Pauly chuckled. "But you don't understand. If the critters get to them, you might not be able to recognize 'em. And they'll have to be recognized for me to draw any bounty that might be offered for 'em."

"Bounty?" Lana asked, with a confused tone in her voice. "Don't tell me you're one of them man hunters!"

"Yes, ladies, the handsome man the three of you have been cavorting with, is a bounty hunter."

AFTER THE TRAIN PULLED AWAY, Pauly found the two horses the outlaws had been riding, just standing where they had been left.

"You're a couple of good horses," Pauly said. "I don't blame you for what your riders did, but you're going to be carrying them one more time. I don't know who belongs to who, but since they're both dead, it shouldn't make any difference to either one of you."

12

The remaining four men who had attacked the train, rode into the town of Boliver, then took their horses into the stable.

"What's Chiles goin' to say about us showin' up empty-handed?" one of the riders asked as he removed his saddle and put it on a bench with some others.

"You let me handle Chiles," Tanner replied as he stroked his chin whiskers in contemplation.

"If you want to deal with Chiles you ain't goin' to get no lip from me," one of the other riders said. "I'd as soon stay out of his sight for a while."

Tanner turned his horse out into the pen, then started across the street to the saloon. He could hear piano music and loud laughter and conversation spilling out into the street.

When Tanner stepped into the saloon, he saw Chiles just where he knew he would be.

Chiles had big shoulders, a barrel chest, and a bald head with a protruding brow. He was drinking a beer when Tanner came in, and he brushed the foam away, then waved him over.

"How much did you get?" he asked in a deep, rumbling voice.

"Nothin'," Tanner said as he lowered his gaze.

Chiles set the mug down on the table so hard, the beer spilled out. He stared at Tanner.

"Are you trying to say there wasn't a red cent on that train?"

"No, I couldn't say that, I don't know whether there was or not. We didn't get a chance to look."

"Didn't you stop the train?"

"We stopped it all right, but we couldn't get on board."

Tanner went on to tell how someone got off the train and began shooting at them from the dark.

"He got Coolidge and Jenkens," Tanner said.

"Let me get this right," Chiles said. "There were six of you, and one of him, but he kept you from gettin' on the train."

"It's like I said, he was in the dark and nobody could see him. We was lit up by the light from the train winders, 'n he was a damn good shot."

"Damn," Chiles said. "Sure as a gun is iron, that train was carryin' money."

"We shoulda taken up a rail, instead of just settin' a fire on the track," Tanner said.

Chiles waved Tanner's suggestion off. "Forget it. There'll be other trains. And we'll still be here."

STATE PENITENTIARY—HUNTSVILLE, TEXAS

Rufe Sawyer was in the last days of what had been a five-year sentence. He had stolen twenty-five dollars. Twenty-five dollars and he had been given five years.

"Damn, that works out to five dollars a year," he told one of the other inmates. "That sure as hell ain't much of a salary to be drawin'."

Actually, he had been tried for murder, seeing as how he had killed the man from whom he had stolen the twenty-five dollars.

Sawyer recalled the trial. He had been defended by Russell Malone who was, everyone agreed, the best lawyer in Weatherford.

Sawyer recalled Malone's closing argument.

"The state has tried to make a case for murder, but they have no witnesses, and they have no evidence. They have only supposition, and you can't convict a man on supposition."

Before sending the case to the jury, Malone had requested a meeting with the judge and prosecutor. When Malone returned to the defense table, he had a smile on his face.

"I proposed a plea bargain, and the prosecutor accepted it," Malone had said. "He had no choice; he couldn't make the murder case."

"You mean you got me off?" Sawyer asked.

"From the murder charge," Malone said. "You'll be getting a sentence of five years for robbery."

"Five years for twenty-five dollars? Hell no!" Sawyer said, angrily.

"Sawyer, they were going to continue the murder charge, and had you been found guilty, you would hang," Malone said. "This was the best I could do. And if you ask me, it's damn near a miracle."

Sawyer's time in prison had been marked with episodes of increased punishment, such as time in "the hole" as the prisoners called solitary confinement. He had also been put on a week of bread and water a couple of times.

Right now, he was pacing back and forth in his cell, expecting a guard to show up at any moment. Earlier this morning he had hit a prisoner with some rudimentary brass knuckles he had fashioned in the prison shop from a couple of links of a heavy chain.

He had the links hidden out in the prison yard. This way they could search his cell all they wanted, and find nothing.

Two guards arrived at his cell then.

"Sawyer, I want you to come over here, and turn your back to the bars, stick both of your arms through," one of the guards said.

Sawyer did as he was instructed, and he felt a pair of handcuffs being applied. The handcuffs not only kept him from using his hands, they also kept him secured against the bars so that his movement was restricted.

"What are you doin' this for?" Sawyer asked.

"Don't worry, we'll just keep you there until we find the brass knuckles you used to break Leonari's nose."

"I didn't need anything like that to help me, I broke that son a bitch's nose with my bare knuckles."

"Sure you did," one of the guards said.

The guards continued their search, then gave up in disgust. They removed the handcuffs so that, once again, Sawyer had freedom of movement in his cell.

After the guards left, Sawyer had a little laugh. They hadn't found the brass knuckles, and they weren't going to find them until after he was discharged from prison.

He had only a few days left, and he thought of the

plans he was going to make with Godfrey, Dumey, and Coleman who had already been released. He intended to make up for the time he had been in prison, and he planned to get enough money to move to California. He'd always wanted to go to California.

Later, that same day, Sawyer was taken to the warden's office.

"What did you do with those brass knuckles?" the warden asked.

"What brass knuckles?"

"Don't try and lie out of it, we have half a dozen witnesses who saw you with them," the warden said. "Two weeks solitary confinement."

"Damn, I don't have that much time left," Sawyer complained.

"If the rules would allow it, I'd keep you in solitary for a whole month," the warden said. He glared at Sawyer for a moment, then with a disgusted sigh and a wave of his arm, he spoke to the two guards who had brought him to his office.

"Get his sorry self out of my sight."

"Come on, Sawyer."

"Two weeks," Sawyer said. "Only two more weeks, and I'm out of here."

As the guards led him away, Sawyer laughed at the prospect of solitary confinement. What the warden didn't know was that Sawyer could do that time while standing on his head. He didn't like people and wouldn't miss being around anyone. Also, while he was in, Sawyer continued to daydream about California. He had heard that the women there were beautiful, and he would have enough money to get any woman he wanted.

The two weeks went by quickly, then he returned to his cell.

THE NEXT DAY, Sawyer was taken to the warden's office.

"I'm telling you the truth, Sawyer, if it was up to me, you'd be in here for fifteen more years. No, on the other hand I'm glad to see you go, you've been nothing but a pain in the ass for the whole time you've been here," Warden Donald Gibson said.

"I'm not going to give you the warden's wish for a better life because it'd be wasted on you."

The warden looked up at the guard who would walk with Rufe Sawyer to the front gate.

"All right, Raiser, just get 'im the hell out of here," Gibson said with a dismissive wave of his hand.

"Come on, Sawyer."

"Yeah, let me tell the warden goodbye first. Goodbye, Warden, and may you rot in hell."

"Get him out of here now!" Gibson said, barking the words.

"Come on, Sawyer," Raiser said again.

Grinning at the warden's displeasure, Sawyer left the office with the guard. He chuckled as they walked across the yard toward the gate.

"What are you laughin' at?" Raiser asked.

"While we were in there, did you come by the idea the warden don't like me all that much?"

"Hell, Sawyer, there ain't nobody in the whole prison—guards, cooks, or even other prisoners—that gives a hoot about you. We're all glad to watch you go. We just wish you was goin' to the gallows instead of the gate."

When they reached the front gate, Raiser showed the guard Sawyer's release papers.

"Open the damn gate," Sawyer demanded.

"Gladly," the gate guard said. "As much as I'd like to see you rot in here, I'd rather see you gone."

The gate was opened, Raiser handed Sawyer twenty dollars and his release papers. Sawyer stepped outside of the prison for the first time in five years. He heard the gate close behind him as he walked away. He planned to make up for lost time.

13

After Lucas left Eastland, he made it a little over halfway on the first day. There was no hotel, but there was a boardinghouse that rented rooms on a nightly basis. There were four bunks in the room he took, and one of the bunks was already occupied. It also had a kitchen. The fare, strips of salt pork and beans, was not any better than what he could cook on the trail. But at least, this time, he didn't have to cook it.

Lucas knew that the three men he was looking for would not be in Palo Pinto, but he was hoping he could get some kind of a lead on where to go next.

He reached Palo Pinto by noon the next day. His first stop was with the sheriff. He told the sheriff who he was, then asked him about Crawford, Rogers, and Hanson.

"I hope you catch up with the sons of bitches," Sheriff Kern said. "They hit Ellie May Ferguson so hard that it kilt her."

"Was the robbery successful? Did they get away with any money?"

"Mr. Dempster says they got away with a little over four thousand dollars," Sheriff Kern said.

"That's good," Lucas said.

"Good? That money belonged to the people. What do you mean, good?"

"If they've got money, they're going to want to spend it. And that means they won't be in some hideout."

Lucas talked to several other people in town, including the bank manager, the teller, and the two customers who had come into the bank while it was being robbed. None of the conversations provided any revelation as to where the three bank robbers may have gone.

DALLAS, TEXAS

Crawford, Rogers, and Hanson bought a change of clothes, then checked into the best hotel in Dallas.

"We'd like a room," Crawford said.

"Yes, sir. One room. I'll arrange to have a cot sent up, that should accommodate the three of you," the hotel clerk said.

"What are you talkin' about, sendin' up a cot. We want a room to our ownself," Crawford said, harshly.

"Oh, I'm sorry, sir, I misunderstood," the clerk said obsequiously. "Of course, that'll be three rooms."

"And I'll be wantin' a bathtub sent up, 'n some hot water for bathin'," Crawford said.

"That won't be necessary, sir," the clerk said.

"What the hell do you mean it won't be necessary? I plan on visitin' me some women tonight, 'n I don't wanna be smellin' like some hog waller."

"Oh, sir, you misunderstood," the clerk said. "Each of our rooms has their own individual bathroom with a tub and running hot and cold water."

Crawford smiled and looked at the other two. "I'll be damn," he said. "What do you think about that?"

"I tell you what," Hanson said. "We're livin' in high cotton now."

The three men collected their keys, then went up to their rooms, took long baths, put on their new clothes, then set out to "do the town." Half an hour after they had left the hotel, they found themselves standing in front of Sadie's House of Pleasure.

"What do you reckon this place is?" Rogers asked.

"Let's go in and find out," Hanson replied.

When they went inside, they saw a room that was appointed as nicely as any parlor room. But what really got their attention were the women. There weren't nearly as many women as men in the room, and they were dressed in the most revealing garments that any of the three had ever seen before.

"Damn, all the women is with other men," Hanson said.

"That don't matter none," Crawford said.

"What do you mean it don't matter none?" Rogers asked.

"Don't forget, we're rich now," Crawford said, with a smile. "Watch and learn."

Crawford took out a twenty-dollar bill, then holding it up, walked over to the nearest woman who was leaning on the table in a way that showed a generous amount of cleavage.

"Hey, darlin'. Why don't you leave them men 'n come with me?" Crawford asked.

"Go away," the man said. "She's with me."

"Can you give her this?" Crawford asked. He held the twenty-dollar bill out in front of the girl.

"Are you serious?" the girl asked.

Crawford reached down through the top of her low-cut dress and stuck the twenty-dollar bill between her breasts. "Don't I look serious?" he asked.

With a broad smile the girl left the table, signaling for Crawford to come with her. The man she had been with, looked on with shock and anger.

"Damn, lookie there," Rogers said. "Did you see what Harley Mack just done? He showed her a twenty-dollar bill and she just left that other feller 'n went with him."

"Hell, we can do the same thing," Hanson said. "It's like Harley Mack told us, we're rich now, so twenty dollars don't mean nothin'."

Rogers and Hanson each took out a twenty-dollar bill, and mimicking Crawford, lured the girls away from the other men.

"How the hell can those three throw money around like that?" one of the men grumbled. "Have you ever seen an uglier son of a bitch than that first one?"

"Money does the talkin'," another man said. "In this place, it doesn't make any difference what you look like."

———

THE NEXT DAY CRAWFORD, Rogers, and Hanson went on a shopping spree, buying new hats, boots, gun belts, pistols, and rifles. Other citizens of Dallas took notice, and word of the "crazy cowboys on a spending spree," spread around town. Some even followed the three from store to store to see what they would buy next.

———

WITH THE TRAIL OF CRAWFORD, Rogers, and Hanson having grown cold, Lucas returned to Fort Worth.

He was certain the three would be going somewhere to spend their money, and he knew it would be a town of some size. That would give them more things to spend their money on, and less chance of being recognized. He decided they could even be in Fort Worth.

He hoped that was so. That would be better than them going to some place like Denver or St. Louis.

Lucas knew that if Crawford and his two cohorts were in town, they would be spending a lot of time in the saloons. There were twenty saloons in the part of Fort Worth known as Hell's Half Acre, so Lucas started his search. Using the wanted posters, Lucas showed them to all the bartenders and bar girls in all twenty saloons. In addition to visiting the saloons, he also took his search to the many bordellos.

When the saloon and bordello searches proved to be futile, he started asking some of the customers until he realized that all he was doing was antagonizing them, so he quit the search.

That night he went to the Double Eagle Saloon, not to ask questions, but merely to take a break from his search to determine what he should do next. He sat alone, quietly nursing his beer.

"You shoulda seen them crazy sons a bitches," someone said. "Damn, they're offerin' the girls more for one night than they make in a whole month. It ain't no wonder that girls is all a-followin' 'em like they're a-doin'. I ain't never seen nothin' like it before."

Lucas listened in on the conversation.

"They's three of 'em, 'n they're goin' around, spending money liken they was a-throwin' confetti around."

That has to be them, Lucas thought.

"Is that here, in Fort Worth?" someone asked.

"No, man, it's over in Dallas."

Upon hearing the three men being talked about were in Dallas, Lucas left the saloon, went to the livery where his horse was kept, saddled him, and started toward Dallas.

When he reached Dallas, he tied Charley Two off at the hitching rail in front of the Full House Saloon. It was late afternoon, and the saloon was busy.

"What'll it be?" the bartender asked.

"I'll have a beer," Lucas said.

While the bartender was drawing the beer, Lucas turned his back to the bar to have a look over the room. There were several customers sitting at tables or standing at the bar. None of them looked anything like the drawings on the wanted dodgers.

"Your beer," the bartender said, setting a mug before him.

Lucas saw an empty table and started toward it. He was met by a bar girl.

"Would you like some company?"

"Yeah, that would be nice. Get yourself a drink and join me," Lucas said, giving the girl a dollar.

As the girl started toward the bar, Lucas sat at the table. He didn't intend to start questioning her right away. Deciding it would be nice just to enjoy the company of a pretty girl.

A moment later she returned, carrying her drink.

"My name is Camille," the girl said, as she joined him at the table. Her smile eased the harshness of the dissipation that her occupation had caused. "What will I call you?"

"I'm Lucas."

They talked for a few minutes, then Lucas posed the question.

"You know, I heard that there are three guys going around spending money like it's water. Is that true?"

"Yeah, they've been in here a couple of times, but I haven't spent any time with 'em. I guess they just want the younger, prettier ones."

"They'd have to be awful pretty, to be prettier than you," Lucas said.

Camille smiled. "Well, aren't you sweet?"

"The names of the men I'm looking for are Crawford, Rogers, and Hanson. Have you heard those names?"

Camille shook her head. "No, I don't think I have."

"What are the names of the three who are spending so much money?"

"Johnson is the only name I can recall."

Damn, Lucas thought. He was sure he was on the right track. "Can you describe any of them?" he asked.

"One of 'em is a pretty big man, the other two I'm not —wait, one of 'em has a dark red mark on his cheek. I don't know if it's a scar or a birthmark, or what it is. It's about this big around," she said, making a circle with her thumb and forefinger.

Lucas smiled. "Thank you, Camille." He handed her a five-dollar bill. "Take the night off."

"I might just do that," Camille said. "And, honey, anytime you want some company, you just let me know."

14

George Hager was sitting alone at the table next to Camille and Lucas. Swallowing the rest of his drink, Hager left the saloon. He knew who the pair was talking about, and he was pretty sure he knew why they were talking about them. Johnson, Jones, and Smith, if those really were their names, couldn't be spending money like they had been, unless they had come into a lot of money somewhere. He suspected the man at the next table was the law, and he thought the threesome might pay a lot of money for that information.

As it so happened, Hager knew where the three men were, because he had just seen them in the Lone Star, not more than fifteen minutes ago. The Lone Star was only three buildings down from the Full House.

He saw them as soon as he stepped inside. The three were sitting together, playing poker. They were playing for such high stakes, that nobody else could afford to join the game.

Hager walked back to stand by the table.

"Go away," the big one said.

"I've got some information that you're gonna want to hear," Hager said.

"What kind of information?"

"Like maybe somebody is lookin' for you guys."

"Why would somebody be lookin' for us?" Crawford asked.

"I don't know. He's got the look of a lawman about him, 'n the way you three have been spending money, maybe he thinks you robbed a bank or somethin'."

Crawford's eyes narrowed as he studied Hager. "Is that what you think?"

"It doesn't matter what I think. It's what Lucas Cain thinks. And he knows you're in town. He just don't know where you are."

"Why are you tellin' us this?" Crawford asked.

"It could be that when I do a favor like this, you might want to grease my hand a little—say, five hundred dollars."

"We ain't givin' you no five hundred dollars," Crawford said, his voice little more than a growl.

"Are you sayin' it's not worth five hundred dollars?" Hager asked.

"That's what I'm sayin'."

"Then perhaps I'm takin' my information to the wrong buyer. Could be that feller with the badge who's lookin' for you would pay five hundred dollars to someone who could tell 'im just where you are."

Hager had barely finished his threat when he heard the sound of a gunshot, concurrent with a bullet going deep in his chest. He felt the pain, an instant of fear, then he felt nothing.

Even as he was pulling the trigger, Crawford pulled a derringer from his pocket and dropped it on the floor beside Hager's crumpled form.

Everyone else in the saloon looked over in surprise, their attention drawn by the sound of the shot.

"What the hell happened here?" someone asked.

"The son of a bitch pulled a gun on us, said he would kill us if we didn't give him the money that was on the table, one hundred 'n twenty dollars," Crawford shouted out to all those who had turned at the sound of the gunshot.

"That's right," Hanson shouted. "Me 'n Jones seen it, 'n it happened just the way Johnson said it did. The sum' bitch was goin' to shoot us. You can see the gun there on the floor right beside him."

"Where's the sheriff's office?" Crawford asked. "I expect we better go see him about this."

"It's down on Preston," someone said.

"Thanks, we'll go see 'im, 'n bring 'im back down here. Don't nobody touch nothin', he needs to see the gun so's it'll prove what happened."

"We won't touch nothin'," replied the man who had told them where the sheriff's office was.

"Come on, let's go," Crawford said to the other two.

Rogers and Hanson followed Crawford outside.

"Harley Mack, you ain't really plannin' on us goin' down to see the sheriff, are you?"

Crawford chuckled. "Hell, no. It was just a way of gettin' us out of there without a bunch of people a-followin' us."

Rogers and Hanson laughed.

"Damn, you're a smart 'n all right," Hanson said.

"Let's go down to the livery and get our horses," Crawford said. "If there's somebody here lookin' for us, we need to get out of town."

Lucas was checking all the saloons, one of which was the Lone Star. When he went inside, he saw that there was a degree of agitation and nervous tension being exhibited by the customers, the bar girls, and even the bartender. Lucas saw a body lying on the floor.

"What happened here?" Lucas asked the bartender.

"That feller lyin' dead on the floor there, is George Hager. The one that shot 'im said that Hager pulled that little derringer that's lyin' there alongside 'im 'n tried to steal the money that was on the table. They was quite a bit of money there, but truth is, I never know'd Hager to have it in 'im to go agin' three men like that, even if there was a lot of money."

"Three men, you say? Do you know them?"

"Not really. One of 'em calls hisself Johnson, but I don't know the names of the other two."

"Do you have any idea where they went?"

"Yeah, I know exactly where they went," the bartender said. "They went down to see the sheriff. That's why they told us not to touch nothin', so the sheriff could look over the scene when he gets here."

"How long ago was that?" Lucas asked.

"I don't know. Half an hour or so, I suppose."

"What did they look like? Did one of 'em have a mark on his face, here?" Lucas put his hand over his cheek where the scar would be.

"Yeah, how'd you know?" the bartender replied. "Do you know them boys?"

"They didn't go to the sheriff."

"Why do you say that?"

"You really think it would take the sheriff half an hour to come check out a murder?"

"Murder? Who said anything about murder? Like I told you, the way it happened is, Hager pulled a gun on 'em and told 'em to give 'im all the money, but one of 'em shot 'im."

Lucas turned to leave.

"Where you goin'?"

"To see the sheriff."

THE SHERIFF LOOKED up when Lucas went into his office.

"Sheriff, I don't suppose three men came in here to say they killed someone down at the Lone Star, did they?"

"What? No, what are you talking about?"

"There was a man killed in the Lone Star about half an hour ago. The bartender said his name was George Hager, and whoever killed him said he was coming down here to see you and report it."

The sheriff stood up. "This is the first I've heard about it. George Hager, you say?"

"That's the name the bartender gave me, yes."

The sheriff left his office and started walking toward the Lone Star. Lucas walked with him.

"I'm not surprised it would be him. Hager has been in and out of jail half a dozen times since I've been sheriff. Never anything serious, but always skating around the edge. Who are you, by the way?"

"I'm Marshal Lucas Cain."

"U.S. Marshal, or town marshal."

"U.S. Marshal. And you are?"

"Ray Kyle. What brings you to Dallas, Marshal?""

"I'm after the same men you are, the men who killed Hager."

Kyle looked up toward Lucas. "Look here, do you know who killed Hager?"

"I know that it was one of three men, and since they are always together, it doesn't matter which one of them pulled the trigger. Harley Mack Crawford, Cole Rogers, Gene Hanson."

"Damn, those are the three men who robbed the bank in Palo Pinto."

"Yes."

"And they're here in Dallas?"

"No."

"Wait a minute. I thought you said they were the ones who killed Hager. How could they do that if they aren't in Dallas?"

"They were in Dallas, but I'm positive they aren't now. I'm sure they left town as soon as they killed Hager."

"How do you know that's who it was?"

"I'll show you," Lucas offered.

When they pushed their way through the batwing doors they saw some of the morbidly curious standing around the body.

"Ah, Sheriff, here you are," the bartender said. "Johnson come down to get you, I see."

"Who's Johnson?"

"There is no Johnson," Lucas said. "I'm pretty sure that it was Crawford."

Lucas hung around to listen as everyone told Sheriff Kyle their version of what happened. When they mentioned that one of the men had a scar, or blemish of some kind on his cheek, Sheriff Kyle, like Lucas, was convinced that it was Crawford, Rogers, and Hanson.

Leaving the sheriff to further investigate the shooting, Lucas rode down to the livery.

"Yes, sir, are you looking to board your horse?" the liveryman asked.

"No, I'm looking for some information. Did three men come here to get their horses within the last hour or so?"

"Three men? Mister, this is a busy livery, what do you mean, three men? Hell, I've had ten or twelve come through in the last hour."

"All right, let's put it this way. One of the men I'm looking for would have had a scar on his cheek." Lucas raised his hand in demonstration.

"Now, there was someone like that come through. He was a rude sombitch, but then all of 'em was. What are you lookin' for 'em for?"

"One of them, and I don't know which one it was, just killed somebody named George Hager."

"Hager? Yeah, well he was a no a'count, but I don't hold with killin'. Wayland, maybe."

"Somebody named Wayland?"

"No, that's the name of a town. I heard 'em talkin' about Wayland. I don't know as that's where they was a-goin' or not, but they was talkin' about it."

"Thanks."

15

WAYLAND, TEXAS

C rawford, Rogers, and Hanson were having supper in Wayland.

"What we need is some insurance," Crawford said.

"That don't make no sense," Hanson said. "Why the hell would we need fire insurance? We ain't got nothin' to burn down."

"I'm not talkin' about fire insurance, you dumb fool. I'm talking about some way to keep this here Cain offin us."

"Sounds good to me, but how do we do that?" Hanson asked.

"We'll grab us a woman 'n put out the word that anybody comes lookin' for us, we'll kill 'er," Rogers said.

"Where we goin' get a woman?'" Hanson asked.

"Hell, it'll be easy," Rogers said. "We'll just pay some whore to make her come with us 'n grab her."

"No," Crawford said. "There ain't nobody what gives a damn 'bout a whore. If we're goin' to do that we need to grab us someone that folks cares enough to make a deal with us."

DENTON, TEXAS

Rufe Sawyer met up with his former prison mates, Moe Godfrey, Chris Dumey, and Amos Coleman. They were sitting around a table in Coleman's shack.

"With all of us out now, we need to go into town and celebrate," Godfrey said.

"How much money you got, Moe?" Sawyer asked.

"I got a dollar 'n eighty cents left out of the twenty they give me when they let me outta prison."

"And I don't reckon either one of you two have much more'n that," Sawyer said.

"I got four dollars," Coleman said, proudly.

"What about you, Chris?"

"Two dollars and thirty cents," Dumey said.

"I've got ten dollars," Sawyer said. "That's less than twenty dollars, all told. Now, can any of you tell me how we can celebrate with less than twenty dollars?"

Godfrey laughed. "That don't help none."

"All right, so the first thing we need to do, is get money," Sawyer said.

"You got 'ny idea how we might go 'bout gettin' this money?" Coleman asked.

"Not yet. I'll come up with somethin' though. I just need to make certain that we're all in this together."

"Hell, yeah," Godfrey said. The other two agreed with him.

LUCAS CAIN WAS unaware of Rufe Sawyer and the three men that made up the outlaw gang that he was assembling. That was because, though their intentions were evil, since being released from prison none of the four had broken any law.

Lucas's attention was directed toward Harley Mack Crawford, an outlaw he did know. The liveryman in Dallas had suggested the three had headed for Wayland, so Lucas was headed that way.

MEANWHILE, Crawford and the other two were in Wayland near the school. They had rethought their idea of grabbing a woman and decided to take a child.

"If it's a grown woman we grab, there'll be some that won't give a damn. But if we take a kid, the whole town will be a-worryin' about it."

BILLY BATEMAN WAS a seventh-grade student in the Wayland School. He was Miss Sidwell's biggest challenge, and this morning he had dropped a frog down Mary Beth Stokes's dress. Mary Beth screamed, the other girls in the classroom recoiled in horror, and all the boys laughed.

"Billy John Bateman!" Miss Sidwell said in her sternest tone of voice.

"Uh-oh, Billy, she used all three of your names. You're in trouble now," one the other boys in the room teased.

Miss Sidwell wrote a note and gave it to Billy. "I want you to take this note to your mother, asking her to meet me after school today. If she doesn't show up, I'll know that you didn't give her the note."

"All right," Billy said as he took the note and started back to his seat.

"Now, Billy," Miss Sidwell said. "I want you to take the note now."

"Yes, ma'am," Billy said, smiling. He would take the note to his mother, but he would get in a little fishing first.

"Harley Mack," Cole Rogers said. "Lookie there, a kid just come out of the school all by his ownself."

"It'd be better iffen it was a girl, but we'll grab 'im," Harley Mack said. "But let's wait 'til he leaves the school-yard, so if he yells out, why they won't nobody hear 'im."

The three waited until Billy was well off the school grounds before they started following him, their horses moving no faster than Billy was walking.

"Where's he goin'?" Hanson asked.

"Looks to me like he's goin' to that crick," Crawford said. "That's good, 'cause there won't nobody hear him down there."

Billy had seen the three men, and he wondered why they were riding their horses so slowly. But other than that, he paid no attention to them.

Billy always carried line and a hook in his pocket. When he got to the stream, he would break off a tree limb, tie his line on it, dig up a worm, and he would be fishing. A big smile spread across his face. He should have thought to drop a frog down Mary Beth's dress a long time ago.

He was busy tying the line to the little branch he had broken off, when the three men came up to him.

"Boy," Crawford said. "You're a-comin' with us."

"What do you mean I'm coming with you? Goin' where?"

"It don't make no difference where we're goin'. You'll be with us."

"No, sir, there ain't no way I'm goin' anywhere with ya'll."

Crawford drew his pistol and pointed it at Billy. "Oh, I think you will."

Billy ran out into the stream to get away from them, but the water was waist deep, which slowed him to a walk.

Crawford aimed at him and pulled the trigger. He saw blood fly from the back of the boy's head, where he hit him. The boy fell forward, face down into the water, then began floating down stream.

"Maybe takin' a hostage warn't that good an idea," Crawford said, as he returned his pistol to the holster.

Miss Sidwell was upset when Mrs. Bateman didn't show up for her meeting after school. She knew that Mrs. Bateman wouldn't just disregard the note, which meant that Billy never gave it to her in the first place.

"Well, young Mister Billy John Bateman, if you didn't give your mother the note to come see me, I'll just go see her," Miss Sidwell said, speaking to herself.

"No, Billy didn't give me a note," Nonnie Bateman said. "As a matter of fact, he hasn't come home yet. I thought, perhaps, you were keeping him after school."

"No, not at all. I dismissed him at two o'clock this afternoon, with instructions to bring you a note asking for a meeting."

"What has he done this time?" Nonnie asked, with a long-suffering sigh.

"He dropped a frog down Mary Beth Stokes's dress," Miss Sidwell said.

"Oh, dear, that isn't good."

"No, it certainly is not. It was a total disruption of the class, to say nothing of what it did to Mary Beth."

"I assure you, he will never do that again. And, I will make certain that he apologizes to Mary Beth and the whole class. He should be home by now, but I have no idea where he is."

"That's quite all right, we've had our meeting, and I'm satisfied that Billy will never do that again."

"Oh, I can promise you that," Nonnie said.

When Colin Bateman came home from his blacksmith shop that evening, he was met by a very anxious Nonnie.

"Billy hasn't come home yet," she said.

"Where is he?"

"That's just it. He didn't come from school. Miss Sidwell sent him home at two o'clock."

"Oh, dear, what did he pull this time?"

"It doesn't matter," Nonnie said. "I'm worried about our boy."

They were upset when Billy didn't arrive for supper.

But when he wasn't home by ten o'clock, they took their worries to see Sheriff Watters.

"Well, I'm pretty sure he isn't in one of the saloons," Watters said, with a little chuckle. He realized, right away, that the Batemans were too worried to react to one of his jokes. "Have you checked with his friends?"

"Yes. We did that before we came to see you," Colin Bateman said. "You were sort of our last hope."

"Well, I wouldn't worry about it too much," Watters said." How much trouble could he get into here? Wayland is a small town, after all."

Having left it in the hands of Sheriff Watters, neither Nonnie nor Colin slept a wink that night.

16

Lucas got an idea as to how to locate Crawford and the others. But for his idea to work, he would need the cooperation of a newspaper. And he smiled as he thought about that, because he knew just where he would go.

He was greeted by Maggie McKay when he went to the *Eastland Journal.*

"I'll bet I know why you're here," Maggie said. "I'll bet you're here to see my sister."

"I do want to see her, but I want to see your father, too," Lucas said.

"You're going to ask him if you can court Carolina," Maggie said with a broad smile.

Lucas chuckled. "Well, that's not quite why I want to talk to him."

Hearing them talking, Carolina came from the press-room, and greeted Lucas with a big smile.

"Hello, big brother," she said. "What brings you back to Eastland?"

"I have an idea as to how I might be able to locate

Harley Mack Crawford," Lucas said. "But I'll need your help. Well, you and your father's."

Carolina got an expression of curiosity. "How could we help?"

"I want you to publish an article to make Crawford think that the bank in Fort Worth is using a courier to send ten thousand dollars in cash to the cottonseed oil mill here in Eastland."

"I don't understand, why do you want them to know...?" Carolina paused in midquestion. "Wait a minute, there isn't going to be a shipment, is there?"

"No."

"But you are going to be the courier."

"Yes."

"Oh, Lucas, you'll be by yourself?"

"Yes."

"All right, if you think that's what you have to do, I'll write the article," Carolina said, "but I won't like it."

Carolina went to her desk, picked up a pencil and began to write as Lucas dictated.

From the Eastland Journal*:*

Carlyle Announces Money Transfer

William Carlyle, president of the Board of Trade, announced today, that money is being transferred from the Fort Worth Bank and Trust to the Eastland Cottonseed Oil Mill to cover the cost of machinery that will be needed to process the cottonseeds.

The Cottonseed Oil Mill project suffered a serious setback when the three Fort Worth businessmen were killed, and the draft guaranteeing payment was nullified.

The Fort Worth Board of Trade and the Fort Worth Cottonseed Oil Mill will establish a memorial fund to honor the service of William Kirby, Mason Poppell, and Woodrow Knox. Details are being set up for the community to contribute to this fund.

According to Carlyle, ten thousand dollars is being transferred by bonded courier from Fort Worth, and will be in the Eastland Bank by Tuesday, next.

"Look at this," Crawford said, thumping the article in the *Fort Worth Democrat Gazette* with his fingers. "Them folks who's a-wantin' that cottonseed oil mill in Fort Worth are at it again. This here article says they're spendin' ten thousand dollars to get equipment."

"So, what does that have to do with us?" Hanson asked.

"It says here, one man is 'a gonna be takin' that money to Eastland," Crawford said. "Now, what do you think's gonna happen to that money?"

"Damn," Rogers said. "We got to take it."

"How are we gonna do that?" Hanson asked.

"The money'll be comin' from Fort Worth. All we got to do is keep an eye on the Fort Worth road," Crawford said.

"But how will we know who it is?" Hanson asked.

"I got me an idea," Rogers said. "We can keep an eye on the bank in Fort Worth, 'n if someone comes out, then starts ridin' toward Eastland, we'll know he's our man."

"That's a good idea," Crawford said.

"I CAN'T SEND ten thousand dollars to Bill Gillespie," Scott Montgomery, president of the Fort Worth Bank and Trust, said to Lucas. "I'd like to help the Board of Trade, but there's no way I could do that."

"I don't actually need the money," Lucas explained. "Just an empty bank bag."

"What good would that…" Montgomery started, then he smiled. "You're using that as bait, aren't you?"

"You got it," Lucas said.

"Wait a minute. Actually, you'll be the bait, won't you?"

"Like I said, you got it."

CRAWFORD, Rogers, and Hanson had been sitting on a bench in front of Chips Shoe Alley since before the bank opened. They noted the arrival and departure of every bank customer so far but hadn't seen anyone who could even remotely be a courier.

Lucas left the Fort Worth Bank and Trust carrying a bank bag, which he took great pains to tie to his saddle horn.

"That's him," Crawford said. "Let's go, we'll get ahead of 'im, and wait on 'im."

The three mounted their horses and rode slowly until they got out of town. Then, they broke into a trot, covering the first two miles rather quickly. Alternating the trotting and walking, they went about twenty miles before turning around and heading back toward Fort Worth. It was there they planned to meet the courier.

So far, Lucas had met quite a few travelers on the road, both mounted and in wagons or buckboards. He was well past halfway to Eastland and was beginning to think that his ruse wasn't going to work.

Then, just as he rounded a curve, someone shot at him, and he heard the pop, as the bullet fried the air beside him.

Lucas dismounted and slapping Charley Two on his rump, he sent his horse out of the way, and then jumped into a ditch that ran parallel to the road.

"Mister, give us that money you're a-carryin', 'n we won't shoot you," someone called.

"No, I don't think so. You're going to have to come get it, Crawford."

"What the hell? How did you know my name?" Crawford yelled back, in an agitated voice.

"I just know. Why don't you three boys throw down your guns now, so we can get this over with?"

"I ain't throwin' my gun down for nobody," Crawford called back.

Crawford had lifted his head to see where Lucas was, and that was all the opening Lucas needed.

Lucas pulled the trigger and saw a hole appear on the forehead of the man who had taken the shot at him.

"Son of a bitch! He just kilt Harley Mack!" one of the other two men shouted.

From Lucas's position, he could see that by keeping below the road elevation, he could circle back and get around the curve. He knew he would be able to cross the road without being seen. He heard two or three shots being fired toward where he had just been.

"What are you shootin' at?" one of the men asked.

"I don't know, but if we can make him keep his head down, he can't shoot us from over there."

"No, but I can shoot you from here," Lucas said, coming up behind them.

One of the two men shot at Lucas, but he was frightened and hurried his shot. Lucas returned fire and hit the man in his gun hand. With a little cry of pain, he dropped the gun.

"Don't shoot! Don't shoot no more! I give up!" the other said, dropping his pistol, and putting his hands up.

Lucas whistled loudly and Charley Two came trotting back toward him.

LUCAS MADE QUITE an entry into Eastland. There were two riders in front of him, and one of those riders was leading a second horse over which lay a body.

The little procession stopped in front of the sheriff's office, and Sheriff Dozier, who had already been alerted, was standing out front.

"Well, well, what do we have here?" Sheriff Dozier asked.

"These are the men who killed the three men on the train and robbed the bank in Palo Pinto," Lucas said, as he dismounted. "Get down," he ordered both Rogers and Hanson.

"Did you recover any of the money they took from the bank?" Sheriff Dozier asked.

"What's left, is in the saddlebags," Rogers said.

"Cole, what the hell did you tell 'em for?" Hanson asked.

"What good would it do us now?" Rogers replied. "If we tell 'em where the money is, they might go a little easier on us."

Lucas opened each of the saddlebags and took out the money.

"Who's the dead one?" Sheriff Dozier asked.

"Look at his face," Lucas replied.

"Crawford?"

"Yes."

"If one of 'em is goin' to be dead, I'd just as soon it be Crawford," Sheriff Dozier said. "Simmons?" he called out to one of the men gathered around the excitement. "Take Mr. Harley Mack Crawford to the mortician for me, would you?"

"Gladly," Simmons answered. He took the horse's lead and started toward the undertaker's establishment.

Once inside, Rogers and Hanson were put in the same jail cell. That done, Lucas and the sheriff began counting the money that was recovered.

"One thousand, two hundred and twenty-seven dollars," Sheriff Dozier said. "They sure went on a spending spree."

"Do we get any deal for tellin' you where the money was?" Rogers called from the jail cell.

"Why should you? It isn't like we weren't going to look in your saddlebags."

"See there, you just gave away the money for nothin'," Hanson said.

"I didn't give the money away," Rogers said. "It's like the sheriff said, they was gonna look in there anyway."

"I know somethin' that might help us," Hanson said.

"What's that?"

"Sheriff?" Hanson called out.

"What do you want?"

"You're probably goin' to get word that a schoolboy is missin' in Wayland. He ain't just missin', he's dead.

Harley Mack shot him, and he floated off down the crick."

"Where are Hanson and Rogers going to wind up?" Carolina asked Lucas, later that afternoon. "Fort Worth for the three businessmen they killed, or Palo Pinto for robbing the bank and killing that woman, or Wayland for killing that little boy?"

"I don't know, probably Fort Worth," Lucas said.

"I think it should be Wayland," Carolina said.

"Why?"

"Because you know the whole town is grieving the killing of a child. And if they're found guilty, they'll probably hang, and that should satisfy both Fort Worth and Palo Pinto."

"But what if the court in Wayland doesn't sentence them to hang?"

"Then they can be taken to Fort Worth and tried again," Carolina said.

"What about the law of double jeopardy?"

Carolina smiled. "It won't be double jeopardy. It would be a new crime in each place."

"I'll be damn," Lucas said with a little chuckle. "That's right, you're a pretty smart woman."

"Well thank you, sir, for not only making that observation, but also saying it aloud."

When Lucas left Carolina, he went to the sheriff's office.

"I've got to make arrangements for Hanson and Rogers to go back to Fort Worth on the train," Sheriff Dozier said.

"Sheriff, let's take 'em to Wayland," Lucas said.

"To Wayland? Why? They killed three of Fort Worth's leading citizens, and they robbed a bank and killed a woman in Palo Pinto."

Lucas shared Carolina's reasoning with Dozier.

"That's a good idea," Dozier said. "I'll let Sheriff Watters know that we'll be bringin' Rogers and Hanson with us."

17

The entire town of Wayland had been looking for Billy John Bateman, who had been gone for over a week. Sheriff Watters was sitting at his desk when the telegraph delivery boy came into the office.

"I have a telegram for you."

"Thanks, Danny," Watters said, holding out a dime as he took the little yellow sheet.

CRAWFORD HANSON ROGERS CONFESS MURDER OF BILLY BATEMAN STOP U.S. MARSHAL CAIN ARRIVING TODAY WITH PRISONERS HANSON AND ROGERS FOR TRIAL STOP

Watters read the telegram, then bowed his head, and pinched the bridge of his nose.

"Damn. I'm not at all surprised. It's going to be hard tellin' that boy's parents."

"They found the Bateman boy?" Deputy Steward asked.

"No, they haven't found him, but they've got a confession to his murder. Marshal Cain will be here today."

Sheriff Watters picked up his hat.

"You're goin' to tell the boy's mama?" Steward asked.

"No, I'm goin' to tell Colin, and let him tell her. That'll be easier," Watters said. "I think," he added.

When Watters reached the blacksmith shop, Colin was holding a glowing red horseshoe with long handled tongs and was raising sparks from it as he brought the hammer down on it. Watters waited until the shoe was dipped into a pan of water and laid aside.

Colin looked up at Watters, and the expression on the sheriff's face was one of concern.

"You've got something for me, Dale?"

Sheriff Watters held out the telegram, and Colin laid the tongs and hammer aside as he reached for it.

He read the telegram, gave a little gasp, and his eyes glazed over with tears.

"Has Nonnie seen this?" he asked in a choked voice.

"No. I thought it might be better coming from you."

Colin nodded his head.

Watters watched as Colin took off his apron, then started a slow walk from the shop to his house.

When Lucas arrived in Wayland with his prisoners, there was a mixture of sorrow and anger.

"Ever'one is glad Crawford is dead, and they're all wantin' Rogers and Hanson to hang," Sheriff Watters said, as he took charge of the prisoners.

"That's probably what will happen," Lucas said. "But now I'm going to help find Billy's body. It won't take away the grief, but I'm sure the Batemans would rather have him buried."

TWO MILES SOUTH OF TOWN, the creek had a very sharp bend to the west, and there hung up in some willows, they found Billy Bateman's body.

Practically the whole town turned out for the funeral. Lucas did as well, even though he had no direct connection to Billy or his parents. After the funeral, as Lucas was about to leave, Billy's parents came to talk to him.

"I want to thank you for finding Billy's body," Nonnie said. "Without it, I don't think I would ever have accepted that he's gone."

"And I especially thank you for killing the son of a bitch that shot my boy," Colin added. "I just hope the other two hang for what they did."

THE WHOLE TOWN turned out to jeer and hurl curses at Rogers and Hanson who were now behind bars.

"We're goin' to be hanged, you know," Rogers said.

"I know," Hanson replied.

"So you rattin' out Harley Mack didn't do nothin' for us."

"It did for me," Hanson said.

"Yeah? Well just what the hell did it do for you?"

"It cleaned my conscience."

"You're really somethin', you know that, Gene? I wouldn't be surprised if you didn't start prayin' to Jesus when you're standin' on the gallows."

"Why not? One of the thieves on the cross did."

THE TRIAL WAS HELD two days later, and there wasn't an empty seat in the saloon that had been converted to a courtroom. Sheriff Watters had held open two seats up front, for Colin and Nonnie Bateman. Lucas was also seated there because he would be the principal witness.

When Sheriff Watters brought in the two defendants, they were booed by the people in the gallery. They shuffled to the defense table because they were in shackles.

The people in the gallery were still muttering when the bailiff came in.

"All rise. This court is now in session, the Honorable Manfred Egleton presiding."

Judge Egleton was an average-sized man, with gray hair, and a prominent nose. He took his seat behind the bench, then rapped the gavel. "You may be seated."

There was the muffled sounds of pants and skirts as the gallery took their seats.

"Mr. Bailiff, for what purpose is this court assembled?"

"Your Honor, there comes before this court, Gene Hanson and Cole Rogers, charged with the act of murder, in the case of the death of Billy John Bateman, a boy twelve years of age."

"Is counsel for the defense present?" Judge Egleton asked.

A short man, nattily dressed, and with glasses, stood at the defense table.

"Nolan Goodridge for the defense, Your Honor." Goodridge sat back down.

"Counsel for the state?" Judge Egleton asked.

A tall, very thin man, wearing a cutaway coat stood.

"Your Honor, Benjamin Cassidy for prosecution."

"Your opening statement, Mr. Cassidy."

Cassidy approached the twelve men who made up the jury.

"During *voir dire*, I asked if there was anyone in this jury as it is assembled, who opposed the death penalty. There was no response as to anyone being opposed, so I tell you now, that this is a capital trial and a finding of guilty, will inevitably lead to the imposition of the death penalty."

Cassidy sat back down.

"Your opening statement, Mr. Goodridge," the judge said.

Goodridge stood but did not leave the table. "Your Honor, I have no remarks to offer at this time." He sat back down.

"Mr. Prosecutor, make your case."

"Billy John Bateman was but twelve years old, a schoolboy. He was at the creek, fishing when these two men," he pointed to the defendants, "and another approached him. He was shot and killed. These two men will say that it was the third man, who is now dead, who shot Billy. Prosecution will accept that, but you must understand, that is tantamount to a plea of guilty, because it makes no difference who pulled the trigger. These two men, by their very presence participated in the murder of an innocent child."

"Call your first witness," the judge said.

"Prosecution calls U.S. Marshal Lucas Cain."

Lucas testified repeating the statement given to him by Hanson and Rogers. After he stepped down, Miss Clara Sidwell was called to the stand.

Miss Sidwell was identified as Billy's teacher, and she told what a good student he had been. She said his absence from school had been authorized, because she had sent him to deliver a letter to his mother.

Nonnie and Colin Bateman both testified about what a good boy Billy was, and how they were going to miss him. Nonnie cried during her testimony, and nearly every woman in the gallery shed tears with her.

That was exactly what Cassidy wanted.

Goodridge offered no cross-examination.

"Defense may call your witness."

"Your Honor, we have no witnesses to call," Goodridge said.

"Very well, you may make your closing statement."

"Your Honor, gentlemen of the jury, my clients admit to being present at the killing of Billy John Bateman. But neither of them fired the fatal shot. That shot was fired by Harley Mack Crawford. And I would remind the jury that it was information provided by my clients that enabled Billy Bateman's body to be found, thus providing closure for his parents. Defense rests."

"Closing statement, Mr. Prosecutor?"

Cassidy stood but didn't leave the table.

"No closing statement is needed, Your Honor. By admitting that his clients were present at the time of the murder, Mr. Goodridge has made my case. Prosecution rests."

THE JURY DIDN'T LEAVE the jury box but caucused in place. It took fewer than five minutes to find Gene Hanson and Cole Rogers guilty of murder in the first degree.

"Would the defendants please stand?" Judge Egleton said.

Goodridge stood and urged Rogers and Hanson to do so as well.

"Cole Rogers and Gene Hanson, you have been found guilty of murder in the first degree. It is the order of this court that you be put to death by hanging, execution to be carried out as soon as it is possible to do so."

———

THE SCAFFOLD WAS BUILT in one day, and two days later, practically the entire town turned out to watch the hanging. There was some discussion as to whether or not to let school out, because it was one of their own who was murdered. The decision was finally made to allow those students who wanted to watch, do so if it was approved by their parents.

Finally, Rogers and Hanson were brought out, with their hands cuffed behind their back. They climbed the thirteen steps up to the platform, and there took their position over the trapdoor that would take them to eternity.

The only church in town was nondenominational, and the preacher, E.D. Snellgrove, waited on the platform with the hangman. He stepped over to Hanson.

"Would you like a prayer?"

"No, I don't want no prayer," Rogers said with a growl. "I want to go to hell to kick Harley Mack Crawford's ass, 'cause he's the one that got us into this mess in the first place."

Hanson accepted the prayer.

18

The bounty for Crawford, Rogers, and Hanson had grown. It was one thousand dollars for Crawford, and five hundred each, for Rogers and Hanson. That two thousand dollars, added to what he already had in the bank, gave Lucas a nest egg of a little over five thousand dollars. That would be enough money for him to buy some land and start a small ranch. He thought about that for a while. Did he really want to settle down? There was something that could be said for herding cows over dodging bullets. On the other hand, he liked the freedom of being a deputy U.S. Marshal, free to pursue outlaws for the bounty that had been placed on their heads.

He considered his possibilities over supper one evening, and as he was thinking about what the future might bring, Carolina McKay popped into his mind. Why was he thinking about Carolina?

It didn't take him long to answer his question. Carolina was a very attractive young woman, and he had enjoyed his time with her and her parents and sister.

Thinking of Carolina brought up an unexpected memory of Rosie, and he remembered their wedding.

Rosie was popular, not only because of her work at the newspaper, but also because she had grown up in Cape Girardeau and the family had many friends. As a result, the First Presbyterian Church on Broadway was filled with well-wishers.

For their honeymoon, Lucas had arranged a trip, by riverboat, down to New Orleans.

"Ha, after the Sultana, *I wouldn't think you would ever want to get on a riverboat again," Dan Lindell said.*

Dan was referring to the riverboat that was carrying Union soldiers who had been prisoners of the Confederacy during the Civil War. The boiler had exploded and the boat sank, with the loss of more than eleven hundred men.

"Think about it, Dan," Lucas replied with a wide smile, "sitting out on the hurricane deck with you and two thousand, four hundred other unwashed, uncouth men, or being in a private stateroom with a beautiful young woman who is my wife. Do you really see any comparison?"

Dan laughed. "Enjoy the trip, my friend."

It took the *Delta Mist* three days to go downriver. After a week in New Orleans, enjoying all that the city had to offer, they returned to Cape Girardeau on board the *Mississippi Queen*, this trip taking four days. Lucas could truly say that it was the most wonderful two weeks of his entire life.

But his memories of Rosie came at a terrible price to pay.

Unbidden, the terrible memory returned. He saw again, the expression on Dr. Brandt's face.

"Doc, what is it?" he asked.

"I'm sorry, Lucas," Dr. Brandt said, with a sad shake of his head.

"You're sorry? What is it? What happened?" This time Lucas shouted the question.

"Childbed fever."

"What? What do you mean?"

"I'm afraid we lost her, Lucas. Rosie died during childbirth. The baby, a girl, was stillborn," Dr. Brandt said in a voice that was quiet, and heavy with sorrow and regret.

"No! My God, no!" Lucas shouted.

He had rushed by the doctor, into the bedroom where he saw Rosie lying on the bed, her legs spread upon a sheet stained with blood and the afterbirth. Her eyes were open, and unseeing.

"Rosie!" Lucas said, kneeling beside the bed and grasping her hand.

"ROSIE." This time, Lucas said the name aloud as the memories faded.

He was going to Eastland.

The first thing he did when he arrived in Eastland, was stop in a saloon to have a beer.

"They robbed the Milner store, 'n kilt both of 'em," somebody said. "Frank and his wife."

"Who did it? Do they know?" another asked.

The first man chuckled. "Well they know who one of 'em was. See, there was this guy named Paul Coker, 'n he was workin' in the back so the robbers never saw 'im. When he heard the shots, he looked through the door 'n seen 'em. One of 'em was a feller by the name of Rufe Sawyer. Coker know'd him, on account of Coker was in prison with 'im."

"Have they caught this Sawyer guy yet?"

"No, but ever' body sure as hell is a-lookin' for 'im."

Lucas listened to the exchange, and filed it away. He chuckled. The way he listened so closely to this bit of information told him he wasn't about to buy land and settle down.

After Lucas left the saloon, he walked down the street to the sheriff's office. Sheriff Dozier was sitting at his desk, and he looked up when Lucas came in.

"Lucas Cain," Sheriff Dozier said with a wide smile. "What brings you back to our fair city?"

"What do you know about Rufe Sawyer?" Lucas asked.

"Only that he, and three other men, one of whom might be Moe Godfrey, robbed a store and killed the man and his wife who owned it."

"Is there paper out on him?"

"Oh yeah, fifteen hundred dollars. Why do you ask? Are you going after him?"

"I don't know. I just heard someone mention him, when I was at the saloon."

After leaving the sheriff's office, Lucas walked down to the newspaper, which was the original reason for his visit to Eastland.

When he went into the office of the *Eastland Journal*, Maggie was sweeping the floor.

"Daddy," she called. "Lucas is here."

"Well hello, big brother," Carolina said warmly, as she came up front to greet Lucas.

"Hello, sis."

"So you came to look me up, did you?" Carolina said with a teasing smile.

"I guess so, if you're the one I need to see to put an ad in the paper," Lucas replied.

"What? You came here to buy an ad?" The tone of her voice was one of disappointment.

Lucas laughed, and Carolina realized that he was teasing.

"Oh, you," she said, laughing as she hit him on the shoulder.

"Lucas, my boy, I just ran a story about you, yesterday," Cephus said, coming out of the pressroom. He wiped his right hand on his apron, then extended it to take Lucas's proffered hand.

"Oh?"

"Yes. You stopping the Harley Mack Crawford crime wave, has appeared in every newspaper in Texas. And beyond our state lines, I'm sure."

"I had no idea," Lucas said.

"Why, boy, they're goin' to be talking about you, the way they talk about Wyatt Earp or Bat Masterson," Cephus said. "What brings you to Eastland? Are you on the hunt for Rufe Sawyer?"

"No. I mean, not necessarily. I just heard about Sawyer for the first time about an hour ago."

"Well, I hope you go after him. He's every bit as evil as Harley Mack Crawford was."

"Actually, I'm here to pay back a debt I owe."

"Who do you owe the debt to?"

"To Carolina. Well actually to you, Mrs. McKay, and Maggie as well."

"I don't understand," Cephus said.

"You had me over for a wonderful supper," Lucas said. "I would like to repay that debt by taking all of you out to supper at the nicest restaurant in town, whichever one that is."

"That would be Eastland's Pride," Carolina said, excitedly. "And we would love to go."

"Carolina, don't you think we should give your mother a say in this before we make a commitment?" Cephus asked.

"Daddy, you know she's going to want to go," Maggie said. "And even if she doesn't, you and Carolina and I want to go, so we can outvote her, three to one, then she'll have to go."

Cephus laughed. "Lucas, it looks like you're going to be out the price of five meals."

BECAUSE HE WAS the publisher of the *Eastland Journal*, there was no one in town who didn't recognize Cephus McKay. He was warmly greeted when they went into the restaurant.

"You have a choice of any of the empty tables," the waiter said.

"Oh, I don't care that much, Murray. I guess…"

"That one back in the corner," Lucas said.

Cephus smiled. "That's the one we want."

As they approached the table, Lucas made the comment. "I hope you don't mind, but I'd like the chair that's back in the corner."

"I gathered as much," Cephus said with a little chuckle.

When they reached the table, Lucas pulled out a chair for Carolina, then to Maggie's delight, for her as well. After the two were seated, he sat down. Where he was sitting was absolutely in the corner, with walls behind and on either side of him.

"Wow, nobody has ever pulled out a chair for me before," Maggie said.

Cephus held the chair out for Ethyl, and she smiled. "Lucas, I wish you spent more time around us. My husband might well learn some manners from you."

After Cephus took his own seat, he looked across the table to Lucas. "I apologize for not requesting this table first. I should have realized that you being a bounty hunter wouldn't want your back to the door."

"A bounty hunter?" Ethyl said in surprise. "I thought you were a U.S. Marshal."

"Technically I am," Lucas said. "But I serve without pay, and that allows me to collect bounties on the men I bring in."

"And, I expect you got a pretty good bounty for Harley Mack Crawford," Cephus said. "Or at least you should have."

Lucas smiled. "Let's just say that I can quite easily afford the price of this supper."

Cephus laughed. "Modesty becomes you."

It was a pleasant supper, and Lucas found that he was enjoying it more than he thought he would.

"Papa, you and mama and Maggie go on home, I'm going to take a little walk," Carolina said.

"You be careful, you hear? You know I don't like for you to be out after dark," Ethyl said.

Carolina laughed. "Mama, Lucas is going to be with me. What could happen?"

"Can you think of anyone better suited to look out for Carolina during a dark walk?" Cephus asked.

After leaving the restaurant, Lucas and Carolina walked through town, its streets illuminated by gas lamps. Then, at Carolina's urging, they left the town and walked down a road that passed through open country.

"This," Carolina said. "This is what I wanted you to see. It's my favorite spot in the whole town."

What Carolina pointed to was the Leon River, a flowing body of water about forty feet wide. The river was shining silver in the reflected moonlight.

"I can see why you like it here," Lucas said.

They found a place to sit, and after a few minutes, Lucas picked up a rock and tossed it into the river. They were rewarded with a splashing sound.

Carolina threw one into the river as well. Then Lucas threw another, then Carolina, and they continued to throw stones until they both broke out laughing.

"Look at us," Carolina said. "Are we a couple of kids, or not?"

"When I was a kid, I used to throw flat rocks into the river to see how many times I could make them skip across the top of the water," Lucas said.

"Really? What river would that be?"

"The Mississippi River at Cape Girardeau, Missouri."

"Oh, my, I've read about that river. It's considerably bigger than the Leon."

Lucas laughed. "Yes, I would say it's a little bigger than this."

"Now you're patronizing me."

"I'm sorry, I didn't mean to."

Carolina smiled, then leaned closer to him. "That's all right. You can make up for it with a kiss."

Carolina put her hand behind Lucas's head and pulled him to her. She kissed him, and the kiss deepened.

Lucas felt something he hadn't felt in a long time, and he allowed it to go on.

Then he thought of Rosie, and he pulled back from the kiss. Carolina looked at him with a pained and confused expression on her face.

"Why did you pull away like that?" she asked.

"I'm sorry, Carolina," Lucas said. "This was the first

meaningful kiss I've had since my wife died, and I guess I'm not over her yet. I hope I haven't upset you."

"Oh, no, not at all," Carolina said with a warm smile. "I admire a man who can love so deeply."

"Maybe I should walk you back home," Lucas suggested.

"All right."

Lucas stood first, then reached down to help Carolina up. They walked in silence for a few minutes, then Carolina chuckled.

"What is it?" Lucas asked.

"I was just thinking, I had no business kissing my brother like that in the first place."

Lucas laughed as well. "Yeah, what were we thinking about?"

19

FORT WORTH, TEXAS

Carl Lewis and Ben Carson were tossing horseshoes in the livery yard of the Rasher and Hall Stagecoach Line. Carson was a driver and Lewis a shotgun guard. This wasn't just any horseshoe match. There had been a tournament among all the drivers, shotgun guards, and hostlers. Lewis and Carson had risen through the sets to become the last two undefeated contestants in the tournament.

Everyone who worked at Rasher and Hall, except the few who couldn't get away, joined with the townspeople and waiting passengers to watch the match. Several of the onlookers had even placed bets on the outcome.

Carl Lewis, who was about to toss, held the horseshoe up to his mouth and spit on it.

"Whoa now, Carl, you weight that thing down with spit, 'n it's goin' to go all cattywampus on you. You don't want to do that, do you?" one of the watchers called out.

"Don't pay him no mind, Carl," another called. "He's

bettin' on Ben, so what he's doin' is tryin' to make you throw a bad one."

Lewis tossed the shoe. It hit the post, made one whirl around it, then dropped as a solid ringer.

It was Carson's turn to toss the shoe. He held it just in front of his chest for a moment, rubbing on it with his left hand, then tossed it. It, too, was a ringer.

The game would consist of each player tossing the horseshoe fifty times. Both Lewis and Carson had tossed the shoe forty-eight times, and as they prepared for the final inning, they were dead even.

Lewis made ringers with tosses forty-nine and fifty.

"It's up to you now, Ben, don't let me down," someone called. "I've got two dollars ridin' on you."

Ben made a ringer with toss number forty-nine, but his fiftieth toss was a leaner.

There were mixed reactions from the onlookers, some groaned in disappointment, others cheered the winner, but there were also shouts of "good game!"

Lewis and Carson met in the middle of the ring and shook hands. Even though they were competitors in this game of horseshoes, they were good friends and were often paired on stagecoach runs.

"Don't feel bad," Lewis said. "You played one hell of a game."

"I did, didn't I?" Carson replied. "By the way, we'll be making a run together next week."

"You sure you want to be making a run with someone who beat you so bad?" Lewis asked.

"Surely, you ain't goin' to be braggin' 'bout beatin' me for the whole trip, are you?"

"Not the whole trip," Lewis replied. "Just about half the time. And who knows, I might even have time to give you a lesson or two on how to toss the shoes," he added with a little chuckle.

"Well, I ain't goin' to be spittin' on no horseshoes, I can tell you that, right now," Carson said.

Lewis laughed. "Damn, I didn't know I'd given that secret away."

"You're full of it, Carl," Carson said with a laugh. "Come on, let's go have a beer. I'm buyin'."

WITH RUFE SAWYER:

"This money was good, but it spends too fast," Sawyer said.

Sawyer was in Decatur in the Bull's Head Saloon with Moe Godfrey, Chris Dumey, and Amos Coleman. "What we need, is a bigger score."

"You got that right," Coleman said. "I don't have much left."

"That's 'cause you wasted all your money on bad women," Dumey teased.

"Huh-uh, they weren't all bad. Just that 'n up in Queen's Peak."

Godfrey laughed. "What was her name? Dinah? Lord, ole' Dinah had a lot of miles on her. She looked liken she coulda been your grandma."

"Yeah, well there's prob'ly some grandmas that still look pretty good," Coleman said. "Only thing is, Dinah ain't one of 'em."

Dumey laughed. "You got that right."

"Come on, fellas, let's get our attention back to what I said. I want us to make a big score, 'n we have to come up with what it'll be."

LUCAS HAD BEEN in Eastland for two weeks. It wasn't the longest he had ever stayed in one place, but it was pretty long, and he had to be somewhere. Fortunately, the last job provided him with enough money to stay in a hotel without any thoughts about it.

Lucas was spending a lot of time with Carolina, but he justified it by telling himself he was checking the newspaper for any situation he might want to pursue.

The time he spent with Carolina was a double-edged sword. He enjoyed his time with her, but he didn't want to lead her on. He had a feeling that she was expecting more from him, but his way of earning his living didn't lend itself to marriage, or even a long-term relationship.

Lucas thought of Sue Ellen Foley. He had saved the ranch for her mother, and Sue Ellen's relationship with Lucas had grown to be more than one of gratitude. He had left Higbee, Colorado, even though he could have been comfortable there. He was afraid if he had stayed any longer, he wouldn't be able to leave Sue Ellen, and just as it was now, he knew it was time to leave Eastland and Carolina.

WEATHERFORD, TEXAS

Anna Malone was preparing supper, and her seven-year-old daughter, Jennie, was peeling potatoes.

"How many do you want, Mama?"

"Oh, I think three will do."

"I think four," Jennie said.

"Why four?"

"Because Daddy can eat two all by himself."

Anna laughed. "Well maybe he can, but I don't think he should."

"They're going to be cut, so we won't tell him it's only three, and maybe he won't know," Jennie said.

"Yes, I think that's a good idea," Anna agreed with a little laugh.

"Mama, when I grow up, will I get married?"

"Well, I suppose you will. Most young ladies do."

"When you were my age, did you think you'd grow up and marry Daddy?"

"Did I think I would grow up and marry your father? Why no, I don't think so."

"Why not? Didn't you like him?"

"Oh, I suppose I would have liked him if I had known him. But I didn't know him."

"But you like him now."

"Yes, I love him now."

"I love him too."

"I don't think that is a problem. I know that he has enough love for both of us."

"I'm glad," Jennie said.

AFTER HEARING about the murder of the Milners, Lucas did some research. He learned that Frank Milner and his wife had operated a little store that was halfway between Fort Worth and Dallas. After telling everyone goodbye, he headed for Fort Worth.

"HELLO, Lucas, I see you're back home," Sheriff Michael Moore said by way of greeting when Lucas stepped into his office.

Lucas chuckled. "I guess Fort Worth is as much my home as anywhere else. It's either Fort Worth or Charley Two's saddle."

"So what brings you back?"

"What do you know about Rufe Sawyer?"

"Hmm, I was wondering when you would get around to looking into that. Rufe and his bunch robbed the Milner Emporium and killed Frank and Zetty Milner. That's pretty close to home. Frank and Zetty were two of the nicest folks you'd ever want to meet."

"Their place is about halfway between here and Dallas, isn't it?"

"Yes, it is. And you can't miss it, the building is pretty big, and there's a big sign on top." Sheriff Moore laughed. "I asked Frank once why he built his store out in the middle of the country like that, and he said, 'This way I can get customers from Dallas and Fort Worth.' He was a pretty smart fella, all right."

"Is there anyone out there now?" Lucas asked.

"Yes, Paul Coker's there, and he's running the store all by himself," Sheriff Moore said. "Frank and Zetty had a daughter down in San Antonio, but she's married to a lawyer there, and he doesn't want to come back to what he considers Podunk. Thing is, that little store, probably makes three times more money than any two-bit lawyer makes in San Antonio."

"I think I'll ride out and see Mr. Coker."

"Cain, just so you know, Paul Coker is an ex-con. He did two years in the state pen for branding a few cows that already had brands. He said he thought they were mavericks, and it being winter at the time, the brands were hard to see through the long hair. I believed him, and thought he would get off, but the prosecutor was damn determined to make a case out of it.

"I think the judge believed him, too, 'cause he only gave Paul two years, when he could have given him ten."

"Thanks for the information," Lucas said, and straightening his hat, he left the sheriff's office.

———

LUCAS HAD BEEN RIDING for about an hour when he saw the store. Set back from the road, there was room for a stagecoach or a large farm wagon to park without interfering with traffic on the road. Lucas rode up to the front of the store and tied Charley Two off at the hitching rail.

The man who greeted him was relatively short, about five feet, six inches tall. He had a well-trimmed mustache and thinning hair that was between brown and blond.

"Yes, sir, what can I do for you?"

"You would be Paul Coker?" Lucas asked.

"That's me."

"Mr. Coker, I'm Deputy U.S. Marshal Lucas Cain." Lucas showed his star. "I'm looking into the robbery and murder of Frank and Zetty Milner. I understand you were a witness."

"Well, sort of. I was in the back, but when I heard the commotion, I looked around."

"And you're able to identify the people?"

"Only one for sure, him being Rufe Sawyer," Paul replied. "Another one might have been Moe Godfrey, but I'm not a hundred percent sure of that. "

"What about the other two? You didn't recognize them?"

"Oh, I recognized them all right, I just don't remember their names."

Lucas laughed. "I don't understand, Mr. Coker. You say you recognized them, but you don't know who they are? How can that be?"

"The thing is, you might not know, I spent two years in prison," Coker said as he ran his hand through his hair. "I remember seein' all four of 'em in the prison yard, but even then, I knowed they wasn't the kind of people I wanted to be around, so I steered clear of 'em."

"Well, tell me what happened here."

"Like I said, I was back in the storeroom, so I didn't see 'em come in. First time I saw 'em was when I heard loud talkin'. I was about to come back out front, and soon as I opened the door, I saw all four of 'em, pointin' their guns at Frank and Zetty.

"Frank give 'em what money was in the cashbox, then they just commenced a-shootin' 'til both him and Zetty went down. After that, Sawyer and the others left. I hurried over to check on 'em, but they was both dead."

"You said you knew Sawyer in prison. Were you friends?"

"Oh, hell no," Paul said. "Sawyer was a mean son of a bitch, someone who bullied all the others. There warn't nobody in the whole prison who liked the son of a bitch, 'ceptin' maybe Moe Godfrey 'n them other two who I can't remember their names."

"Apparently they did," Lucas said. "You say there were three men you had seen in prison."

"They might be with him, but I'd be willin' to bet you that even they don't like him."

20

STATE PENITENTIARY—HUNTSVILLE, TEXAS

Warden Donald Gibson greeted Lucas when he was shown into the warden's office.

"Thanks for seeing me, Warden," Lucas said.

"What can I do for you, Marshal?"

"I'm doing some research on Rufe Sawyer," Lucas replied.

"Why? I'm sure you know he left us some time ago."

"There were some men who held up a small country store, the Milner Emporium. They killed Milner and his wife."

"And you think it might be Sawyer?" Gibson asked.

"There was an eyewitness who identified him. He was an employee of the store, and was in the storeroom at the back of the Emporium, so he wasn't seen."

"How did an eyewitness just happen to be able to identify Sawyer?"

"The witness says that he served time here with Sawyer, and recognized him."

"I don't know, that makes it a bit more suspect in my mind. If your witness is an ex-con, he may have known that Sawyer had been paroled, and just decided to take advantage of the opportunity."

"That could be true, I suppose. But I'm pretty good at reading men, and Mr. Coker came across as pretty credible to me."

"Coker? Paul Coker?"

"Yes, he said he had been in prison with Sawyer."

"No, not in prison with Sawyer. He was in at the same time. There's a difference. 'With,' suggests that Coker is just as bad as Sawyer, and that's not the case. Coker was a model prisoner, well-liked by convict and guard alike. If Coker identified Sawyer, you can count on that being the truth."

"Good. As I said, there were three others who were with Sawyer, and Coker thinks one of the other three may have been someone named Moe Godfrey."

"Godfrey, yes, it well may have been. And did you say there were two more?"

"Yes, Coker said he could remember seeing them in the yard, but he couldn't remember their names."

Gibson nodded. "My guess would be Chris Dumey and Amos Coleman. Those four spent a lot of time together, and all 'em were always getting into some sort of trouble."

"Do you think any one of the four would be capable of the cold-blooded murder of an innocent man and his wife?"

"Hell yes," Gibson said. "Sawyer served time for armed robbery, but he stood trial for robbery and murder. And as far as I'm concerned, the son of bitch should have been hanged. A smart lawyer got him off."

"Would you say that Sawyer would be the leader of the men?"

"Absolutely. Sawyer's a natural leader. If he was an honest man, he would've made a good army officer."

Lucas visited with the warden for over an hour, and when he left the prison, he felt like he had a pretty good understanding about the men he was looking for.

WEATHERFORD, TEXAS

"Mr. Morris, Mr. Fitzhugh will see you now," the bank clerk said.

"Thank you."

He followed the clerk to the office of the bank president. Fitzhugh was standing when he went to the office, and he extended his hand.

"What can I do for you, Mr. Morris?"

"Well, sir, it's what I hope I can do for you."

"And what would that be?" Fitzhugh asked.

"I've recently left the army, and I believe the experience I had could be of use to you."

"What experience was that?"

"I was an army finance officer and was often required to transfer large amounts of money. So I'm wondering if you might be able to use that experience as a courier to transfer funds for your bank."

"Hmm, that's an interesting proposal, Mr. Morris, and I know that some banks do utilize couriers, rather than stagecoaches or trains," Mr. Fitzhugh said. "Of course, any hire I might make has to have board approval, so I would need some background information. If you could provide endorsements from the army, then I believe we might be able to use you. It's too bad we didn't cross paths last week."

"Why is that, sir?"

"We're about to make a rather significant transfer of funds to a bank in Fort Worth."

"When will you be doing that? Maybe I'll have time to get all the endorsements you'll need to hire me as a courier."

"Oh, heavens, I don't see how that's possible. We'll be shipping the money to Fort Worth on the morning stage."

"That is a bit too soon," Morris said. "I'll see to it that you get my endorsements. Perhaps I could be on your payroll by the time you need another transfer."

"I'll be watching for the paperwork, Mr. Morris," Fitzhugh said. "I've always believed that it's much more efficient to use private couriers rather than a stagecoach, because we can keep better control of the transfer if we don't let it get out of our hands. Of course, we always keep the transfer schedules secret, especially when the money transfer is handled by stagecoach, so I trust you will keep our discussion this morning on the quiet."

"Of course I will, and thank you for seeing me, Mr. Fitzhugh."

———

LEAVING THE BANK, Amos Coleman rode northeast out of Weatherford to the small town of Springtown. There he rode up to the Ace High Saloon, dismounted, and went inside. He saw the three men he was meeting sitting in the corner and he headed toward them.

"What did you find out?" Sawyer asked.

"There'll be a money shipment on the Fort Worth

stage, tomorrow," Coleman said with a triumphant smile.

A big smile also spread across Sawyer's face. "Men, we have hit the jackpot."

───────────

Russell Malone had been assigned by the state to defend Arnold Pittman, an indigent defendant who was being tried for stealing from a grocery store. The case had been tried, and was just about concluded, lacking only the closing statements.

Malone was near the end of his closing argument.

"As this trial comes to a close, I ask you, what did Mr. Pittman do? He stole from a grocery store. Did he steal money? Did he hurt anyone, or even brandish a gun during the robbery? The answer to all those questions would be no. Mr. Pittman could not have brandished a gun, because he doesn't own one.

"The sad truth is, Mr. Pittman was a man on the verge of starvation. He stole a loaf of bread, a can of beans, and a pickle from the pickle barrel. The guilt belongs, not to Mr. Pittman, but to the town of Weatherford. A poorhouse, where the starving can be fed, has long been discussed in our town council. But so far, it has only been discussed; it has not been put into effect. Would it be asking too much for those of us present in this courtroom today, to take up a collection to pay Mr. Beamus for the food that was taken from his store? It would be but pennies a person. Defense rests."

Barry Westfall, who was prosecuting this case, stood and addressed not the jury, but the judge.

"Your Honor, prosecution withdraws its argument,

and asks the court to show mercy to Mr. Pittman, and direct a verdict from the bench, of not guilty."

Judge Noah Craig picked up his gavel. "This court finds the defendant, not guilty." He struck his hammer one time.

The gallery applauded, as Russell Malone and Arnold Pittman stood. There was a huge grin on Pittman's face. "Thank you, thank you!"

"Mr. Pittman, Jim O'Dell has said that he will give you a job working at his ranch. Will you consider that?" Russell asked.

"Yes, sir, I'll do anything to make an honest dollar."

"Do you know where his ranch is?"

"Yes, sir, I know."

"Also, some fine folks have taken up a collection, and they gave it to me to give to you. It amounts to thirty-seven dollars. I suggest you use it sparingly until you get your first pay from Mr. O'Dell. Don't spend it on whiskey. You were once a productive citizen, then you started drinking. It was whiskey that betrayed you."

"I'm goin' to give it up, Mr. Malone, I swear I will."

"Good. Now I want you to go over there and meet Mr. O'Dell, who is waiting for you. Don't let us down."

"I won't," Pittman said. "I promise I won't. This has sure taught me a lesson."

After court adjourned, Russell Malone returned to his office. Though he sometimes pleaded in court, such as the Pittman case just finished, most of his work dealt with documents. He had a good reputation for drawing up business contracts, property titles and other land issues, powers of attorney, and wills. Today he had done a power of attorney and prepared a will. That meant he was caught up with his work, and he smiled as he thought of the surprise he had for his wife.

Leaving his office, he walked the three blocks to his house. Anna's birthday was next week, and he looked forward to telling her what he had planned.

As soon as he opened the door, he heard Jennie call out. "Daddy's home!"

"Hello, my little angel, what have you been up to this day?" Russell hugged his daughter to him.

"I've been workin' all day, Daddy. I helped Mama cook supper."

Anna came into the living room then to greet her husband with a kiss. "That's right," she said. "Jennie has been a big help. She dusted the stairway, and she peeled the potatoes."

"Uhmm, well whatever is cooking sure smells good."

A few minutes later, as they were having roast beef with carrots and potatoes, Russell looked across the table to Anna.

"I bet you thought I'd forgotten that next Tuesday is your birthday."

"Oh, I thought you'd remember it. You always do— even if it's after I've had to give you a hint," Anna said as she began clearing the table.

"Yes, ma'am, you'll be fifty years old."

"What?" Jennie shouted. "Daddy, Mama's not that old."

"Maybe not," Russell said with a little laugh. "But when she is fifty, I'll still love her just as much as I do today. Anyway, I have an idea as to how we can celebrate your birthday."

"What do you have in mind?" Anna asked.

"How would you like to go into Fort Worth? We'll spend your birthday with your parents."

"Goodie!" Jennie said. "We're going to see Grandma and Grandpa."

21

WEATHERFORD, TEXAS

"Yeah, Sawyer is from here, all right," Sheriff Patterson said. "But I haven't seen the son of a bitch since he got out of prison, and I don't want to see him. He should have been hanged; he was tried for robbery and murder. He had a good lawyer in Russell Malone, and Malone was able to get him off the murder charge. But no matter what the jury said, there's no doubt in my mind but that he murdered Amon Belcher and got away with it. I don't really blame his lawyer. Russell is a good lawyer and a good man, and once he was assigned the case, he was honor bound to do the best he could."

"I don't think they've had time to put out any posters on him since he was identified as the killer of Frank Milner and his wife. You think you could tell me what he looks like?" Lucas asked.

"I can do a little better than that," Sheriff Patterson

said. "I've got some old wanted posters from when he killed Belcher. He's older now, of course, but I can guarantee you, he'll still be just as ugly as he always was."

The sheriff opened the bottom drawer of his desk and pulled out a binder of old dodgers. He thumbed through them until he found the one he wanted.

"Here's the one you're looking for," Sheriff Patterson said as he removed it and handed it to Lucas.

"Thanks," Lucas said. "This will help. By the way, do you know if he has any friends from when he used to live here?"

"I don't think he has a friend in town. He had some people he used to drink with, but I don't think any of them would call themselves Sawyer's friend."

"Where could I find any of them?"

"You might start with the Brown Spur Saloon. Muley Sutton is the bartender there. Tell him I said you should talk to him."

"Thanks for your help, Sheriff."

"No, thank you for going after the bastard."

LUCAS PINNED the marshal's star to his vest, so that it was visible when he went into the saloon.

"Hello, Sheriff," the bartender said. Then, taking a closer look at the badge, he corrected himself. "I mean Marshal. What can I get for you?"

"I'll have a beer," Lucas said.

The bartender got a mug, then held it under the spigot of a beer barrel to fill it.

"You would be Muley Sutton?" Lucas asked.

The bartender chuckled. "Yes, I am, and I don't mind

telling you that, because I'm sure as hell not wanted anywhere."

"That's good to know," Lucas said with grin. "Sheriff Patterson suggested I talk to you."

"About what?"

"Rufe Sawyer. He used to live here, didn't he?"

"That he did," Muley said. "But I can tell you one thing. The whole town cheered when he went to prison."

"Have you heard he was released?"

"Oh, yeah, I forgot. I did hear somebody sayin' that. You know Russell Malone got him off the murder charge for killin' Amon Belcher, but ever'body in town knows he done it. They put him in prison for stealing what? Twenty-five dollars I think it was."

"If he didn't come back to his hometown, do you have any idea where he might have gone?"

"No, not really, but you might want to talk to old Burt Cox. I guess he knew Sawyer about as well as anyone did."

"Where can I find him?"

"He runs the livery stable."

"Thanks," Lucas said. He left a quarter on the bar and didn't wait for the change.

Lucas rode down to the livery and was dismounting when a bald man, with a flowing white beard, came out to meet him.

"Yes, sir, will you be needin' to board your hoss?"

"No, I'm after a little information."

"Information? I ain't sure I can help you there."

"Are you Burt Cox?"

"Now, that I know," Cox replied, somewhat guardedly.

"Mr. Cox, I'm U.S. Marshal Lucas Cain, and I'm

looking for information on Rufe Sawyer. I was told that you and he were friends."

"Yeah, we were, when we were kids. His dad and my dad both rode for the Double Y brand. Rufe was always gettin' into trouble for first one thing then another. Then he got the idea to steal a couple of cows from Mr. Yancey, and he wanted me to go along with him on that. But I wouldn't do it, and I told my dad about it. Dad told Rufe's dad and him and me ain't been friends since."

"You know he's been released from prison, don't you?" Lucas asked.

Cox stroked his beard. "I heard that. The whole town's prayin' he don't show up here."

"Do you have any idea where he might have gone, once he got out of prison?"

"I don't have the slightest idea."

"Do you think he might try and get in touch with you?"

"Lord, I hope not," Cox replied.

"If he does try to contact you, would you make sure you let Sheriff Patterson know?" Lucas asked.

"Yes, sir, in a heartbeat I would. I've got me a family, and I don't want that son of a bitch anywhere near 'em."

"All right, well, thanks for talking with me, Mr. Cox."

"I'm sorry I couldn't tell ya much," Cox said.

Lucas nodded. He decided it was too late to ride back to Fort Worth, so he had supper and checked into a hotel for the night.

THE STILL-MORNING QUIET was invaded by the sound of the hoof beats of six horses, the rushing sound of the rolling wheels, and the rattle and squeak of the coach rocking on the thoroughbraces.

"We seem to be making pretty good time," Carl Lewis said. Lewis was riding as shotgun guard for the Rasher and Hall Stagecoach Line. This run was from Weatherford to Fort Worth.

"Well, we got away a little early," Ben Carson said. He snapped the reins over the six-horse team, to keep them trotting at a good pace.

"Are you still a little sore at me 'cause I beat you in horseshoes?" Carl asked.

Ben chuckled. "Are you still on that? You know I let you win."

"You what?" Carl shouted.

"I let you win," Ben repeated.

"Now just why, in heaven's name would you do that?"

"Because I consider us friends, and I knew it was more important to you than it was to me," Ben said. "Didn't you think it was strange that I got a leaner on the fiftieth throw?"

"You're full of it, Ben."

Ben laughed. "Does that mean you won't come to supper tonight?"

"Supper?"

"Yeah, Tillie told me to invite you over for supper tonight."

"Well, yeah, of course I'll come. Your wife's the best cook I know."

"You ain't got no argument from me on that," Ben said.

"That's a cute little girl back in the coach," Carl said. "She reminds me of your daughter, when she was about that age."

Ben chuckled. "Yeah, she does, doesn't she?"

They rode in silence for about a mile, then Ben spoke again.

"I wonder how much money is in that shipment we're carryin'."

"Quite a bit," Carl answered.

"Oh, yeah, you signed for it, didn't you? How much?"

"Twenty-five hundred," Lewis said.

"Whoowee! That's a lot of money," Carson said.

THERE WERE three passengers in the coach. Russell Malone was dozing while his wife, Anna, and daughter, Jennie, were talking.

"Mama," Jennie said. Since she was riding on the seat across from her parents, and had the seat all to herself, she spoke out rather loudly.

"Shh," Anna said, holding her finger across her lips. "Daddy's sleeping."

"Mama," Jennie whispered.

"Oh heavens, sweetheart, you can speak louder than that, just try not to wake up Daddy."

"We're goin' to see Grandma and Grandpa, aren't we?"

"Yes, we are."

"Why do we call them grand? Is that because they are so grand?"

Anna chuckled. "Well, honey, don't you think they're grand?"

Jennie clapped her hands and flashed a big smile. "I knew I was right."

"You know what?" Jennie asked.

"What?"

"You're grand, too."

"I am?"

"Certainly. You are a 'grand' daughter, aren't you?"

"Yes!" Jennie said with a happy smile. "I am grand, too, and you know what? Even though you and Daddy don't have grand in your names, I think you're both grand, too."

"Well, thank you, sweetheart," Anna said.

Jennie turned her attention back to a paper she was drawing on.

"What are you doing?" Anna asked.

"I'm drawing a picture of a flower for Grandma."

"Oh, I know she's going to like that," Anna said with a big smile.

"Do you want to see it?" Jennie asked.

"I'd love to see it."

Jennie showed her mother the picture.

"That's lovely. Your grandma's going to love it. I'll bet she puts it in a frame."

"May I see this masterpiece?" Russell asked.

"We thought you were asleep, Daddy."

"I was asleep, until somebody started talking about how grand they are, and what a pretty picture they were drawing," Russell said. The smile on his face showed that there was no censor in his words.

"Well, now, that is the most beautifulist flower I've ever seen."

Jennie laughed. "Beautifulist isn't a word, Daddy."

"It isn't? Hmm, how about it's the most beautiful flower I've ever seen."

"Beautiful, that's a word. Thank you, Daddy."

"You're welcome, honey." Russell turned his attention to the view outside the coach. He figured they were no more than half an hour from Fort Worth.

JUST AHEAD, Sawyer, Godfrey, Dumey, and Coleman were waiting on the Weatherford-Fort Worth road. They were behind some trees so they couldn't be seen from the road, unless someone was specifically looking for them. On the other hand, they had an unobstructed view of the road.

"Are you sure the money shipment is on this coach?" Godfrey asked.

"That's what Fitzhugh said, and him being the president of the bank, I don't think he would lie to me."

"Why not?" Dumey asked with a little chuckle. "You lied to him."

"I guess I did, didn't I?" Coleman replied, with a chuckle of his own.

"Here it comes," Godfrey said.

"Huh, uh, that's not the right one," Sawyer said. "It's going the wrong way. The one we want will be coming from Weatherford, going to Fort Worth."

TEN MINUTES LATER, the Weatherford-bound coach met the coach on its way to Fort Worth.

"That's ole Crack and Jeb," Lewis said.

The two coaches passed with greetings exchanged as they met.

"MAMA, a little boy in that coach waved at me," Jennie said.

"Careful there, Jennie," Russell said with a smile on his face. "You're too young to be flirting with men."

"Daddy, he wasn't a man, he was a little boy."

"One of these days you'll be a young lady, and I won't want you to be flirting with men, so I might as well start training you now."

Jennie laughed. "Mama, did you hear Daddy? He doesn't want me to be flirting with men."

"Well, I think that's a good idea."

"Mama?"

"What?"

"What does flirting mean?"

Anna chuckled. "I'll tell you when you're older."

"Why does everything have to wait until I'm older?"

"Because we don't want you to grow up too soon," Russell said. "We want you to enjoy being young while you still can."

"But I want to grow up now," Jennie said.

"Oh, I don't want you to grow up," Anna said. "Your daddy and I like having you as our little girl."

"HERE COMES A STAGECOACH NOW, and it's going the right way, so I know this is the one we want," Coleman said.

"All right, everyone get mounted and get ready," Sawyer said. "When it gets about fifty yards away, we'll ride out and block the road."

ON THE APPROACHING COACH, Carl looked at his pocket watch. "It won't be long now."

"No, it's like you said earlier, we've made good time today," Ben said.

"That beer's goin' to taste awful good when we get in," Carl said.

"You got that right."

"What are those four men doing spread across the road like that?" The tone of his question reflected Carl's concern.

"I don't know, but it don't look good," Ben said.

Carl reached for his shotgun.

"Leave it," Ben said. "There's four of 'em, and you've only got two shells in that gun."

Ben stopped the coach.

Back in the passenger section, Russell registered surprise when the coach stopped. "Wonder why we stopped out here in the middle of nowhere?"

"Maybe an animal or something in the road?" Anna offered.

"Oh, I hope it isn't hurt," Jennie said. "Maybe it's a cow."

"You're blocking the road," Ben said to the four men.

"Is that a fact? Well, we won't be here long," Sawyer replied. He raised his gun and shot the guard. The other three started shooting as well, and within a moment Ben and Carl both lay dead in the footwell.

"RUSSELL! WHAT WAS THAT?" Anna asked, her voice breaking with fear.

"I don't know, but it can't be good," Russell answered. "And I don't have a gun with me."

"DUMEY, you climb up there and get the money shipment," Sawyer ordered.

"Godfrey, you come with me. We're going to take care of whoever's in the coach."

"What do you mean, take care of?" Coleman asked.

"I mean kill 'em."

Godfrey and Sawyer walked back to the coach and looked inside.

"Rufe Sawyer," Russell said. "I heard you were out of prison."

"I'll be damn," Sawyer said. "Godfrey, do you know who this is?"

"No, I don't. But he sure knows you, don't he?"

"He was my lawyer. Lot of good he was, I wound up goin' to prison for stealin' twenty-five dollars."

"You served five years for murder," Russell said. "All things considered, I got you a pretty good deal. You could have been hanged."

"Yeah? Well you were supposed to get me off, but you, you son of a bitch, you cut a deal with the prosecutor."

"Sawyer, please watch your language in front of my daughter," Russell said.

Sawyer laughed. "Ha, there ain't no need for you to be a-worryin' 'bout my language in front of your daughter, when it won't make no difference."

"What do you mean it makes no difference?"

"Because we're goin' to kill all three of you."

Anna had been looking on with a face drawn in fear. When she heard Sawyer's words, she called out.

"Oh, Russell!"

Sawyer and Godfrey began shooting.

———

"You know, I sort of hated to kill the little girl," Godfrey said, as they walked away from the coach. "But since we were a-killin' her mama and papa, you might even say I did her a favor."

Sawyer laughed. "Moe, you're the only one I know who could kill a little girl and say you're doin' her a favor."

By the time the two men returned to their horses, Dumey was mounting his own horse. He was also holding the express bag containing the money.

"What are we gonna do with the stagecoach?" Godfrey asked.

"Don't worry about it. It ain't goin' nowhere," Sawyer said.

What Sawyer did not realize, was that as they rode away, the team of horses started out again, continuing their journey. Also, Godfrey had been wrong. They had killed Jennie and her mother, but Russell was still alive.

"Anna?" Russell called in anguish. "Jennie?"

Russell checked both of them, and to his intense sorrow, found that they were dead.

"Lord, let me die, take me too," Russell prayed. Then, he saw the blood-spattered paper on which Jennie had been drawing. The pencil was beside it, and he picked up the paper and pencil.

He felt himself growing weaker and weaker and

knew without a shadow of doubt that he was going to die, too.

"Lord, let me live for one more minute," he prayed.

With a shaking hand, he began to write: *Rufe Saw...* that was as far as he got.

Though there was no longer anyone to guide them, the team of horses continued their journey.

22

The stagecoach came into town with the team at a full gallop. This was not all that unusual, because from time to time, drivers made such an entry to make an impression. What made this arrival unique was that there was neither driver nor shotgun guard on the driver's seat, and the coach itself appeared to be empty.

The horses, because they were trained to do so, and knew they would be fed when they completed the trip, galloped up to the stagecoach depot, then stopped. They stood there as the trailing dust wrapped the coach in a wraith-like cloud. Elmer Lingle, the chief hostler, started toward the coach, then stopped and stared at it, wondering where Ben and Carl were. When he came closer, he saw blood running from the footwell. He stepped up on the wheel and found both men lying dead.

Stepping down, he hurried back and opened the door of the coach.

"Oh, my God," Elmer whispered. A man, a woman, and a little girl, no older than six or seven years old, lay dead.

"What in the hell happened?" Elmer asked, awestruck by what he was seeing. He hurried into the depot where Clyde Prescott was processing tickets for the departing passengers.

"How many of the incoming passengers will be going on through, Elmer?" Prescott asked. "I need to know how many I can put on this stage."

"None of 'em are goin' nowhere never again, Mr. Prescott."

Prescott looked up, puzzled by the strange reply.

"What do you mean none of them aren't going anywhere? They're either getting off here, or going on."

"Huh, uh," Elmer said, his face ashen. "They ain't none of 'em goin' nowhere. All of 'em, is dead—Ben 'n Carl 'n all the passengers."

"What?" Prescott shouted the word. "What do you mean?"

"I mean dead."

Prescott hurried out to see for himself. By now a dozen or more townspeople and waiting passengers, drawn by the arrival of the coach, were gathered around, looking on in shocked horror.

"Who done this, Prescott?" one of the onlookers asked.

"I don't have any idea," Prescott replied.

"Well, don't you think you ought to get the sheriff?"

"Yeah," Prescott replied. "Elmer, go get Sheriff Moore."

"What about the outbound stage?" Elmer asked.

"Have Skeeter get the reserve coach out, and pull this one around back until the sheriff gets here," Prescott said. "He'll want to see this before we move the bodies."

Skeeter drove the coach around back, then unhitched the six horses and took them into the livery.

The horses were skittish, and Skeeter had to work to control them.

"I don't blame you fellas for bein' a little upset," Skeeter said. "That was quite a thing you had to come through."

Behind Skeeter, the blood-spattered picture of Jennie's flower, and Russell's cryptic note, lay unnoticed under his body.

From the Fort Worth Democrat Gazette*:*

Ghost Coach Arrives in Fort Worth

Yesterday, May 11th, a coach from the Rasher and Hall Line generated a great deal of commotion upon its arrival.

The shock experienced by those who witnessed the arrival of the coach, was caused by the discovery that everyone aboard had perished by gunshot wound.

A money shipment is also missing. It appears to be obvious that robbery was the motive for this terrible crime.

The coach had been driven by Ben Carson. Carl Lewis was the shotgun guard. Residents of Fort Worth will recall the spirited competition by these two in the recent horseshoe contest.

The three passengers, residents of Weatherford, were well-known attorney Russell Malone, his wife, Anna, and their seven-year-old daughter, Jennie. It has been reported the family was en route to Fort Worth to celebrate Mrs. Malone's birthday with her parents, Mr. and Mrs. Chancy Gordon of this city.

Sheriff Moore says he has no leads on who committed this foul act and asks that anyone who can shed light on who the perpetrator may be, should contact his office.

This newspaper will keep its readers aware of all facts learned about the Ghost Coach as they develop.

Lucas Cain was still in Weatherford when he learned of this bizarre event. Having exhausted all avenues for Sawyer's whereabouts, he decided to return to Fort Worth.

When he arrived in Fort Worth, he was aware of the anger and fear that permeated the town. It was his intention to call upon Sheriff Moore, but on his way, he happened to see Ezra Karg coming out of a hotel.

"Lucas," Ezra said as he extended his hand. "I expect you're here to investigate the Ghost Coach that everyone's talking about."

"As a matter of fact, that has piqued my interest. Are the Karg brothers looking into it?"

"No, Wyatt is in New Orleans, and I'm heading out tomorrow," Ezra said. "You might want to call on Clyde Prescott. He's the depot manager of the Rasher and Hall Stagecoach Line. You can imagine how devastating this whole thing has been for them."

"Thanks, Ezra, I'll go there now. And good luck in New Orleans for you and Wyatt."

Lucas headed for the stagecoach depot.

"Marshal Cain, am I ever glad to see you," Prescott said. "I suppose you know about the stagecoach that arrived with everyone dead? Sheriff Moore is on the case, but there's not much to go on."

"That's why I'm here," Lucas said. "I saw the article in the paper. Has anyone stepped up with a suggestion as to who could do such a thing?"

"No, and that's the thing. With everyone dead, there

are no witnesses to tell us anything. Are you going to go after them?" Prescott asked.

"What do you mean?" Lucas asked.

"I mean, you being a U.S. Marshal, you can go anywhere, can't you?"

"That I can," Lucas agreed.

"Then I want you to find out who did this, and to recover any money that they took."

Lucas took a deep breath. "Right now, I'm looking for Rufe Sawyer and his associates for the robbery and murder of Frank and Zetty Milner," Lucas said. "I'll do what I can on this case as well, but like you said, there aren't any witnesses, so I'll be starting with nothing to go on. I'm sure the sheriff is doing all he can, too, so I'll need to coordinate with him. There's no sense in the two of us working against one another."

"You know I'm worried about the money because Rasher and Hall is responsible," Prescott said. "But I'm even more upset by the senseless murder of my two friends, and the innocent passengers. Especially the little girl. So please, Marshal, do whatever you can to find whoever did this, and send them to hell."

Lucas nodded but didn't speak as he left the depot.

SHERIFF MOORE and Deputy Campbell were both in the office when Lucas went in to see them.

"I thought you might be coming to see me. Have you talked to Prescott yet?"

"Yes," Lucas replied.

"I figured you probably had. We've been talking ever since the Ghost Coach, as they're calling it, arrived. I explained to them that we'll do what we can, but you know we can't leave Tarrant County, so if we figure this out, it's going to pretty much be up to you."

"I rather thought you might say that," Lucas said.

"But, if you think there's anything my office can do for you, feel free to ask," Moore said.

"I will, and you can count on that," Lucas replied.

THE ENTIRE TOWN turned out for the funeral. Ben's wife, Tillie, and their sixteen-year-old daughter, Hannah, sat in chairs that had been provided for them. Both were dressed in black and both were crying.

Russell, Anna, and Jennie were also being buried in the Fort Worth cemetery because they had no relatives in Weatherford, and Russell's parents were deceased, but Anna's parents were still living in Fort Worth.

Chancy and Myrtle Gordon occupied the other two chairs that were in the front row. And though neither was crying, the expressions on their faces reflected their sorrow over the loss of their daughter, granddaughter, and son-in-law.

Although Carl had many friends in town, he had no relatives to attend the funeral.

The murder of five people had made a huge impact on the citizens of Fort Worth, and as a result, every business in town was draped in funeral black.

AS LUCAS BEGAN HIS INVESTIGATION, he realized that the team had brought the coach in without a driver, because the horses knew where to go. That meant the team had to have been changed at the way station, so that's where Lucas decided he would start.

Lucas waited until after the funerals, then he went back to the office of the Rasher and Hall Stagecoach Company to have another talk with Clyde Prescott. There was black bunting around the door and windows.

"This was the saddest day this company has ever seen," Prescott said.

"I can understand that," Lucas said.

"Is there anything I can do to help you?" Prescott asked.

"As a matter of fact, there is. I was wondering if you had a route map from here to Weatherford that would show me everywhere the coach may have stopped during its trip here."

"I can help you with that," Prescott said. "If you'll just wait here for a minute, I'll get it for you."

"Thanks."

23

L ucas thought hard about where his efforts should be placed. On the one hand, he was after Rufe Sawyer for murder and robbery. On the other hand, the case of the Ghost Coach was occupying everyone's mind, so it seemed sensible to him, to put the Sawyer case aside. Because of that, he left the depot with his thoughts and efforts directed toward solving this mystery.

He decided that his best way of getting any information about the Ghost Coach would be to retrace its travel from Weatherford. There was only one way station between Weatherford and Fort Worth. If the murders had occurred before the way station, the team would have stopped there on their own.

That gave Lucas the reasonable expectation that whatever happened, occurred between the way stop and Fort Worth. That narrowed the immediate investigation down to no more than fifteen miles. The only way to check his theory would be to visit the way station.

As Lucas rode toward the way station, he kept his eyes open for anything that might be useful. He was reasonably certain that he wouldn't find shell casings or anything like that. But he might be able to discover where the robber, or robbers, waited for the coach.

He checked three sites that he thought may have been a good place to stay out of view, but none of the sites offered anything he could use.

He had ridden just over fifteen miles when he came to the way station, and as it so happened, there was a coach standing there waiting to proceed on its journey.

In addition to providing a change of horses, the way station also had a restaurant, not only for the passengers, drivers, and guards of the stagecoaches, but also for the occasional lone traveler that might come through.

Lucas dismounted, tied Charley Two off at the hitching rail, then went inside. Some of the passengers were waiting out front, and a few more were inside. It wasn't yet time for a meal, but they had to leave the coach while the team was being changed. There were six passengers—four men and two women.

"Sir?" Lucas called, holding up his hand to get the proprietor's attention.

"Yes, sir, what can I do for you?" the proprietor asked.

"I am Deputy U.S. Marshal Lucas Cain, and I was wondering if you could answer a few questions?"

The man who replied to Lucas had a protruding belly, thinning hair, and red-blotched skin. He sauntered over toward Lucas.

"I'm not the brightest feller in Texas, but if I can answer your questions, I will," the man said with a chuckle. He stuck out his hand. "Abe Pounders. What is it you're wantin' to ask about?"

"Mr. Pounders, you know about the Ghost Coach," Lucas said.

The smile left Pounders's face. "Just awful. I reckon I

might have been the last person to see them folks alive. I can't help thinkin' about that poor little girl. What kind of low-life creature would kill a little girl like that?"

"That's something I'm trying to find out. Did you see the coach leave?"

"Just through the window. I wasn't outside when it left," Pounders said.

"Was anyone else here at the time?"

"A couple of old ladies is all. They took the coach for Palo Pinto, but that was going west."

"Who's your hostler?"

"That would be H.W. Ford," Pounders said. "He was outside the whole time. He might have seen somethin'."

"Could you tell me where I can find him?"

"I can do better than that, I'll take you to him."

Pounders walked with Lucas over to the stable, where Ford was rubbing down a horse.

"H.W., this man would like to talk to you," Pounders said.

"What about?" Ford replied without looking up from his task.

"About the coach that Carson and Lewis were driving."

"Ben 'n Carl was friends of mine, 'n I don't care to talk to someone who don't want to do nothin' but walk on their graves. Them was good men."

"He's a U.S. Marshal, 'n he's after whoever it was that done it," Pounders said.

Ford turned away from the horse. "Why didn't you say so?" he asked. "But I don't know why you want to talk to me; I don't know who done it."

"Mr. Pounders said the only other people who were here when the coach left, were a couple of women who were waiting to catch the westbound stage," Lucas said.

"That's right, there warn't nobody else here."

"Did you see anyone out on the road?" Lucas asked.

"Well, yeah, I mean it's a busy road. They's most always folks out there."

"Nobody that looked unusual?" Lucas asked.

Ford shook his head. "I'm sorry. My job is takin' care of horses, 'n that's what I do."

"I can understand, and I thank you for your time," Lucas said.

Lucas turned away from the stable and started toward his horse, when Ford called out to him.

"Marshal, wait a minute."

Lucas turned back toward the hostler.

"You might want to talk to Crack Stilman 'n Jeb Taylor."

"Who are they?" Lucas asked.

"Stilman is a driver, and Taylor rides shotgun," Ford said. "And not long after Ben 'n Carl left, headin' toward Fort Worth, Crack 'n Jeb come by, headin' for Weatherford. It's more 'n likely they seen the Fort Worth coach, 'cause their times was so close together that I don't see how they couldn't a-seen 'em."

"How would I find Crack and Jeb, so I could talk to them today?" Lucas asked.

"All you got to do is wait about half 'n hour," Pounders said. "They'll be comin' through here, headed east."

"Thanks, I'll wait."

THE COACH, driven by Crack and Jeb was early, and arrived within the next ten minutes. That worked out well, because the normal layover was for half an hour, and this would give Lucas a little more time to interview them.

Pounders came out to speak to the two men as they arrived.

"Crack, Jeb, would you step inside? I have someone who wants to talk to you."

"Well, yeah, we're goin' to be here for a little over an hour anyway, so me 'n Jeb was plannin' on gettin' us some coffee," Crack answered.

"Who is it you're a-wantin' us to talk to?" Jeb asked.

"It's a U.S. Marshal. I'll introduce you to him inside."

Once inside and the introductions made, Lucas asked his question.

"I wonder if the other day you might have met the coach being driven by Carson and Lewis?" Lucas asked.

"Yeah, we seen 'em," Crack said. "They was about fifteen minutes this side of Fort Worth. Wait a minute. That prob'ly means we was the last ones that seen 'em, don't it?"

"Yes, except for the people who murdered them," Lucas said. "And that helps, because it narrows the window quite a bit as to where it might have happened."

"Oh, you're wantin' to see where it happened?" Taylor asked.

"Yes, I do."

"Why didn't you just ask me? I can show you exactly where it happened," Taylor said.

"All right, where did it happen? And how is it that you know?"

"On account of I seen four men just waitin' alongside the road, 'n I pointed 'em out to Crack. 'What do you think them men is doin' there?' I asked."

"Yeah, Jeb 'n me talked about it some, after we

learned what had happened to Ben 'n Carl 'n we figured they must o' been the ones what done it," Stilman said.

"Wait a minute, four of them you say? Were they hidden? How did you happen to see them?"

"Well, that's it. They weren't none at all hid from someone goin' west. I mean, we could see 'em just real easy. But if you was goin' east, 'n if you wasn't lookin' for 'em, you wouldn't of seen 'em at all, on account of they was sort of waitin' behind some bushes 'n trees 'n such," Taylor said.

"What can you tell me about the four men?" Lucas asked.

"Well, one of 'em was a big man, as big as you are," Taylor said.

"Yeah, which is some funny, 'cause they's another 'n that's a real skinny lookin' little bastard," Stilman added.

"Thank you, you've been very helpful. I'm sure I'm on the right track, now," Lucas said.

"You're saying that me 'n Crack was right in thinkin' them four men is the ones that kilt Ben 'n Carl?" Taylor asked.

"I would bet money on it," Lucas said. "And I thank you two gentlemen more than I can say."

"Hey, if it helps you find those sons of bitches what kilt Ben 'n Carl, I'm glad we could talk to you," Stilman said.

"If you don't mind, I'll ride alongside the coach when you leave here, and you can point out where you saw those four men."

"Sure, come along," Stilman said.

WHEN THE COACH resumed its trip to Fort Worth, Lucas rode alongside, so they could show him where they had seen the four men. They had been on the road for about fifteen minutes, when Crack called out to Lucas.

"You see them trees up there, on the left side of the road?" Crack asked.

"Is that where you saw the four men?"

"Yeah, it is. And if you notice, you'll see there ain't no place for you to hide on this side of them trees. They was just waitin' there pretty as you please."

Crack was quiet for just a minute. "It was my fault, you know."

"What do you mean, it was your fault?" Lucas asked.

"It's my fault on account of I seen them four men just a-standin' there, 'n I didn't say nothin' about it. Iffen I had 'a said somethin' to Ben 'n Carl, they might coulda kept a eye open or somethin'."

"You had no way of knowing, so there's no sense in blaming yourself," Lucas said.

Lucas halted there and watched as the coach continued on its way to Fort Worth. After the coach left, he examined the site where the four men had waited, but found nothing, other than a few horse droppings that indicated they had stayed there for quite a while. That indicated that whoever was here was waiting for the stagecoach.

But, who were they?

***

LUCAS DECIDED to continue his search in Weatherford, and the first place he went to when he arrived was the sheriff's office.

"Hello, Marshal Cain. What can I do for you?" Sheriff Patterson asked.

"I would like to talk to you about the Ghost Coach incident."

"Russell and Anna Malone, and their little Jennie. What a wonderful family they were, and this town is sure going to miss 'em."

"Yes, it was a shame," Lucas said.

"Everybody liked 'em. I sure hope they catch the sons of bitches that done this."

"Oh, I will," Lucas said.

"I wish I could help you, but I don't have the slightest idea where to start."

"If you hear anything, please get word to Sheriff Moore. I'll be checking in with him from time to time," Lucas said.

"Oh, I'll do that," Sheriff Patterson said. "You can count on me. I'll for sure do that."

"Thank you," Lucas said as he bade the sheriff goodbye.

24

It had been two weeks since Lucas had started his search for whoever robbed the coach and killed the driver, the guard, and the three passengers. Two weeks, and he was no closer to finding the four men who did it, or even their names. He was, however, convinced it was the four men who had been seen by Crack Stilman and Jeb Taylor when they met Ben and Carl on that last fateful trip.

He was in Wayland now. He hadn't gotten any clues to draw him here, but Wayland was a pretty good-sized town. He reasoned that the four men would want a larger-size town rather than one with few businesses.

Currently he was in the Frying Pan restaurant, enjoying a meal that he didn't have to cook. He hadn't seen the sheriff yet, but he would go there right after he ate. From the sheriff's office, he would start a tour of the four saloons. He had seen four of them as he had ridden into town.

"Would you like some apple pie, sir?" the waiter asked. "It's awful good, I can tell you that."

Lucas had planned to see the sheriff as soon as he finished his meal, but the allure of apple pie convinced him to delay his visit for a few more minutes.

After dinner, he checked in with the sheriff.

Sheriff Watters looked up as Lucas stepped into his office.

"Marshal Cain, what brings you to my town?"

Lucas smiled. "Well, I could say the apple pie at the Frying Pan."

Sheriff Watters chuckled. "Martha Lee can take an ordinary apple and turn it into something you'll want to write home about, all right. But I have an idea that it's something more than that."

"Yes, it is," Lucas said, and the smile left his face to indicate the seriousness of his visit.

"Sheriff Watters, have you heard anything about the stagecoach that showed up in Fort Worth with everybody dead?"

"You mean the one they're calling the Ghost Coach?" Watters asked.

"Yes. I don't particularly like that name, though. In my mind, it tends to trivialize what is a real tragedy for the families of those people who were killed," Lucas said.

"Yes," Sheriff Watters agreed. "Do you have any idea who did it?"

"Well, we don't have an eyewitness, of course, and no real clues. But a driver and a shotgun guard who were on a coach headed to Weatherford saw four men waiting beside the road. There is no doubt in my mind but that those four men are the ones who did this."

"Were they able to give you any descriptions?"

"No, not really. They described one of them as being a man about my size, and another who was very thin."

"But no facial features," Watters said. It was more of a declaration than a question.

"Right."

"So, what you're saying is, you don't have the slightest idea who did this."

"No, that's not true. I do have an idea, or maybe it's just a gut feeling."

"Oh? And what would that be?" Sheriff Watters asked.

"I've been looking for Rufe Sawyer. The description fits him, as far as size goes. And what also fits him is the way this happened," Lucas said. "Sawyer killed Frank Milner and his wife, and Paul Coker could definitely identify him. He said there were three men with him, and in my mind, it stands to reason that this could be Sawyer and his bunch."

"I can see how you might believe that," Sheriff Watters said. "But if Sawyer goes on trial, you would need something more than your gut feeling to get him convicted. You know he cheated the hangman once, already."

"That may be true, but I'm already looking for him for killing Frank and Zetty Milner, and for that, we do have an eyewitness."

"You do know that Paul Coker is an ex-con, don't you?"

"Yes. Do you know him?"

"I reckon I do. I'm the one who got him sent to prison. He took a few cows that weren't his."

"Yes, I know about that. But as I understand it, his claim was that they were mavericks without brands."

"That was the claim."

"Tell me, Sheriff, do you think Coker was lying to me about Sawyer, and that it was Coker who robbed and killed the Milners?"

"No, I don't reckon I think that," Sheriff Watters said. "He may have branded a few cows that weren't his, but he's not the kind of man who would kill anyone."

"I'm glad you agree with me."

"Where are you going now?" Watters asked.

"I'm going to visit all the saloons and see what I can find out."

OVER THE NEXT THREE WEEKS, Lucas extended his search to the counties that surrounded Tarrant County, to include Dallas, Parker, Johnson, and Denton. Since he didn't even know who he was looking for, his search turned up nothing.

BACK IN FORT WORTH, the Ghost Coach was sitting behind the depot livery. It had been there since the killings, because Prescott was afraid nobody would want to ride in it. But it had been there long enough, and Prescott needed another coach, so he told Elmer Lingle to clean it up, and roll it out for the next departure.

"Make sure there's no blood anywhere," Prescott said.

The first thing Lingle did was clean the driver's seat and the footwell. Then he washed down the outside of the coach where blood had run down.

As soon as he opened the passenger door, he saw the blood-spotted sheet of paper lying on the floor, and he picked it up.

"Huh, flowers. The little girl must have been..." Lingle stopped in midsentence when he saw what else was on the paper.

"I'll be damn," he said. There was more wonder in the words than profanity.

Lingle ran into the depot to show Prescott what he had found.

"What's the matter?" Prescott asked.

"I found this on the floor of the coach," Lingle said, as he handed the drawing to Prescott.

Prescott saw the blood spots, the incomplete drawing of a flower, then the words at the bottom of the page.

Rufe Saw

"Oh my God! I'm going to take this to Sheriff Moore right now," Prescott said.

"I'm not surprised," Sheriff Moore said when he saw the paper. He showed the paper to his deputy.

"Ray," Sheriff Moore said to Deputy Campbell, "I'm going to write a message, and I want you to send it to the sheriffs of every county that borders Tarrant. No, make it a ring two counties deep around us. I know that Cain always checks in with the local sheriff. Hopefully, one of them will get the message to him."

"Sheriff Kern?" the Western Union delivery boy said to the sheriff of Palo Pinto. "I have a telegram for you." He handed the message to Kern.

"Thanks, Syl," Kern said. He gave the boy a dime as he took the message.

FOR MARSHAL LUCAS CAIN STOP NOTE FOUND IN GHOST COACH PROOF RUFE SAWYER GUILTY OF GHOST COACH MURDERS STOP

Kern chuckled as he read the telegram, then he folded

it up, put it in his pocket, and started toward Uncle Billy's Restaurant. As it so happened, Marshal Cain was in Palo Pinto, and had checked in with him less than an hour earlier.

A few minutes later, he entered the restaurant and saw Cain at a table, eating his supper.

"There you are," Sheriff Kern said with a grin, as he approached Lucas.

"This was a good suggestion," Lucas said.

"Enjoying your supper?" Sheriff Kern asked.

"Yes, quite a bit."

"Here's something you might even enjoy more."

"What is it?"

"I just got this telegram, and it says they found proof of the Ghost Coach killing. I thought you might be interested in seeing it."

Lucas read the telegram aloud, then smiled, and struck the paper with his fingers.

"Yes," he said enthusiastically. "I knew it, it had to be Sawyer."

Lucas thought, but did not speak aloud, that this would take away any sense of guilt he might have felt about choosing the stagecoach case over that of Milner's store. Now he knew they were the same perpetrators. Yes, this was the first good news he had had about the case.

"So, what are you going to do now?" Sheriff Kern asked, when he saw that Lucas had finished reading the telegram.

"I'm going to find Sawyer and whoever is with him, and I'm going to bring them in, dead or alive."

"You sound pretty positive."

"I am absolutely positive."

"Do you have any idea where to start?"

Lucas chuckled. "Well, I intend to start now, and that means I'll be starting from here. But where I'll go from here, I have no idea."

<hr />

SHERIFF KERN WASN'T the only one listening to Lucas's words. In the same restaurant, and having just eaten his supper, was Moe Godfrey. Godfrey left the restaurant, got on his horse, and rode away.

Half an hour later he stopped where Sawyer and the others were camping.

"Did you get the stuff we needed?" Sawyer asked.

Godfrey held up the sack. "It's all here."

"Including some Arbuckles?" Dumey asked.

"And whiskey?" Coleman added.

"Coffee, whiskey, and some news we need to know."

"What's that?" Sawyer asked.

"The stagecoach we held up? They found a note that says you were the one who robbed the coach."

"A note?" Sawyer asked.

"That's what they're saying. That someone stayed alive long enough to write a note saying it was you."

"It had to be that bastard Malone. I know damn well he's the one who would do that," Sawyer said. "I should have made sure that the son of a bitch was dead."

"Yeah, well there's somethin' else, too. You know who it is, that's lookin' for us?"

"Some sheriff?" Sawyer asked.

"No, it's Lucas Cain. You've heard of him, haven't you?"

"Damn, Lucas Cain?" Coleman said. "I've heard of him."

"Me too," Dumey said.

"I've heard of him, too," Sawyer said. "He's supposed to be a marshal, but all he really is, is a bounty hunter, hunting people down for the reward money."

"It's too bad there ain't nobody ever put a bounty on his ass. Then we wouldn't have to worry about him," Godfrey said.

"I'll be damn!" Sawyer said, with a wide smile on his lips. "That's it, Moe. You ain't so dumb after all. We'll put a thousand-dollar bounty on him, then get the word out to ever' one we know. We'll see how Cain likes it, having a price on his head."

"A thousand dollars?" Dumey asked. "Does that mean we have to come up with the money?"

"If we put the reward out on him, then who would you expect to put up the money if not us?" Sawyer asked.

"That would be two hundred fifty dollars from each of us," Dumey said. "And if you remember, we only got a little over six hunnert dollars each from robbin' that stagecoach. Hell, you're sayin' we're gonna to have to pony up damn near half of what we've got to put out the reward."

"What would you rather do? Spend half your money or hang?" Sawyer asked.

"Yeah, I see what you mean. But damn, I hate to give up the money."

Sawyer smiled again. "Don't worry about it," he said. "I've got something in mind to take care of that. But for now, if Cain is here in Palo Pinto, then we need to be somewhere else."

"Where?" Godfrey asked.

"Anywhere but here."

25

For the next three weeks, Lucas wandered from town to town, looking. Now, at least, he knew who he was looking for. He also had a new photograph of Sawyer, taken shortly before he was released from prison. Because of the photo, when he questioned people, he had something to show.

"Yeah, I seen 'im," a man in Breckinridge said. "He was with three other men. Are you tellin' me they was the ones that kilt ever' body on that coach, includin' the little girl?"

"Yes, that's what I'm telling you."

"I sure hope you find 'em. There ain't a one of them sorry bastards that's fit to live."

Lucas Cain wasn't the only bounty hunter whose name struck fear in the hearts of the wanted. Deke Pauly was another bounty hunter with a reputation that rivaled that of Lucas Cain. While Lucas was in Breckenridge,

Deke Pauly was in Jacksboro in Jack County. There, Sheriff Buck Alexander was counting out seven hundred and fifty dollars. The money was the reward for Kit Chiles, a prisoner Pauly had brought in the day before. Chiles was in one of the cells, dealing with some anger issues, angry for being caught and angry with Pauly for catching him.

"Thank you," Pauly said as he gathered in the money.

"You know what you should do if you want some real money, like a thousand dollars or more," Sheriff Alexander said.

"Who do you want me to kill?" Pauly asked with a chuckle.

"You joke, but the truth is, he is wanted dead or alive, and I expect there's just a whole lot of people who would prefer you bring him in dead. Last time he was brought in for murder but he got off with only five years in prison."

"Murder, you say? And only five years? How the hell did that happen?"

"He had a good lawyer," Sheriff Alexander said.

"I see now why folks are wantin' him brought in dead," Pauly said. "They're afraid he'll get that lawyer again."

"That's not very likely," the sheriff said. "Seeing as that same lawyer is one of five that was killed when Sawyer and his men robbed the stagecoach and killed everyone on it."

"You're talking about the one they're calling the Ghost Coach, aren't you?" Pauly asked. "The one that came on into Fort Worth with everyone on it dead?"

"Yep, that I am."

"You said a name. Sawyer?" Pauly asked.

"Yes, Rufe Sawyer and three others," the sheriff said.

"They aren't sure who the others are, but one of them is believed to be Moe Godfrey."

"How'd they find that out?" Pauly asked.

"Apparently, one of the victims in the coach left a note saying that it was Rufe Sawyer."

"All right, thanks for the tip. I'll start lookin' for him."

THE MEN LUCAS, and now Pauly, were looking for—Sawyer, Godfrey, Coleman, and Dumey—were in the Red Palace Saloon, in Jacksboro, Texas.

"Two thousand, five hundred dollars," Coleman said, with a sigh of disgust. "I still can't believe that's all the hell they were carrying. And now we've got to hold on to two hundred 'n fifty dollars so as to have enough money to pay the reward to whoever kills Cain."

"It's better 'n what we started out with," Godfrey said.

"Yeah, but what money we did get is goin' down fast. Especially if we have to be puttin' out a bounty on Cain," Coleman said. "I mean, you'd 'a thought there would be more money, wouldn't you? Because they was takin' it to a bank, 'n a bank is where all the money is, ain't it?"

"Banks," Sawyer said, with a smile. "You're right, Amos. That is where the money is."

"What are you smilin' about?" Godfrey asked.

"Banks," Sawyer replied, his smile bigger than before. "It's like Amos said. That's where the money is."

"Yeah, but what's that got to do with us?" Godfrey asked.

"Ha, I see it," Dumey said.

"What do you see? 'Cause I sure as hell don't see nothin'," Godfrey said.

"Well, think about it, Moe," Dumey said. "If we know

where the money is, we can also know where the money won't be."

"You ain't makin' no sense a'tall," Godfrey said.

"I get it," Coleman said. "If the money was in the bank, and then it ain't in the bank, it means it could be with us."

Godfrey stared at the others for a moment, his face drawn up in confusion and frustration. Then the thought came to him, and a broad smile replaced the confusion that was on his face.

"Oh, I get it now, we're goin' to…"

"Don't say it," Sawyer sharply interrupted him.

"What?" Godfrey asked.

"Don't say what you were about to say. We're in a saloon," Sawyer said. "And we ain't the only ones that's in here."

"When are we goin' to do it?" Coleman asked.

Sawyer looked around at the others in the saloon to make certain no one had overheard them. "We'll talk about it later."

"We're goin' to get to spend some of our money here, though, ain't we?" Coleman asked. He was looking at one of the saloon girls.

"Well, hell, that's what it's for, ain't it?" Sawyer replied with a big grin.

Coleman waved the girl over. She approached, smiling at everyone at the table.

"What's your name, honey?" Coleman asked.

"Why, my name is Suzy," she said.

"Well, Suzy, I need to tell you what's on my mind," Coleman said.

"I think I know. You boys want a drink, don't you?" she asked.

"No, I don't want no drink," Coleman said. "I got me somethin' else in mind."

"Oh?" Suzy said, thrusting her hip toward Coleman. "And just what would that be?"

"I thought maybe me 'n you could go upstairs for a little while."

"You got two dollars, honey?"

"Yeah, I got two dollars."

Suzy backed away a few steps, then with a seductive smile, held her hand out toward him, and crooked a finger.

"You guys wait here," Coleman said. "This won't take me very long at all."

EASTLAND

Lucas was going through the morgue file Cephus McKay kept of his old newspapers. He found a story that was a little over five years old.

Rufe Sawyer to Get Five Years

In what must be described as a twisted application of the law, Rufe Sawyer, on trial in Weatherford for the robbery and murder of Amon Belcher, was found guilty on the robbery charge, only.

Russell Malone, the court-appointed defense council, pled the case arguing that without witness or absolute evidence of the murder, the jury could not suspend reasonable doubt.

Amon Belcher, employed as a salesclerk for Falkoff Men's Clothing store, was making preparations for the nightly deposit when he was killed, and the money, $25.35, was never *deposited. The exact amount of the money taken is known, because Belcher had made an entry for that amount in the ledger that he kept for the store.*

It is believed that Mr. Belcher attempted to prevent the robbery but was shot and killed in the process. However, Lawyer Malone advanced the hypotheses that relieved of the money, Belcher may have experienced a sense of failure, and thus killed himself.

This theory was supported by the fact that a pistol, with one shot fired, was found at the scene. Merlin Matheny, the prosecuting attorney, argued that the gun may have been left behind by Sawyer, specifically to create a question of doubt.

Though this newspaper recognizes the brilliance of Russell Malone in his construction of the defense, it is our belief that Sawyer is guilty of murder, and justice was not served.

"It's ironic, don't you think, that Sawyer killed the very man that saved his life," Cephus said.

"More than ironic," Lucas said. "It is just plain evil."

Carolina walked back to the table where Lucas and her father were standing.

"Papa, all the ads are set. Do you want Maggie and me to start setting the copy for the front page?"

"Yes, that would be nice," Cephus replied.

"Carolina?" Lucas called to her as she started back toward the composition table.

She turned back toward him. "Yes?"

"Would you have time to have dinner with me?"

"Well now, I was beginning to think I was going to have to ask you," she said with a smile. "Yes, of course I'll have dinner with you."

No more than fifteen minutes later, Lucas and Carolina took their dinner at a small, corner café called Warner's Place. The food was good, but you had to take whatever they had cooked for the day, as there was no menu. Today was Swiss steak and whipped potatoes.

"This reminds me of home," Lucas said. "My mom used to do round steak like this."

"Tell me some more about you," Carolina said. "I know you grew up on the Mississippi River. Do you have any brothers or sisters?"

"I have two sisters."

"Oh?" Carolina said with a bright smile. "Tell me about them."

"Well, they are both pretty, but both of them are a little sassy if you let them get away with it."

Carolina chuckled. "Sassy. I like that."

"Oh, I'm sure you do."

"What are you sisters' names?" Carolina asked.

"Oh, you'll like their names. One of them is named Maggie."

"Really? You have a sister named Maggie?" Carolina raised her eye in surprise.

"Yep. And the other one is named Carolina."

"Oh, you!" Carolina said, reaching across the table to playfully hit him on the arm.

"Lucas, tell me about your wife."

"You want to know about Rosie?"

"Yes. Unless it's too painful for you to talk about."

"No, it isn't too painful to talk about. Not anymore," Lucas said. "I told you before, like you, she worked at a newspaper. Actually, not quite like you. You do almost everything. All Rosie did was write articles."

"I'll bet she was a good writer, too," Rosie said.

"She was the best the newspaper had. That's how I

met her, you know. She wanted to do a story about my time in Andersonville, and to be honest, I never wanted to speak about it, or even think about it again. But she brought it all out, and you know what? It actually acted as a catharsis. I'm not really haunted by the terrible memories as much as I used to be."

Carolina reached across the table and placed her hand on his. "I know you miss her terribly."

"I do. I'm sorry, Carolina, I didn't mean to put a pall on things. And to be honest, one of the reasons I like being with you, is because you make me feel good."

Carolina smiled. "I like being with you, too."

"But, I'll be leaving town this afternoon," Lucas said.

"Leaving town? Why? You just got here."

"I know. I got the idea of looking up any old newspaper stories about Sawyer and figured the *Eastland Journal* was the best place to start."

"Will you come back?"

"I'll be back sooner than you think. I kinda like this little town," Lucas said.

Carolina smiled. "You know what? There are people in this town that kinda like you, too."

26

Two weeks later, Sawyer and Godfrey rode into the town of Breckenridge, approaching from the east, while Coleman and Dumey entered from the west. There were some people out on the street—a man loading a wagon, two older men playing checkers, two women looking through the window of the Elite Shop. There were two boys playing marbles who had gathered half a dozen kibitzers, both boys and girls. Sawyer and the others met in front of Planters Bank, and all but Godfrey dismounted. Godfrey was left to hold the reins of the other three horses.

Sawyer had timed it so they arrived at the bank just as it was opening. Sawyer, Coleman, and Dumey went inside.

"My, you gentlemen are bright and early this morning." The man who greeted them was sitting behind a desk. "My tellers have just gotten their cash drawers full."

Sawyer and the two with him drew their pistols.

"I'm glad they got their cash drawers full, because we are about to empty them," Sawyer said.

"What?" the man who had greeted them said. "Here, what is this?"

Sawyer laughed. "You mean you work in a bank, and you don't recognize a bank robbery when you see one?"

"This is outrageous, it simply isn't allowed."

Coleman and Dumey stepped up to the tellers' windows and handed each of them a cloth bag.

"Empty your drawer, put the money in the bag."

Nervously and with shaking hands, the two tellers complied. It took but a minute for the bags to be filled.

"We've got the money," Dumey said.

"All right, finish the job," Sawyer said.

Three gunshots sounded, and the two tellers and the bank manager fell to the floor.

As they left, they turned the *open* sign in the doorway to *closed.*

When they got outside, nothing had changed. The man was still loading his wagon, the two old men were still playing checkers, and the two boys were still demonstrating their skill at marbles.

"I don't think anyone heard anything," Godfrey said.

"Good, that makes getting out of here, real easy," Sawyer said.

"Chris, you and Amos go back out the same way you came in. Go no faster than you did comin' in, unless you're chased. We'll meet where we were this morning when we separated."

The four men left town without anyone paying any attention to them.

RICHARDSON, TEXAS

Sam Harris stood over the bed, looking down at his sleeping wife. He and Sally had been together for a little over two years.

Sally had brought a small ranch into their marriage, having inherited it from her father.

At the time of their marriage, Sam had just been released from prison. He brought less than one hundred dollars into the marriage. The result of that dissimilar contribution to their assets left Sally in charge of the money. That was not an arrangement Harris liked, but there was nothing he could do about it. Sally had opened a bank account with her name as the only one authorized to make a withdrawal.

But Sally wanted to leave Richardson and go somewhere else, so she sold the ranch to get eight hundred dollars for them to make the move. And because it was her money, the decision to move, as well as where to move, was Sally's.

"We're going to California." Sally had said excitedly, talking about everything she wanted to do and see when they got there. "I want to see the ocean before I die."

Harris was worried that she might be so excited that she couldn't sleep. And for his plans, she had to go to sleep tonight.

Earlier in the day, he had seen her open the ginger jar, put something in it, then put the top back on. He knew damn well she was hiding the money there. He could do a lot with eight hundred dollars, even more if she wasn't with him.

But nothing could happen until she went to sleep.

Then, about an hour after they went to bed, he heard

her snoring quietly. She was asleep. Harris felt a sense of excitement.

Now, standing over the bed, and looking down at Sally, he thought about what he was going to do.

"It's your own fault," Harris said, speaking quietly, so as not to awaken her. "If you hadn't been so damn selfish, we coulda shared the money, 'n ever' thing woulda been fine."

Harris leaned down over his wife. "Good enough for you. If you hadn't been such a bitch."

Sally suddenly awakened with a sharp pain. When she put her hand to her neck, it felt wet, and pulling it away from her throat, she saw that it was covered with blood. Looking up, she saw a smiling Sam Harris, holding a bloody knife.

Her last conscious thought was that her husband had just killed her.

Harris stood there watching until she took her last breath. Then, with an increased state of excitement and a feeling of satisfaction, he went over to the ginger jar, lifted the lid, and stuck his hand down into the vase for the money.

There was no money. There was only a note.

I thought you might look in here for the money, but I haven't taken it out of the bank yet. Be patient, we will be out of here soon with money to spend. It will be like a second honeymoon.

"You bitch!" Harris shouted. He threw the jar on the floor, breaking it into pieces.

Harris carried his wife's body outside and buried her in the garden. After that, he burned the bloody bedsheets, then burned all of her clothes.

THE NEXT MORNING, Harris went to the bank. "How much money is in the Harris account?" he asked.

The teller checked the book then said, "Nine hundred and twenty-eight dollars."

"Good, I'm closing the account. I'll take it all."

"Oh, I'm sorry, sir, Mrs. Harris is the only one who can withdraw from this account."

"We're moving to California, and she's already gone ahead of me. She told me to come get the money," Harris said. He smiled. "And you know how wives are. If they tell you to do something, you damn well better do it."

"I'm sorry, sir, it's like I said. Only your wife can draw from her account."

"But she's not here. She's gone on to San Francisco, and I'm supposed to get the money and join her there."

The teller, and even the bank president, told Harris that unless his wife came in to personally withdraw the money, it would have to remain in the account.

"The only way you could get it, would be after her death. She has a codicil to her account saying that in the event of her death, the money would pass to you."

Harris was stunned. Sally was dead, so the money was now, his. The problem was that he would have to prove that she was dead and that would be the same thing as confessing to her murder.

Harris left the bank and knew he would have to leave town. He had forty-two dollars to his name, and that would have to do.

AFTER THE BANK robbery in Breckenridge, Sawyer and the others rode fifteen miles south to the town of Gunsight. There, they went into a saloon, ordered a bottle of whiskey and four glasses, then chose the most remote table.

"Eight thousand dollars—that's more like it," Godfrey said, happily. "That's two thousand dollars apiece."

"No, it's one thousand, seven hundred, and fifty dollars," Sawyer corrected.

"Here, where do you get that?" Godfrey asked.

"We're putting a one thousand dollar reward out for Lucas Cain, remember?"

"Oh, yeah, I forgot."

"Rufe, how are we going to put this thing out?" Dumey asked. "It ain't liken we can print posters or nothin'. I mean liken them's that's out on us."

"We're goin' to put it in the paper," Sawyer said. "Once it comes out in the first paper then pretty soon after that, ever' paper in the entire state will pick it up."

"We can't put no ad in the paper. We'd get caught."

"It won't be an ad, it'll be a news story," Sawyer explained. He smiled. "And like I say, just about every other paper will want to do a story about outlaws puttin' a reward out for the law. That switches things around, you see, and it'll be what they call a people's interest story."

"Yeah, but once they kill Cain, how will they collect the reward?" Coleman asked.

Sawyer chuckled. "Now, that will be up to whoever it is that done it, won't it?"

"How do we get it put in the paper?" Coleman asked. "I mean if one of us go to the paper to tell 'em to write the story, what would keep 'em from going to the sheriff?"

"I've already wrote the story. We'll find some kid and give him a dollar to take it to the newspaper. The kid won't see anything but the dollar."

IT HAD BEEN LESS than two weeks since Lucas had left Eastland, and the first place he visited when he came back was the newspaper office. Cephus McKay looked up from the composition table.

"Lucas," he said. "What brings you back so soon?"

"I thought maybe I might check in on you and see how you're doing."

"Is that the only reason you came? To see how we're doing?" Carolina asked, with a mischievous smile.

"Oh, I don't know, I thought I might also see if you were still as pretty as you were the last time I was here."

"Oh?" Carolina said, striking a pose. "And what have you decided?"

Lucas held the palm of his hand out and rocked it back and forth. "Oh, I guess you'll do."

"Lucas!" Carolina said, feigning irritation, as she playfully doubled her hands to fists and hit him on the chest.

Lucas laughed, caught her fists in his hands, then raised them to his lips and kissed both of them.

Lucas looked around the office. "Where's Maggie? I thought she would come greet me as well."

"She's helping Mom today," Carolina answered. She smiled. "Now don't tell me I have to be jealous of a twelve-year-old."

"I'm told she's almost thirteen," Lucas said with a little laugh.

"Lucas, are you still looking for Rufe Sawyer?" Cephus asked.

"Yeah, I am, but so far I don't have a clue as to where he might be," Lucas replied.

"Well, don't worry about it, since he's trying to find you, maybe you won't have to look for him."

"What? Mr. McKay, what are you talking about? What do you mean, he's looking for me?"

"Oh, my. You don't know that he's looking for you, do you?"

"No, I don't know."

"Then that means you don't know about the reward," Cephus said.

"Yes, I know about the reward. It's been raised to three thousand dollars for Sawyer, and a thousand dollars each for the other three."

"No, you don't understand. I'm talking about the reward that's been put out for you."

"What?" Lucas nearly shouted. "Cephus, what are you talking about? Why would the law put out a reward for me?"

"It's not the law that's doing it. It's Sawyer. He's put out a reward of one thousand dollars to anyone who will kill you."

"I've heard of no such thing. How did you hear about it, and even if it's true, how does he expect to get the word out?"

"It's already out," Cephus said. "The AP has sent it out to every newspaper in the state, and dozens of them are running the story, even though the reward is being offered by a known murderer. I didn't print it, of course, and I wouldn't have printed it, even if I didn't know you. But there are those editors who will print anything they think will be read. And I'm sure there will be many who read this." Cephus looked around on his desk, then picked up a newspaper. "This ran in the *Belle Plain Herald*."

Lucas took the newspaper, then read the article Cephus had pointed out to him.

TABLES TURNED ON REWARD

Wanted murderer and robber, Rufe Sawyer, has offered a reward of one thousand dollars to anyone who kills the noted lawman, Lucas Cain. This newspaper thinks the offer is despicable, but we also believe we must honor the first amendment, thus we bring Sawyer's offer to you in his own words:

To anyone who wants to make themselves a thousand dollars, all you got to do is kill Lucas Cain, then cut off his head and bring it to Rufe Sawyer, and I'll give you a thousand dollars for it.

Those were Sawyer's words as written in the note delivered to the newspaper, and certainly not the words of this newspaper, and we disavow any connection with the offer.

Lucas handed the paper back to Cephus.

"That's a hell of a thing, they say they disavow any connection with this, but yet they printed it," Cephus said.

"I wonder how anyone plans to collect on the reward?" Lucas asked. "I've been looking for Sawyer for weeks, and I can't find hide nor hair of him."

"Well, they," Cephus started, then he stopped and chuckled. "That's a good point. Just how do they expect to collect, unless they know where he is?"

"I hope somebody does try and collect the reward," Lucas said.

"Lucas, no! What are you saying?"

"Think about it, Carolina. If someone did try, they might be the connection I would need to find Sawyer. That is, if he doesn't kill me first," he added with a teasing grin.

"Oooh, you're awful," Carolina said.

"Too awful to have supper with tonight?" Lucas asked.

"Well, maybe not that awful."

27

Eastland's Pride was just as Lucas remembered. They were shown to their table, which the waiter remembered would be in the back corner. Lucas pulled out the chair and held it for Carolina until she was seated.

"I wasn't sure I would ever see you again," Carolina said.

"Oh? What made you think that?"

"You made it fairly clear that I was moving too fast."

Lucas sighed. "Carolina, don't come to any conclusions too quickly. It's just that...well, I know it won't make sense to you, or anyone else for that matter. I know that Rosie is dead, and if I'm with another woman, it's almost as if I'm being untrue to her. It's something that I'll get over, and soon, I hope."

Carolina reached across the table and placed her hand on his. "Lucas, I know you told me about this before. And I hope you remember what my answer was."

Lucas smiled. "I think you told me that you admire a man who could love so deeply."

"I did say that. And I mean it."

"Good," Lucas said. "I hope that means that you won't give up on me while I work this out."

"I'll never give up on you, Lucas."

RICHARDSON, TEXAS

Frustrated and angry that he had been unable to withdraw money from Sally's bank account, Sam Harris came home to decide what he should do next. He gave some thought to robbing the bank, but he wasn't sure he could pull it off by himself, and because he was known by nearly everyone in Richardson, he was certain he wouldn't be able to get away with it.

Over the next few days, friends and acquaintances would inquire about Sally.

"Where is Sally? We haven't seen her in several days," one of Sally's friends asked.

"Well, you know how Sally has always been smarter than me," Harris replied. "She made up her mind that we should live in California, so she took a train to San Francisco to find a place for us to live. She'll send word when she's ready for me to come out there."

"Please let us know when you hear from her."

"I will."

ONE WEEK LATER, Harris went to Greenville and sent a telegram to himself in Richardson.

ARRIVED SAFELY STOP JOIN ME SOON AS YOU CAN

Harris hurried back to Richardson to receive the telegram. Then he took it around to show it to some of Sally's friends.

"Oh, I'm so glad that she made it safely. When will you join her?"

"I've been anxious to go ever since she left. But I knew she'd be better getting us all set up."

"You tell her to be sure and write and tell her how much we all miss her."

"You can count on it," Harris said.

TWO DAYS LATER, Harris was in Fort Worth. That was when he read the article about Rufe Sawyer offering a thousand-dollar reward for anyone who would kill the U.S. Marshal, Lucas Cain.

Damn, he thought. *That would be enough money to get me to California, or anywhere else I might want to go.*

In order to collect on the bounty, he would have to know where Lucas Cain might be.

As he pondered that particular dilemma, an idea came to him, and he smiled at the brilliance of his thinking. Cain is a lawman, and who knows better about lawmen than another lawman.

He couldn't just go see a sheriff and ask where Cain might be. He had to come up with some kind of believable story. Then, as he thought of an idea that might work for him, he walked down to the sheriff's office. There was a grin on his face, as he contemplated the one thousand dollars he would get.

He stepped into the sheriff's office, where he saw a man sitting behind the desk, reading a newspaper. The sign on his desk informed him that this was Sheriff Michael Moore.

"Sheriff Moore?" he said.

Sheriff Moore lay his paper down and looked up.

"I'm Sheriff Moore."

"Sheriff, I'm Steven Cain. The last I heard from my cousin, Lucas, he said that he was here in Fort Worth. But he didn't give me an address. Do you know where he lives?"

"You're his cousin, you say?" Sheriff Moore asked, suspiciously.

"Yes. My father was his father's brother, and of course we have the same grandmother, that is, we had the same grandmother. That's why I'm looking for him. Our grandmother died, and since Lucas was so close to her, my father thought it might be better if I came to tell him in person, rather than sending him a letter or a telegram."

"Yes, I can see why it would be. But I'm sorry to tell you that he isn't here."

"By not here, do you mean not here in Fort Worth?"

"Yes, he's trying to find an outlaw we have around here, a man named Rufe Sawyer. I'm sure you've heard of him," the sheriff said.

"No, I've never heard the name. I'm from Missouri."

Sheriff Moore chuckled. "You know, Mr. Cain, I wasn't sure I believed you, until you told me you were from Missouri. I know that's where Lucas is from and I don't think too many people know that, so I'll tell you where he is. Lucas is in Eastland."

"Eastland?"

"It's a little west of here, just a little over an hour by train."

"Thank you very much, Sheriff."

"I'm glad I could help you. And when you see Lucas, give him my condolences for his…and your grandmother."

"I will, Sheriff, and thank you."

Harris left the sheriff's office with a big smile on his face. He had no idea that Cain was from Missouri. It was just something he had come up with, to convince the sheriff that he knew nothing about Rufe Sawyer. In fact, he knew Rufe quite well.

BY TRAIN, it took just over an hour to get to Eastland. The first thing he did after he left the train, was go to a saloon. Stepping up to the bar, he ordered a whiskey, then after getting his drink he looked for an open table.

Having found the table, Harris began thinking about what he should do to find Cain. The sheriff told him that Cain was in Eastland, and in a town as small as Eastland, finding him shouldn't be all that hard. What might be difficult would be finding Sawyer so he could collect on the bounty, once the job was done.

Harris was so deep in thought that he didn't notice someone approach his table, until his visitor spoke.

"Sam Harris, what are you doing here?"

Looking up at the speaker, Harris smiled. "Moe Godfrey, I might ask the same thing of you. I haven't seen you since we were both spending some time in the Huntsville School for Boys." Harris chuckled at the appellation many of the prisoners had for the state penitentiary. "What are you doing here?"

"Oh, I'm just hangin' around," Godfrey said. "What about you? I thought I heard you got yourself hitched."

"Yeah I did. I met her in a whorehouse, but she inherited a ranch, so we got married."

"Some people are just lucky, I guess," Godfrey said. "Get yourself a woman and a ranch."

"Not all that lucky. She kept everythin' in her own name—the ranch, the bank account, everything."

"Damn, that ain't very good. So what happened? Are you still married to her?"

"No." Harris started to tell how he had ended the marriage but decided against it.

"Yeah, I don't blame you for gettin' out of that marriage. There's nothin' worse than a whore with money that she won't share."

"Say, I remember that you and Sawyer were once friends, or what could be passed off as friends with him," Harris said.

"Yeah, we was. What about it?"

"Do you have any idea how I might find him?"

"Why do you want to?"

"For the bounty," Harris answered.

"You want to collect the bounty on Sawyer, and you expect me to find him for you?" Godfrey's hand dropped to his gun, but he didn't pull it. "Now, just why the hell would I tell you that?"

Seeing Godfrey grow tense and drop his hand to his gun, frightened Harris, and he knew he had better tell Godfrey why he was looking for Sawyer.

"When we was in prison together, me 'n Sawyer sure as hell warn't friends. But you misunderstand me. I ain't lookin' for a bounty *on* Sawyer, I'm lookin' for a bounty *from* him. I plan on killin' Lucas Cain."

The angry expression left Godfrey's face. He smiled and moved his hand away from his gun.

"I tell you what," Godfrey said. "I'll take you to see him now."

"I don't have a horse," Harris said.

"That's all right. It ain't that far. We've got a few extra horses, we can ride double 'til we get there, then you can pick up one for youself."

"All right, I'll go with you."

"You think Rufe will remember you?" Godfrey asked.

"I don't know, I was doin' the last six months of my time when he come into prison."

"Maybe he'll remember you," Godfrey suggested.

"Lord, I hope not."

Godfrey laughed.

28

I t took less than an hour to reach the campsite where Sawyer and the others were.

"What the hell do you mean, bringin' someone to our campsite?" Sawyer asked.

"Take it easy, Rufe, you know him," Godfrey said, as he dismounted, and Harris slid down from the horse.

Sawyer examined the newcomer, then nodded. "Harris, ain't it?"

"Yes," Harris replied.

"All right, so I know 'im," Sawyer said. "I still don't know why you brung him here. I don't want to add anyone else to our group."

"I'm not here to join your group, Sawyer. I'm here to collect the reward."

"You killed Cain?" Sawyer asked.

"Not yet, but I will. I just wanted to know where to find you after I do it."

"Yeah, well when you do it, get back to me and I'll pay the reward. There's no need to see you again before that."

"Well if, somehow I lose track of him, you'll want your horse back, won't you?"

"What horse?"

"Uh, he don't have a horse," Godfrey said, "So I told 'im we'd loan 'im one of ours."

"Who give you the right to do that?" Sawyer asked in an angry tone.

"Well, I figured it would be worth it if Harris kills Cain," Godfrey replied, trying to explain his reasoning.

"Yeah, all right, you can borrow one of our horses. But I want it back when you're done, unless you're plannin' on buyin' it."

"I'll buy it with the thousand dollars I'm goin' to make," Harris said with a big smile.

"Yeah? Well have you ever heard of the old sayin', don't count your thousand dollars 'til after you kilt Cain?"

"Uh, yeah, something like that, I guess," Harris said.

Half an hour later, mounted on one of the three horses Sawyer and his men had stolen, Harris rode into Eastland to find Cain. After he killed Cain, he would collect his thousand dollars, then maybe join up with Sawyer and the others.

"Hey, Rufe, I remember Harris," Dumey said, after Harris had ridden away. "He was caught, 'n put in prison for holdin' up only one store. Don't seem to me like anyone who ain't got no more sense 'n that, ain't goin' to be able to kill Lucas Cain."

"I don't expect he will," Sawyer said. "But it'd be good if he did."

"Yeah, I guess so," Dumey said. "It's just that I'd hate to give some son of a bitch like that, a thousand dollars."

"Who said we're gonna give him a thousand dollars?" Sawyer replied.

"Well, ain't we? I mean, that's what the reward is," Godfrey said.

"Not for Harris," Sawyer said. "The only thing he's gonna get is a bullet between his eyes."

"Yes!" Coleman said, excitedly. "That'll save us two hunnert 'n fifty dollars apiece."

Dumey slapped at a mosquito.

"Damn, they's a lot of mosquitos here."

"That's because we're near water," Godfrey said. "And we need to be near water, for us and for the horses."

"Yeah, well, it wouldn't be so bad iffin we was inside," Coleman said. "It ain't fittin' to live outside like a damn animal all the time. What we need is a house."

"You want us to build a house, do you?" Godfrey asked with a little chuckle.

"No," Sawyer said. "Coleman's right, we do need a house, but we won't build one, we'll steal one."

"Steal a house? How do you do that?"

"I know just the one we need," Sawyer said. "Let's close this camp out, then come with me and I'll show you."

IT TOOK LESS than an hour to get to the house Sawyer was talking about. Actually, it was more of a cabin than a house. It was of adobe construction with a tiled roof. It appeared to be well-kept, indicating that it was occupied.

"Do you know who lives here?" Godfrey asked.

"An old man and his wife. I know his name, it's Lopez, but I don't actually know him."

"How are we going to do this?" Dumey asked.

"It'll be simple enough," Sawyer said. "You three wait here. I'll take care of it."

While Godfrey, Dumey, and Coleman waited on a ridgeline that overlooked the Lopez house, Sawyer rode down to it.

THE MAN who answered Sawyer's knock on the door had white hair, a white beard, and wrinkles enough for one to determine by a casual glance that he was an old man. That observation would be correct because Juan Lopez was eighty-six years old.

"Who are you?" Lopez asked.

"I'm just a lost traveler looking for information," Sawyer answered. "Which way is it to Eastland, and how far would that be?"

"It's about eight miles. All you got to do is follow the road that way." Lopez pointed.

"Who is it, Juan?" a woman's voice called from inside the cabin.

"It's just someone askin' for directions," Juan said.

"Well invite him in for coffee. We don't see that many people, it would be nice to have someone to talk to."

"You heard Marica, come on in," Juan invited.

Sawyer went inside and was welcomed by Marica. He had a look around. The house was small, about twenty-by-twenty feet. There was a big, cast-iron cookstove, a small table with two chairs, and a bed.

"So you're going to Eastland?" Marica asked. "Juan has four beehives, and we go into town from time to time to sell honey. I enjoy it when we do go. What will you be doing in Eastland?"

"You won't have to worry about that," Sawyer said cryptically.

"Why, what do you..." Marica's question was interrupted when she saw that Sawyer was holding a gun. "Oh, what..."

Her second question was interrupted by Sawyer shooting, first Marica, then Juan.

Two hours later, Marica and Juan were behind the house, both buried in the same grave. Sawyer, Godfrey, Dumey, and Coleman were no longer camping outside.

BACK IN THE office of the *Eastland Journal*, Maggie was setting type under the direction of her big sister.

"No, no," Carolina said. "It's not T-h-u-r-s-d-a-y, it's y-a-d-s-r-u-h-T."

"Why do you have to set the words backward?" Maggie asked. "I mean that would be really hard for people to read, wouldn't it?"

Carolina chuckled. "It's just backward when it's set in the type chase, but once the printing starts, the words come out frontward on the paper."

"Ha, imagine that," Maggie said as she took up the Thursday, then set it backward as Carolina had said.

"HOW LONG DO you think Lucas Cain will stay in Eastland?"

Sam Harris was standing at the bar in a saloon in Eastland.

"I guess he'll stay around as long as Carolina McKay's here," someone who was standing next to him at the bar replied.

"Yeah, I see him in the newspaper office all the time, and it ain't no secret what's keepin' him there," the man standing on the other side of the first speaker said.

Harris took in the information. So, Lucas Cain was sniffing around some local woman who worked at the newspaper office. That gave him an idea.

Harris tossed his drink down, left the saloon and walked down to the newspaper office. When he went inside, he saw two women. One was setting type, and the other was bending over her, giving directions, pointing out what to do. Actually, a closer examination showed that one of the two was a young girl.

The older of the two looked up when Harris came in.

"Yes, sir," she said with a bright smile. "How may I help you?"

"My name is Sam Harris, and I'm looking for Marshal Cain," Harris said. "I'm told that he spends some time here."

"That's because he's in love with my sister," the young girl said with a broad smile.

"Maggie!" Carolina scolded. "What a thing for you to say."

"Well, we both know it's true," Maggie said with a big grin.

Carolina turned her attention back to the man who had just entered.

"I'm sorry. Pay no attention to my little sister. Now, what can I do for you?"

Harris pulled his pistol and pointed it at Carolina. "You and your sister can come with me."

"What? Why on earth would I do such a thing?"

"I don't know," Harris said. "Maybe because I'll kill your sister if you don't?"

"Who are you? What do you want?" Carolina asked. "Why do you want us to come with you?"

"Well, let's put it this way. I've been told that Lucas Cain likes you. So, I figure if I hold you and your little sister, he'll come lookin' for you. And when he does, I'll kill 'im."

"What? No, you're insane! I'm not coming with you," Carolina said.

"Oh, I think you will," Harris said. He raised his pistol, pointed it at Maggie, and pulled the hammer back.

"No, no!" Carolina shouted. "We'll go with you; we'll go with you!"

Harris lowered the pistol and let the hammer back down. "I thought you might see things my way," he said. "Come on."

"Where are we going?" Carolina asked.

"Oh, I have a room in the Dunn Hotel," Harris said.

"The Dunn?"

"Yes, I figure if you two are going to be with me, then I'm going to get a room in the nicest hotel in town."

"How are we going to get there?" Carolina asked.

"Why, we're gonna walk. It's only a little over a block away," Harris answered.

"How do you know we won't run as soon as we get outside?"

"Oh, you don't understand. I don't care whether you run or not," Harris said. He smiled an evil smile. "Because whichever one of you runs, I'll kill the other one."

"You," he yelled at Maggie, who had not left the composing table. "Ain't you been listenin' to me? Get over here now."

"I can't right now," Maggie said. "Papa wants me to set this story for the paper."

"That ain't your problem no more," Harris said. He waved his pistol, making a come here motion. "Now! Get over here now! We're goin' to the hotel, where I've got a nice room for us."

"Okay, but Papa's going to be mad at me for not finishing the story," Maggie said.

"Which would you rather have? Your papa mad at you, or your sister dead?"

When Maggie got up from the composing table, she spilled several pieces of type on the composing table and on the floor. She started to pick them up.

"Leave it," Harris ordered in a stern voice.

Harris walked over to Maggie and motioned for her to come with him. He happened to look at the type frame where Maggie had been working.

"What the hell?" he said. "This don't make no sense a'tall. What is this?"

"You have to read it backwards," Maggie explained. "Here, I'll read it to you. *The Women's Club of Eastland will meet on Thursday to…*"

"That's enough," Harris said, interrupting Maggie's reading. "Get over here with your sister."

Maggie walked over to stand beside Carolina. Carolina put her arm around her.

"All right, here's what we're gonna do," Harris explained. "When we get outside, we'll just have a nice walk, looking into the store windows, just enjoyin' ourselves. And remember, if one of you tries to run, I'll kill the other one."

The three of them stepped out into the street.

"If you see anyone you know, just say hello, nothing else," Harris said.

The hotel was only a block and a half down the street, and they didn't meet, or pass any other pedestrian.

When they reached the hotel, they walked through the lobby without arousing the attention of anyone.

As soon as they were upstairs and in his room, Harris brought his gun butt down, first on Carolina's head, then Maggie's. When both were unconscious, Harris got to the next part of his plan. He took the clothes off first Carolina, then Maggie.

"Hmm, too bad I didn't meet you before I met Sally," he said. "You're one good-lookin' woman."

He put both of them up on the bed, then stuffed a rag in their mouths, to keep them from calling out. Then, using a small rope, he tied their hands and feet to the bedstead. He waited until the two were awake.

Both Carolina and Maggie pulled at the ropes that held them, but there was nothing they could do. They tried to talk, but neither of them could make a sound beyond a quiet, unintelligible humming.

"Now, let me tell you what's going to happen," Harris said. "I'm gonna tell Cain that I have both of you tied to a tree just outside of town, and I'll tell 'im I'll let the two of you go, if he'll pay a ransom."

He laughed. "Only, there ain't really gonna be no ransom. That's just the way I can get him out of town, where I can kill him."

Harris laughed, a high-pitched, hacking laugh.

"Then Cain will be dead, and I'll be a thousand dollars richer."

29

Cephus was laughing at something as he and Lucas came back to the newspaper office.

"Hmm, that's strange," Cephus said as he looked around the office. "Where are the girls? It's not like them to leave the office unattended like this."

"The privy is out back, isn't it? I'll take a look," Lucas offered.

"All right, but I can't think of any reason both of them would go out there at the same time and leave the office empty. Damn, and type scattered all over like that."

Lucas started toward the back door as Cephus started to pick up the type. He stared at the type bed.

"Lucas!" he called.

There was a hint of distress in Cephus's voice, and Lucas looked back toward him.

"I know where they are."

Lucas hurried back to where Cephus was standing at the composition table.

Cephus pointed to the type bed. "Harris took them to the Dunn Hotel."

"Who's Harris?" Lucas looked at the type bed. "What are you talking about?"

"Look, they left a message." Cephus read the message.

nnuD ot su sekat sirraH nam eman pleH

"What do mean a message? That makes no sense," Lucas said.

"You have to read it backward. I've been reading backward-set type for twenty-five years. This says 'Help, Harris takes us to Dunn.'"

"I'll be damn, she left it backwards, didn't she? Smart little girl, even if Harris, whoever he is, saw this, he wouldn't know what it said."

"Let's go to the Dunn Hotel," Cephus said.

Lucas held out his hand. "Better let me go alone. It's likely to be dangerous."

"It won't be any more dangerous for me than it already is for my daughters. I'm going."

"All right, let's go," Lucas said, giving in to Cephus's logic.

Lucas and Cephus reached the hotel quickly and spoke to the man at the front desk.

"Hodge, did you see my daughters come in here? There would have been a man named Harris with them."

"No, Cephus, I didn't see anything like that, but I was in the back room most of the morning, so they could have come in without me seeing them. Is there something wrong?"

"Yes, there's something wrong. Harris has taken them against their will."

"Oh, my! Well, we do have a Sam Harris registered with us."

"What is his room number?" Lucas asked.

The clerk started to check the registration book, then he looked up and got a frightened expression on his face.

"There's Mr. Harris now, coming down the stairs."

"Harris, where are my daughters?" Cephus shouted.

"Cain!" Harris shouted as he drew his gun.

Lucas hadn't expected him to draw, and because of that, didn't get his gun out until after Harris had already taken a shot. The bullet energized by Harris's gun punched a hole in the front desk. Lucas's gun sent a bullet into the middle of Harris's chest. Dropping his gun, Harris put his hand over the wound, then fell forward, tumbling the rest of the way down the stairs.

Lucas hurried over to Harris, then knelt beside him. "Where are the women?" he asked.

Harris gasped for breath.

"Where are they?" This time the question was more harshly asked.

"Wait until you see them," Harris replied.

"That's no answer. Where are they?"

Harris drew his last breath without saying another word.

Lucas looked over at Cephus and the desk clerk, both of whom were staring in open-mouthed shock.

"What's this man's room number?" Lucas asked.

The clerk checked the book. "Two thirteen," he said. "All the way in the back, on the right side."

Lucas hurried up the stairs, taking them two at a time. He ran down the hall to room two thirteen, then realized he didn't have the key. It would have to be locked if they were inside. He checked the door and was shocked when it opened. He hesitated for a moment. If they were in the room, and the door wasn't locked, that could only mean that they were...he drew a breath to brace himself against the sight of two bodies, then stepped inside.

He saw them on the bed and drew a breath of relief to see that they were alive, though bound and gagged.

They were also naked.

He moved quickly to the bed, then pulled out the cloth that was keeping them gagged.

"Oh, thank God!" Carolina said.

Lucas took a knife from his pocket and started cutting the ropes, Carolina first.

"Lucas, a man named Harris is wanting to kill you," Maggie said.

"Not a problem," Lucas said. "I killed him."

"That was the gunshots I heard," Carolina said as she removed the cut rope from her arms and legs.

"I'll, uh, get out now so you two can get dressed," Lucas said.

"It's a little late for that, isn't it?"

"I'll be outside," Lucas said again.

As soon as Lucas left the room, he saw Cephus hurrying up the hall toward him. The expression on his face was one of fear and worry. "Are they in there?" he asked.

"They're in there."

Cephus reached for the doorknob, and Lucas stopped him. "I wouldn't go in there just yet."

"Oh, my God! Are they...are they?"

Cephus couldn't finish the question, and Lucas realized then that Cephus must be thinking they were dead.

"They're both fine," he said. "But they are also undressed."

HALF AN HOUR later the four of them were back at the newspaper office.

"Harris was after the bounty that Rufe Sawyer said he would pay to anyone who killed you," Carolina said.

"Carolina, that was smart of you to leave a message the way you did," Lucas said.

"Message? What message are you talking about?"

"The one that you left in the type bed, setting it backward so Harris couldn't read it if he saw it."

"And then spilling type on the floor so I would see the message when I picked up the type," Cephus said. "That was brilliant."

Carolina smiled. "Yes, Maggie is brilliant, isn't she?"

"Maggie?" Lucas said.

"Yes, Maggie, my brilliant little sister. She's the one that left the note and spilled the type. I didn't know anything about it."

"Maggie, thank you, you saved both of your lives," Cephus said, giving his daughter a hug.

"Is it all right if I give you a hug, too?" Lucas asked with a big smile. "You saved my life as well."

Laughing, Maggie went to Lucas for an embrace.

Sheriff Dozier came into the newspaper office then, and seeing everyone in a happy mood, smiled.

"Is this a private party?" Dozier asked. "Or, can anyone join?"

"We're celebrating getting my two daughters back safely," Cephus said.

"And this little girl here, for saving my life," Lucas added.

"I'm not a *little* girl," Maggie insisted.

Lucas laughed. "After what you did today, you can be anything you want. You have certainly earned it."

"I'm sure this has something to do with the body

that's down in the undertaker's place now," Dozier said. "He registered as Sam Harris, but I don't have any other information on him. Is he someone you were after, Lucas?"

"I wasn't after him; he was after me."

"After you?"

"For the bounty. Sawyer has placed a bounty on my head, remember?"

"Oh, yes. That means there will be others coming to town, won't there?" Sheriff Dozier asked. "I can understand why you might want to leave, but speaking as the sheriff, I want you to know you're always welcome here."

"Thanks."

"When will you be pulling out?"

"Not until he has supper with us," Cephus said.

"Cephus..." Lucas stopped in midsentence looking for some way to politely decline the invitation. "I..."

"Accept," Carolina interjected, quickly.

Lucas smiled, and added, "With pleasure."

ETHYL MCKAY WENT ALL OUT for supper that night. She baked a hen, made dressing, corn on the cob, green beans cooked with bacon and onion, biscuits, gravy, and a blackberry cobbler.

"Mrs. McKay, I do believe this may well be the best dinner I've ever eaten," Lucas said as he finished the cobbler. He rubbed his stomach. "I see what you're doing, though. You're feeding me so much that I won't be able to move. Then, I would have to stay in town longer."

"Can you blame me, Mr. Cain? You saved my daughters' lives."

"No, that would be Maggie," Lucas said. "And she saved my life as well."

"Yes," Ethyl said, beaming proudly at her daughter. "She did, didn't she?"

30

"So, instead of killin' Cain, the son of a bitch got hisself killed, is that what you're tellin' me?" Sawyer asked.

"Yeah," Godfrey said. "He was comin' down the stairs at the hotel when Cain shot 'im."

"We're gonna have to find someone else," Dumey said.

"I wish now that I hadn't got that article printed that said I'd pay a bounty. You don't know what you'll get, that way, I mean, look at Harris, and what a loser he was. Chris is right. We need to find somebody our ownselves. That way we'll know whether we have somebody that can actually get the job done, instead of an idiot like Harris turned out to be."

"Where we gonna find someone?" Coleman asked.

"I got a few ideas," Sawyer said. "But first thing we got to do, is get out of here. We're too close to where Cain is, 'n if we stay here any longer, he could find us."

"But they's only one of him, 'n there's four of us,"

Dumey said. "Why are we runnin' from the son of a bitch?"

"'Cause he ain't your ordinary bounty hunter. He's a U.S. Marshal, and like as not, if he decides to come after us, he's likely to have a posse with him. No, sir, we need to play this game by our rules, 'n our rules is that we know where he is, but he don't know where we are. We'll find someone to kill 'im, then he'll be out of our hair."

"Yeah," Godfrey said. "I like the idea of him bein' kilt."

WEATHERFORD

When Deke Pauly rode into town, his eyes made a practiced sweep, not only of each side of the street, but also the balconies and roofs of the buildings. He didn't have any specific enemies, but a few years of hunting for bounties had created several enemies in general.

He dismounted in front of the Brown Spur Saloon, tied his horse off, and went inside.

"You're new, ain't ya?" the bartender asked.

"New enough, I reckon."

"What'll you have?"

"Whiskey."

The bartender took a glass, filled it, then slid it in front of Pauly.

"And some information," Pauly added. He held out a ten-dollar bill, then added, "I'll pay for it."

"What do you expect me to know that's worth ten dollars?"

"Where I might find Rufe Sawyer," Pauly said.

The bartender handed the ten-dollar bill back. "Mister, even if I knew the answer to that question, I wouldn't tell you. It ain't worth gettin' shot for ten dollars."

"Then you do know him. You must know him, or you wouldn't know enough to be afraid to tell me."

"I've got customers to tend to," the bartender said, walking away from Pauly.

As Pauly was drinking his whiskey, one of the others in the saloon came up to stand alongside him.

"You a bounty hunter?"

"You might say that," Pauly replied.

"Make that offer fifty dollars, and I'll take you to him."

Pauly finished his whiskey and put the glass down. "You've got a deal," he said.

"I want the money now."

"You're saying that you will take me to him?"

"Yeah, I'll do that."

"How are you going to do that? Do you know Sawyer well enough for him to trust you?"

"Me 'n him go back a long ways."

"What's your name?" Pauly asked.

"Scobey."

"That's it? Just Scobey?"

"That's all you need to know."

"So, Scobey, what you're telling me, is you're willing to betray your friend for fifty dollars?"

"I told you, me 'n Sawyer ain't friends. I just happen to know 'im, 'n I know where he is, right now. So are we goin' after 'im, or not?"

"Lead on."

The two men left the bar, climbed onto their respective horses, and rode out of town.

Half an hour later, they were following Ash Creek. Pauly had asked Scobey a few questions but his answers, when he bothered to answer at all, were monosyllabic.

"We'll stop here," Scobey said.

"Where is Sawyer?"

"I don't have any idea. I'm just goin' to take your money and…" Scobey raised his pistol but was shocked to see that Pauly already had his gun out, pointing at Scobey.

"I don't think so," Pauly said, pulling the trigger.

Scobey died with a shocked expression on his face.

Pauly thought about leaving the body, but then reasoned that if Scobey was going to kill and rob, there may be a bounty on him. To that end, he draped Scobey across his horse, then started back to town.

When he reached the sheriff's office, he left Scobey's body draped across his horse, then went inside. A man, with a star pinned to his shirt was sitting at his desk, drinking a cup of coffee.

"Are you the sheriff?" Pauly asked.

"Sheriff Patterson, yes. Who are you?"

"Deke Pauly."

"Pauly? You're the bounty hunter, aren't you?"

"I am 'a' bounty hunter, I don't know that I am 'the' bounty hunter."

"What can I do for you, Pauly?"

"I've got a body draped over a horse outside. I want to check and see if there's any paper on 'im."

"What the hell, Pauly? Did you just kill someone on the chance there might be a bounty?"

"It wasn't quite like that. He told me he could lead me to Rufe Sawyer, but when we were a few miles out of town, he drew his gun on me, and tried to rob me."

"Let's see now, he pulled a gun on you, but you drew on him and shot him?"

"Not exactly like that. He was acting a little strange, so I already had my gun out, and when he raised his gun toward me, I shot him."

"What's his name?"

"Scobey is the only name he gave me."

Sheriff Patterson shook his head. "The name doesn't ring a bell with me. Let's take a look at him."

Pauly and Patterson went out front to look at the body. By the time they got outside, half a dozen citizens of the town had gathered around the macabre display. The sheriff lifted the head of the body.

"Who did you say this was?"

"He said his name was Scobey."

"His name is Majors, Newt Majors. And yes, there is a bounty on him. Not much, only one hundred and fifty dollars but he is wanted. Not dead or alive, though."

"Like I said, Sheriff, I didn't kill him for the bounty, I killed him to keep him from killing me."

"There's no way to prove or to disprove your story, so I won't be charging you with anything. I'll have the money for you by tomorrow morning."

"Thanks, Sheriff."

RUFE SAWYER, the three men who made up his gang, and a visitor were in the recently acquired cabin that had become their headquarters.

Rufe Sawyer was engaged in an intense conversation with the visitor to the little cabin.

"One thousand dollars," Sawyer said. He was talking to Stretch Mueller, someone he had met in prison.

"All right," Mueller said. "I'll do it."

"And I want him dead, not just scared off."

"And just who, exactly is it you're a-wantin' me to kill?"

"Lucas Cain."

"You mean the U.S. Marshal Cain?"

"Yes."

Mueller paused for a moment before he responded. "Make it fifteen hundred," he said.

"Are you telling me that a thousand dollars ain't enough for you?"

"You ain't been followin' Cain, 'cause you've been in prison. But I've been out for two years, and I know all about Cain. And one of the things I know is, he takes a heap o' killin'. Once I do it, I'm goin' to have to get far away from here. Maybe as far away as some place like New York."

Sawyer nodded. "All right, do the job, and it's worth fifteen hundred to me."

"I want the money now."

"No," Sawyer said, resolutely. "I'll pay for it when the job is done, and I have proof that Cain is dead."

"All right, that's fair enough, I suppose. By the way, do you have any idea where Cain might be?"

"He's sniffin' around some woman who's the daughter of the publisher of the *Eastland Journal.* You'll as likely find him there, as anyplace else, so all you gotta do is get somewhere where you can keep an eye on the newspaper office until you get the chance to kill the son of a bitch."

"All right, only one more thing," Mueller said.

"What's that?"

"I know you said you ain't goin' to give me the money first, but before I risk my life doin' this, I want to know that you actually have fifteen hundred dollars to pay me. So, I want you to show me the money," Mueller said.

"All right." Sawyer said. He went over to the wall, just under the side window, pulled out a loose board, then stuck his hand in to grab a canvas bag. Reaching down into the bag, he brought out a large wad of money. "I don't know how much is here, but it's a hell of a lot more 'n fifteen hundred dollars."

Mueller smiled. "Sawyer, you just bought yourself a slack man."

"A what?"

"You have some loose ends that need to have slack taken out of 'em. I'm the man that's goin' to do that for you."

Mueller left the cabin with a bounce in his step, got on his horse and rode off.

Godfrey came over to stand by Sawyer and watch as Mueller ride away.

"Is he goin' to do it?"

"Yes."

"How much does he want?"

"I told him we'd give him fifteen hundred dollars."

"What?" Godfrey shouted. "Fifteen hundred dollars?"

"Listen to what I said, Moe. I *said* we would give him fifteen hundred dollars. But I have no intention of actually doing that."

Godfrey laughed. "Yeah, let's see the son of a bitch actually try and collect."

31

"So, Carolina writes the stories, Maggie sets the type, and you do the actual printing," Lucas said.

"That's the operation," Cephus replied.

"This is quite a family business then, isn't it?"

"Yes, and to be honest, I'm not sure I could even publish a paper without them. I'm not making enough money to hire help."

"Anyway, we like doing it," Carolina said. "Don't we, Little Sister?"

"Yes, we sure do," Maggie replied as she was setting type for today's edition.

"Maggie, I want to tell you again how smart you were to leave a message the way you did," Lucas said.

Maggie smiled under Lucas's praise.

"Oh, here's an item in the Associated Press reports that might interest you," Cephus said"Sawyer has been seen inComanche Comanche County."

"Where?" Lucas asked.

"Oh, wait a minute, he's also been seen in Callahan and Stephens County."

Lucas shook his head. "Then that means none of the reports can be counted on."

"You'll find him," Carolina said. "I have every confidence that you will."

Lucas picked up a few of the AP articles and began reading them.

"Oh, I don't like this. Here's an article putting me in Eastland. It's a story about me shooting that man in the hotel."

Cephus held up his hand. "I guarantee you, Lucas, I didn't run that story."

"I know you wouldn't."

MUELLER WAS IN THE SALOON, just down the street from the newspaper office. He wanted to ask about Lucas Cain, but he didn't have to. Cain's name came up in a conversation he overheard.

"He's moved here, he lives here now," one of the men said.

"Huh-uh. Lucas Cain don't live nowhere."

"Yeah? How come, right now, he's in the newspaper office?"

"He's there 'cause he's sweet on Cephus McKay's daughter."

"Yeah, well who wouldn't be? I'd like to take a run at her myself."

"Really? Have you forgotten that he killed a man in the hotel the other day because of what he did to Carolina?"

"No, I haven't forgotten. Come to think of it, I don't think I would be interested in her. You can have her all to yourself."

"No thank you."

"Are you two talking about Lucas Cain, the famous bounty hunter?" Mueller asked.

"Yeah, except he's more than just a bounty hunter. He's a deputy U.S. Marshal."

"But you say he killed someone, just for looking at a woman he likes?"

"No, there was more to it than that," one of the two men said. "Sam Harris, that's the name of the man Cain killed, had kidnapped Carolina and her sister, and was holdin' 'em to draw out Cain. He was reckonin' to kill Cain, onliest thang is, it was Harris who got hisself kilt."

"Thanks for the information," Mueller said. He finished the rest of his drink, put the glass down rather sharply, then turned away from the bar and left the saloon.

"That man has somethin' in mind," one of the two bar gadflies said.

It wasn't hard to find the newspaper office. It was just down the street from the saloon, and the name was painted on a big window in front.

Mueller crossed the street and went into the office. A young girl greeted him.

"Yes, sir, may I help you?" the girl asked.

Mueller paused for just a moment. He couldn't just ask about Cain, without arousing some suspicion, but he needed to know if he was here.

"Yes, I would like…" Mueller stopped midsentence when he saw a man answering Cain's description just coming up from the back of the office. There was a very pretty young woman with him.

"Say, would that be my old friend, Lucas Cain?" Mueller asked.

"Yes, sir, that's him," the young girl said with a big smile.

"Cain!" Mueller shouted, drawing his gun at the same time.

The harsh and hostile tone of Mueller's voice warned Lucas, and with his left hand, he gave Carolina a shove, hard enough for her to go down. At the same time he shoved Carolina, he did two other things. He drew his own pistol as he leaped to the right.

Mueller pulled the trigger, but the bullet whizzed through the air where Cain's head had been just an instant earlier. The bullet brought down the overhead lamps then lodged in the back wall.

Lucas pulled the trigger, the report of his pistol so closely following Mueller's that all those who heard the gunshots were certain that they heard only one.

Lucas's shot hit Mueller in his right eye, leaving a black hole where the eye had been. A spray of blood issued from Mueller's head as he fell, dead before he reached the floor.

Cephus was busy putting out the flames from the burning lantern to keep them from spreading into what could become a major fire. That was a definite possibility, what with all the inflammable material found in a newspaper and printing office. Lucas started to help Cephus, then he remembered that he had pushed Carolina down rather sharply and he looked over at her.

"Are you all right?" Lucas asked, anxiously.

"I'm fine," Carolina replied. Lucas stepped over to help her up, as Cephus continued to fight the flames at the back of the building.

Lucas and Carolina hurried back to help him. They

extinguished the flames rather quickly, then Cephus looked up and noticed that Maggie wasn't with them.

"Where's Maggie?" he asked in an anxious tone.

"Maggie!" Carolina called, loudly.

They looked around but didn't see her.

Carolina hurried to the front and saw Maggie lying on the floor. Carolina gasped, and put her hand over her mouth. Then she saw Maggie move, and she knelt beside her.

"Maggie, my God, have you been shot?"

"No," Maggie said in a groggy voice. "I don't think so."

"Thank God you're all right."

"What am I doing on the floor?"

"You must have passed out."

"I guess I did. Help me up."

Carolina and Maggie were looking at the body of the intruder, with sickly expressions on their faces. There was a dark, bloody hole where his right eye had been. In addition, there was some yellow brain matter on the floor, having seeped from the exit wound.

"I can see why you passed out, sweetheart," Cephus said as he pulled his daughter to his side.

"Me too," Carolina added.

"Lucas, do you know this man?" Cephus asked.

Lucas shook his head. "I've never seen him before in my life."

"If you don't know him, he must be one of the men after the bounty that Sawyer has put on your head."

"Yeah, I reckon so," Lucas replied.

FROM THE *WEATHERFORD PRESS*:

Another Outlaw Falls to the Guns of Lucas Cain

*Deke Pauly was having supper in the Castle Café in Weath-
erford when he read the story of the shootout in Eastland. He
was aware that Rufe Sawyer had put a bounty on the head of
Lucas Cain, and as he read the story, he got an idea of what
he should do. He was going to look up Cain. From what he
had learned, Cain had been in Eastland for some few weeks,
and if Pauly started now, he would be there by midmorning
of the next day. Hopefully he could beat the next person who
would be after the Sawyer-imposed bounty.*

"WE'LL SPLIT THE BOUNTY MONEY," Emmet Peters said.
Peters, Buzz Logan, and Jake Slater had been brought to
Rufe Sawyer with the proposal that the three of them
would go after Lucas Cain.

"It seems pretty obvious that there ain't one man that
can kill Cain," Logan said. "I mean, seein' as a bunch of
men have tried, and a bunch of men have died. It don't
seem like there's any one person what's been able to
kill 'im."

"And you think the three of you can do it?" Sawyer
asked.

"Yeah," Peters said. "Onliest thing is, we don't want
nobody else goin' after him at the same time we are,
'cause it wouldn't be right for us to get ever' thin' all set
up, 'n then somebody else come along 'n take advantage
of what we done."

"All right, if you can get it done, have at it, long as you
understand the bounty ain't goin' to be no more 'n it is
now just 'cause there's three of you doin' the job."

"Yeah, we know, 'n like I said, we're all right with it," Peters said.

DEKE PAULY STEPPED DOWN from the train in Eastland, waited as his horse was off-loaded, then boarded his horse in the livery, and walked down to the Cactus Saloon.

Pauly got lucky as soon as he went into the saloon. He saw three men sitting together at a table in the back corner. Unlike the other customers they weren't flirting with any of the saloon girls, and even sent them away if any of the women would approach their table. They also seemed to be engaged in what appeared to be a serious conversation.

But the real clincher was that Pauly recognized one of them. Jake Slater had a bounty of five hundred dollars on his head, and if Pauly wasn't after bigger game, he would take Slater down to the local sheriff, dead or alive.

But he had a strong gut feeling now, and his history of gut feelings was that they were right, more often than they were wrong. Pauly's gut feeling was that these men were after Lucas Cain.

He nursed his whiskey until he saw the three men leave, then he left right behind them.

"IT'S a double-edged sword with me spending my time here," Lucas said to Cephus. "On the one hand, I'm drawing people here to kill me. On the other hand, they would probably come here whether I was here or not, and at least this way, I'm able to protect you. So it's your call, do I stay, or do I go?"

"I don't know whether I want you to stay here, or not. I'll ask the girls. They have every right to have a say about this."

Lucas and Cephus walked up to the front where the two sisters were working. Lucas posed the question.

"I want you to stay," Carolina said.

"Maggie?" Lucas said. "It's your call. If you don't want me to stay, say so, and I'll go."

"If you hadn't been here, that man wouldn't have taken Carolina and me to be tied up in that hotel room," Maggie said. She left out the part about the two of them having been stripped naked, and Lucas knew that it was because she was too embarrassed to speak of it.

"Well, Carolina?" Maggie said.

"What?"

"Kiss him so he'll stay. You know you want to."

Carolina smiled. "Yeah, I do." She gave Lucas a chaste little brush of her lips on his.

32

W hen Jake Slater and the other two men left the saloon, Pauly followed them while keeping out of sight. When they reached the newspaper office they stopped, then conferred with one another. They were too far away for Pauly to hear what they were saying, but he was able to observe the result of their conference.

Slater stayed out on the street in front of the newspaper office, while one of the men walked through the space to the right between the newspaper office and the leather goods store, while the other went through the space to the left between the newspaper office and the apothecary.

Slater stayed out in the street, but he was looking around as if studying all the businesses on Main Street.

Pauly was curious as to what was going on, so he looked in through the window of the hat shop to cover his real interest, which was to see what Slater and the others had planned. He didn't have to wait too long. The two men who had been with Slater appeared on top of the two buildings that were adjacent to the newspaper office.

Slater exchanged a quick wave with each of them, then the men got down behind the low parapet that lined the roofs of both the leather goods store and the apothecary. Pauly could still see both of them, but that was only because he had seen them before they got down.

Slater turned his attention to the newspaper office. "Cain," he shouted loudly. "Cain, I know you're in there. Come out here and face me like a man!"

It was Carolina who saw the man standing in the middle of Main Street. The man didn't have a gun in his hand, but his hand was resting on the butt of his pistol.

Lucas had been in the back of the shop with Cephus when he heard the shout. He started toward the front.

"Don't do it, Lucas," Carolina said. "His hand is already on his gun, so he could kill you. And, if you kill him, you might be charged with murder."

"I've got to go out there, Carolina. If I don't, he may find a way to come after you or your sister or your papa."

"All right but be careful, Lucas. Please, be careful."

"I'll be as careful as I can in a gun fight."

By now Cephus and Maggie were also in front of the building, looking on, nervously.

"Cephus, get the double-barrel shotgun, and if he kills me, then if he comes in here, don't even talk to him. Just fire both barrels at him."

"Why don't you take the shotgun with you?" Cephus suggested.

"I'm comfortable enough with my pistol. Carolina, you and Maggie get down behind the counter in case any bullets come through the window."

"All right," Carolina replied with a fright-tinged voice.

Lucas opened the door, then stepped outside. The man who had challenged him still hadn't drawn his pistol, but he had backed all the way to the other side of the street. By now, several citizens of the town had figured out what was going on, and they were hanging around to see how it developed.

One of those onlookers was Deke Pauly. As soon as Lucas came out, the two men who had been posted on the buildings, stood up and pointed their guns at Lucas.

"Cain, behind you!" Pauly shouted, shooting at the same time.

Logan, who was the man on the roof of the leather goods store, dropped his pistol, put his hand over his chest, then pitched forward, headfirst, from the roof. He made half a turn on the way down, then fell on his back where he lay motionless.

Slater gave a loud yell then took advantage of the distraction to draw his own gun. "Cain, draw your gun, you son of a bitch!"

Lucas beat Slater to the draw, and Slater pulled the trigger of his pistol, sending his bullet into the ground, as he fell forward.

Even as Lucas was watching Logan go down, a bullet nicked him in the arm, and he turned toward the shooter. Before he could shoot, however, the man who had cautioned him shot the second man off the roof.

"That's it, there were only three of 'em," the man said, putting his pistol away.

"Deke Pauly?" Lucas asked.

"At your service," Pauly said.

"It's good to see you again, particularly good, I would

say. How did you happen to be here at such a fortuitous time?"

"I was in the saloon when I heard them planning to kill you, so I thought I'd follow 'em and take a hand in whatever happened."

"It's a good thing you did," Lucas said.

"I'm not just here by accident, I planned to be here. I figured it might take both of us to track down Rufe Sawyer."

"So, you're after Sawyer too?"

"Yes, as well as Moe Godfrey, Chris Dumey, and Amos Coleman. The bounty on Sawyer is three thousand now, and a thousand dollars apiece on the other three. Also, I wouldn't be surprised if Sawyer hadn't picked up a couple more men besides the three he has now.

"As I see it, that's too much for one person, and the bounty is enough to share, if we do this together."

Lucas smiled and extended his hand. "Welcome aboard, partner."

33

"All three of them?" Sawyer asked. "Are you telling me that Cain killed Peters, Slater, and Logan?"

"Not by himself. He had help," Godfrey said.

"Who helped him?"

"It was a feller by the name of Pauly. I don't rightly know his first name."

"Are they still in Eastland?" Sawyer asked.

"Yeah, that's what I heard."

"All right, here's what we're going to do. You, Chris, and Amos are going to round up two men apiece. That'll give us a total of ten men."

"What are we goin' to do with ten men?" Godfrey asked.

"Whatever it takes to kill Cain and Pauly," Sawyer replied.

WHEN LUCAS LED PAULY into the office and shop of the *Eastland Journal*, they were greeted by Maggie.

"Deke, this young lady is Maggie McKay," Lucas said.

"Young lady, you say?"

"Don't let her age fool you. The bravery and intelligence she showed a week or so ago, probably saved her, and her sister's lives."

Lucas went on to explain how Maggie had left a note by setting the type backward.

"That is pretty smart," Pauly agreed. "But tell me, why isn't a smart young lady like you in school?"

Maggie laughed. "It's summer, silly."

Hearing the conversation, Carolina came up front, where she greeted Lucas, then looked at Pauly in an obvious hint that he should be introduced to her.

"This is Maggie's older sister, Carolina McKay," Lucas said. "This is Deke Pauly."

"This is the man who saved your life?" Carolina asked.

"The same."

Carolina turned to Pauly with a big smile. "Then I'm very glad to meet you."

"That's because my sister is sweet on Lucas, and he is sweet on her," Maggie said.

"Maggie! People don't go around saying things like that," Carolina scolded.

Pauly laughed. "Why not? It will certainly keep me from butting in where I'm neither needed, nor wanted."

"Oh, your friendship is wanted," Carolina said.

"And freely given," Pauly offered.

"Carolina, Deke and I would like to take the two of you to supper tonight," Lucas said.

"Yes, we'll go!" Maggie said, enthusiastically. "It'll be my first social outing with just a man and me."

"Little Sister, it won't be a social outing with just you and Mr. Pauly. We'll be along as well," Carolina said.

ON THE WAY TO, during, and after supper that evening, several of the town's citizens had made congratulatory comments to Lucas and Deke about how they had rid the community of three unsavory visitors.

Later that night after Carolina and Maggie had been escorted home, and over drinks in the saloon, Lucas and Pauly made plans as to how they intended to work together.

TWO DAYS LATER, about eight miles west of Eastland, in the small cabin they had taken from Juan Lopez, Rufe Sawyer looked out over the men that had been gathered.

"All right, now," Sawyer said with an evil grin. "There's ten of us, enough to do what I've got planned."

"What do you have planned?" one of the new men asked.

"The first thing we're goin' to do, is take care of Cain and Pauly."

"How we goin' to do that?" Godfrey asked. "I mean, we ain't been able to do it yet, 'n it ain't like we ain't been a-tryin'."

"What we're goin' to do, is tell the sheriff that if they don't turn Cain and Pauly over to us, we'll burn ever' other buildin', 'n kill ever other person—man, woman, and child—in the town until we've taken control."

"'N what if they do turn Cain and Pauly over to us?" Dumey asked.

Sawyer smiled. "We'll kill 'em, then we're goin' to burn ever' other buildin' 'n kill ever' other person—man, woman, and child—until we've taken control of the town, anyway. Then we're goin' to take ever' cent there is to take. Wait a minute. Chris, how many sticks of dynamite do we have?"

"We have seven sticks left."

A broad smile spread across Sawyer's face. "Yeah, that'll do it. That'll do it just real good."

THAT AFTERNOON, Deputy Sheriff Hastings was sitting at his desk playing solitaire when a boy, about twelve, came into the sheriff's office.

"Is Sheriff Dozier here?" the boy asked.

"What do you need him for?"

"Some man gave me a dollar to give the sheriff a note," the boy said.

Hastings looked up in surprise. "What? He gave you a whole dollar just to give a note to the sheriff?"

"Yes, sir."

"Give it to me, I'll take it," Hastings said.

The boy shook his head. "No, sir, I can't do that, I'm s'posed to give it to the sheriff."

"I'm the deputy, givin' it to me is the same thing."

Hastings reached for the note, but the boy pulled it back to his chest.

"No, sir, I'm s'posed to give it to the sheriff."

"All right, you can wait for him."

"Good," the boy said.

"But you'll be fined one dollar, and have to wait for him back there in a jail cell."

"Uh, I'll give it to you."

Hastings smiled. "I thought you might come around." Hastings held out his hand, the boy hesitated just for a minute, then he turned the note over.

"That was a smart move," Hastings said.

After the boy left, Hastings read the note.

TAKE CAIN AND PAULY TO THE OLD LOPEZ CABIN EIGHT
MILES WEST ON ASH CREEK ROAD TOMORROW. TIE THEM
UP AND LEAVE THEM THERE. IF YOU DON'T DO THIS, WE
WILL BURN EVERY OTHER HOUSE AND STORE, AND KILL
EVERY OTHER PERSON IN EASTLAND.

    RUFE SAWYER

Hastings felt his blood run cold.

"HE WOULDN'T REALLY DO SOMETHIN'" like that, would
he?" Hastings asked when he showed the note to Sheriff
Dozier.

"This is Sawyer we're talking about, remember,"
Dozier said.

"Does that mean we're actually going to take Cain
and Pauly to this place, and leave 'em there, tied up like
Sawyer wants?"

"Tell me, Travis, do you really think we could take
Cain and Pauly to a cabin, then tie them up and leave
them there if they didn't want to do it?"

"Uh, no. So, what are we going to do?"

"We'll see what Cain thinks," Sheriff Dozier said.

"HELL YES, WE'LL GO," Lucas said after reading the
note the sheriff showed him. "The problem we've
had with Sawyer is finding him. So, we'll let him
find us."

"Yeah," Dozier said with a relieved smile. "Yeah, I thought you might want to do that."

An hour later, Lucas and Deke were taken to the cabin. Both men had their wrists bound. When they reached the cabin, they dismounted.

"All right, we'll be untying you now, but then we'll tie your hands behind your backs," Sheriff Dozier said. He was speaking loudly enough to be heard, if anyone was close by, and listening.

Both Lucas and Deke complied with the request and after the task was done, they were led inside where they sat on the floor with their backs up against the wall.

"We'll leave your horses about a half mile back toward town in that little copse of trees that I pointed out to you," Sheriff Dozier said.

"Thanks," Lucas answered.

"Are you two going to be all right?" Deputy Hastings asked.

"Yeah, now that our hands are untied," Deke said.

"We'll leave you to it. Good luck," Sheriff Dozier said.

COLEMAN'S JOB had been to remain on the ridge overlooking the cabin. He had watched them arrive, and now he saw the sheriff and deputy riding away, taking the other two horses with them.

"They did it!" Coleman reported, excitedly.

"What did you see?" Sawyer asked.

"I seen the sheriff 'n that deputy of his'n takin' Cain 'n Pauly to the cabin, 'n both of 'em was tied up. Then, when the sheriff 'n deputy rode off, they was leadin' the other two horses with 'em."

"It's time to go to work. We'll wait here, while you go

down, 'n take care of Cain 'n Pauly," Sawyer said to one of the new men they had recruited. "Shouldn't be too hard of a job, with both of 'em tied up like they are."

"All right," the man said.

———

"HERE THEY COME," Pauly said. "No, wait a minute, there's just one of 'em."

"He must just be checking us out," Lucas said. Lucas was sitting on the floor against the wall with his hands behind his back. There was a coil of rope around his ankles, but, like his hands, his feet were free.

"Better get back down here before he looks in," Lucas cautioned.

Pauly sat down against the wall, looped the rope around his ankles, and put his hands behind his back. Like Lucas, Pauly had a gun in his hand.

They didn't see anyone when the door opened, and they held their breath, waiting to see who came in.

Nobody came in. Instead, whoever it was, tossed something into the room that looked like a stick of wood.

"Why the hell would somebody throw a stick in here?" Pauly asked.

That was when the two men saw the sparks.

"Damn, that's dynamite!" Lucas shouted.

"Out back!" Pauly said.

The two men started toward the back wall, then halted. There was no back door.

The stick of dynamite exploded.

34

From the top of the ridge that looked down on the little cabin, Sawyer, and the nine men who were now with him, saw the explosion. There was a loud, thunderous noise, a flash of light, and a cloud of smoke. The roof tiles blew off, then came fluttering down in dozens of pieces. The front wall collapsed, and the two side walls were pushed out in a rolling gush of smoke and fire.

"Whoooee, them two boys is nothin' but crispy critters now," Sawyer said. "Come on, let's go to town."

Sawyer and the others rode away.

INSIDE THE CABIN, Lucas and Pauly had taken shelter behind the hulking iron cookstove. The stove had shielded them from the effects of the blast, but both men were coughing and wheezing from the smoke.

They stood up, dusted themselves off, then looked around to take stock of the situation.

"Where are they?" Pauly asked.

"You remember the note about how they were going to kill so many and destroy half the town?" Lucas asked.

"Yes, and they have dynamite," Pauly said.

"We've got to get to town right away."

After recovering their horses, they rode hard back toward Eastland, and were less than a mile from town when they heard the first explosion. That was followed by gunshots, then a minute later, another explosion.

When the road made its last curve, they were only about five hundred yards away from a group of armed men who were gathered on Main Street standing just in front of the Dunn Hotel. They could see a man lighting the fuse of a stick of dynamite, preparatory to throwing it into the hotel.

"Hold on a second, Deke," Lucas called over to Pauly. Pauly stopped and looked over at Lucas. With his horse standing still, Lucas had his Winchester out, sighting down the barrel. He pulled the trigger and the rifle kicked back against his shoulder. The man holding the stick of dynamite gave a yelp of pain, and grabbed the bloody hand that no longer held the dynamite.

The dynamite dropped to the ground, right in the middle of the four men who were there.

"What the hell?" one of the men shouted, and that was the only sound before the stick of dynamite exploded. The explosion took all four men down.

The other six men, three on either side of the street, were totally unaware of what had just happened. They were shooting at the few hapless citizens who happened to be outside when the attack started. Now the towns-people were running, darting into the various businesses, or dashing in between the buildings to find shelter.

Bailey's Harness Shop and Alsup's Tinware stores were both showing the effects of a dynamite blast and fire. And on the boardwalks at least seven townspeople were lying facedown. Included in that number were two women and a small child.

Lucas waved for Pauly to take the right side of the street, and he would take the left side. Lucas came upon the first man who was drawing a bead on a woman cowering under the display window of Sheppard's Millinery. The shooter's back was to Lucas, and for just a second, he held off, hesitant to shoot someone in the back. Then, he saw that his target was about to shoot an innocent woman, so Lucas pulled the trigger. He saw a mist of blood fly from the would-be shooter's head, and the man went down, dead before he even knew he was in danger.

Less than a minute later, every outlaw invader lay dead in the street, and the danger Eastland faced had been eliminated.

THE TEN DEAD outlaws were laid out in the alley behind the mortuary. Irvin Welch said that he wouldn't look at an outlaw's body until the innocent people of the town were taken care of.

Lucas, Deke, Sheriff Dozier, and Deputy Hastings were there looking down at the bodies. The four who had been killed in the dynamite blast were so disfigured that they couldn't be identified, even by someone who knew them.

Fortunately, Rufe Sawyer, as well as Godfrey, Coleman, and Dumey could be identified.

"I should have the authorization to pay the reward money to you two by tomorrow," Sheriff Dozier said.

"Yeah, and don't forget, the bank will pay ten percent on the money that was recovered, and that's six thousand dollars," Hastings said.

"Damn, Lucas, we're near 'bout rich," Deke said with a big smile.

"We aren't paupers, that's for sure," Lucas said.

"Have you given any more thought to what we were talking about?" Deke asked.

"You mean about us workin' together?" Lucas replied.

"Yeah. We make a pretty damn good team."

"I think we might be able to work something out," Lucas said. "But I've got something else I have to take care of first."

"Yes, you do. What are you going to do about it?"

"I'm goin' to give it a lot of thought."

THE NEXT DAY, even as the town was recovering from the battle that had been fought in the streets, Lucas and Deke were paid their bounty.

"You still haven't decided?" Deke asked.

"I've decided," Lucas said.

"And?"

"I'll look you up."

EPILOGUE

"What do you mean, you're going?" Carolina asked, when Lucas told her he would be leaving town the next day.

"Carolina, you know who I am, you know what I am. I'm a bounty hunter. More than that, I'm a rambling man. I can't be the man you need."

"I know that," Carolina said with tears in her eyes. "Go." She closed her eyes. "Please, go now, while I can't see you. I don't want to watch you leave…"

Lucas saw the tears streaking down Carolina's cheeks, and he felt his own eyes glazing over. But he knew that this was the right thing to do to keep Carolina from feeling even more pain.

As Lucas rode out of town, he thought about the hurt he had caused Carolina, and he hated doing it, but he knew if he hadn't done it now, it would get much harder at a later time. Telling Carolina goodbye had been a very hard thing to do, but Lucas knew he couldn't become a newspaperman, or even a rancher. There was something in his makeup, something deep in his soul, that made him, always, a rambling man.

A LOOK AT: THE TENDERFOOT

THE COMPLETE SERIES

Master of the Western adventure, *New York Times* best selling author Robert Vaughan is back with another page turner sure to please Western fans of all ages.

When Turquoise Ranch hand Curly Stevens went into Flagstaff to meet a new employee arriving on the train, his first impression of Rob Barringer is of how big and strong the tenderfoot is. Rob's eagerness to learn and his willingness to take on the most difficult jobs wins everyone over, including ranch foreman Jake Dunford, and Melanie Duford, his beautiful daughter.

Rob is well-educated, and his demeanor and intelligence catches the attention of Melanie, causing him difficulty with ranch manager Lee Garrison, who believes he has an exclusive right to Melanie. Garrison makes life difficult for the ranch hands, and Rob in particular.

When Jake Dunford makes a public accusation that the ranch manager is stealing from the ranch, Garrison reacts by firing everyone, but it is Garrison who is in for a big surprise.

"Vaughan offers readers a chance to hit the trail and not even end up saddle sore."—*Publishers Weekly*

AVAILABLE NOW

ABOUT THE AUTHOR

Robert Vaughan sold his first book when he was nineteen. That was several years and nearly five-hundred books ago. Since then, he has written the novelization for the mini-series Andersonville, as well as wrote, produced, and appeared in the History Channel documentary Vietnam Homecoming.

Vaughan's books have hit the NYT bestseller list seven times. He has won the Spur Award, the Porgie Award in Best Paperback Original, the Western Fictioneers Lifetime Achievement Award, the Readwest President's Award for Excellence in Western Fiction, and is a member of the American Writers Hall of Fame and a Pulitzer Prize nominee.

He is also a retired army officer, helicopter pilot with three tours in Vietnam, who has received the Distinguished Flying Cross, the Purple Heart, The Bronze Star with three oak leaf clusters, the Air Medal for valor with 35 oak leaf clusters, the Army Commendation Medal, the Meritorious Service Medal, and the Vietnamese Cross of Gallantry.

Made in United States
Troutdale, OR
01/18/2024

17012596R00176